Divided Loyalties

Keith Thomas

To Mary: ANTHOR'S
COPY

from

Keith.

DIVIDED LOYALTIES

by

Keith Thomas

NEW MILLENNIUM
292 Kennington Road, London SE11 4LD

British Library Cataloguing in Publication Data.
A catalogue record for this book is available
from the British Library.

Printed by Watkiss Studios Ltd. Biggleswade, Bedfordshire.
Issued by New Millennium*
ISBN 1 85845 141 8
*An imprint of The Professional Authors' & Publishers' Association

Acknowledgements

I hereby express my appreciation to those who helped along the way. Firstly, to my wife Meg, for a labour of love in deciphering my hand and typing the original copy. Then to my sister-in-law Sig, for her expert advice on fact and form. Also to friends and colleagues for their interest and patience in reading the final version of the story and correcting late lapses of mine and being kind in their encouragement. Finally to Olive, my sponsor.

Preface

There are those whose lives take a predictable course, they would have it no other way. Indeed, they are comfortable with, and feel safe in, that predictability. There are others who plan their lives and set out to accomplish that plan. Sometimes it is not to be, however, as events and people determine otherwise, as though a stronger hand is at the helm. Yes, like a vessel setting out on a voyage, charting the shortest route, a straight line between the departure point and its destination. It is blown this way and that and touches the original course, but rarely. The vessel may reach its original goal. Or it may, perhaps, find a final haven totally unforeseen.

Chapter 1
1869

The town came into view as he emerged from the foothills. It resembled all the other towns he had ridden into during the past months. The dry, pitted track curving away to his left and disappearing into what, at this distance with the late sun low behind him, could be mistaken for a match-stick assembly, liable to crumble at a breath. He stole a glance behind him at the rugged hills which bore testimony to the tortuous track he had just followed. Often at walking pace, his horse, a grey and aptly named Valiant picked its way precariously among the rocks and boulders. Even after almost a year he still missed the gentle green slopes of England. His mind took flight, as it had on so many occasions, back to his homeland. It had been his accent which had caused most of his problems for no matter how he had tried to conceal his university English he'd had little success in this direction. He smiled to himself as his tutor came into his mind's eye. What a good thing it was that Professor Hobson was not present to witness his attempts to compromise the English language. The name of Richard Shaw had not seemed too 'un-American', in fact he had seen that very name above a store somewhere back on that trail. At the time he had not felt disposed to investigate the similarity, his mind no doubt on the next milestone of his long journey. Later he had regretted his impatience as it would have been an interesting deviation from the routine pattern of his ride.

Putting these thoughts behind him, he set his horse at a canter and followed the arc that led into Randolph.

At close quarters too, the town was like all the others. The wide main street he moved along had side-walks with alleys and streets leading off at right-angles to the right and to the left. On each side of the street imposing frontages stood almost opposite each other. On his left was the Hilltop Hotel and to the right the saloon Emperors Delight. The possible origin of both names eluded him for the moment, but no doubt delving into the town's history would provide an answer. Other shops, bars, and various buildings ranged between these landmarks were on a much more modest scale.

People were much the same here too. The contrast between those scurrying and hurrying about their business and those idly looking on was marked. In each town he never ceased to marvel at the length of time, sometimes hours, that these idlers would lean on anything available, hat tilted forward, alternating between cat-napping and a motionless, lazy observation of the activity around them. The town's predictability was such that he turned down one of the side streets and sure enough found lodgings for his horse a block or so away. He explained to the stableman that he was staying for a spell, but even the use of a local term did not in any way hide his accent. He left the man staring after him as he returned to the main street on foot.

He pondered with amusement on the differing reactions to his educated English in this land of the drawl and considerable inarticulation. Many a skirmish had originated from the locals' failure to accept this strange 'dude'.

Hunger drove him to the hotel where he booked in and stashed his gear. Finding the restaurant and choosing from a limited menu, he sat back in his chair relaxing his long frame and sipping at the beer he had carried from the bar. Glancing to one side he caught his reflection in one of the many wall mirrors of the dining area. He mentally approved of himself as fitting in well with the surroundings. The only deviations from his black outfit were the white ornamentations on his gun handles, and his black and white waistcoat. His muscular body looked deceptively lean in black. These clothes had been selected for him on his arrival in America (was it really almost a year ago?) at the invitation of his good friend Dave 'Yankie' Holland, whom he had met at university. In those first months Dave taught him to fight, shoot and ride. Then the finer points of keeping himself and his horse alive in the wild were learned the hard way during frequent trips into the desert or hills. Richard had used firearms on hunting trips around his country home but looking after a horse had been a completely new experience, as had roughing it out in the open. He had surprised himself by the way he naturally adapted to his new way of life. Then came the day when Dave had said;

"Richard, you're as ready as you'll ever be", and went on with the compliment; "You know all that I know. You wanted a challenge - now you've got one. Ride West my boy". They clasped hands warmly. "Watch out for yourself, friend", Dave had added in a softer tone.

So it was that Richard Shaw and Dave Holland parted company, with an agreement to meet up again on the coast a year hence.

Richard was anxious to see as much of the West as he could in that year and curious to handle all situations which would inevitably arise, drifting as he was from town to town. He smiled to himself as he thought of Dave's prediction that having had the very best training and tuition he would eventually appear unscathed at the year's end, even after a long period on the trail.

His thoughts were terminated by the arrival of his meal. The pretty, smiling blonde whose name, Jackie, was being hollered by every impatient diner, laid his plate before him and withdrew, smoothing her dress with the palms of busy hands. He soon forgot her and the curious looks of the other occupants as he gave the meal his full attention.

3

Much later he stepped into the darkening street feeling good with a full stomach. The feeling was enhanced by the soak in a tub and shave he'd had prior to eating. He decided to keep a low profile that evening, turned down the already familiar alley and found the stable in which Valiant would be spending the night. The horse was obviously pleased by Richard's visit and accepted the hotel sugar with a display of affection that had long been a sign of the bond between man and beast. He resolved to return to his room and spend time on his diary, a routine that was difficult under the stars, and required considerable up-dating in the relative comfort of an hotel room. He congratulated himself for pulling off the main trail and finding this place. He had been pushing himself and his horse; the rigours of the ride and the tightness of the schedule were telling on them both.

Later, before sleep claimed him, Richard calculated that at his present rate of progress he would arrive back at the coast and the Holland household in two months. He imagined that wicked grin on Dave's face as his protege, as he put it, returned unscathed. His final decision that night was that he would ride out of Randolph in two days after he'd rested up, heading Eastward.

Chapter 2

Richard was awake very early the next day and was down at breakfast before Jackie had finished setting the tables. He marvelled at her fresh look after what must have been a late night in the kitchen. They exchanged opinions on the weather, as the night had been a very windy one and items of rubbish had been scattered throughout the town. He gleaned that she was the joint owner of the hotel with her brother, she looking after the catering and cleaning and he the running of the establishment. She brought Richard's fried breakfast and departed, and by the time he had devoured it hungrily the noise level had risen from a murmur to a hubbub as the tables became occupied.

He was glad to leave the diner and escape into the comparative freshness of the dust-laden street. He took a sniff of air and felt a sense of belonging, a strange familiarity with the town, a feeling which had eluded him in other towns, both on his trek West and now as he returned.

Richard took advantage of the empty barber's shop and dropped into a chair, giving the proprietor explicit instructions as to his requirements. This unusual approach took the barber by surprise and he creased his brow in concentration, relieved only as his regular customers drifted in and conversation took off. Richard listened with interest to the parochial tenor of the conversation. He could not have chosen a more informative start to the day. Each fragment of news was broken louder than the last as the bearer strived to remain audible. The price of beef; the lack of rain; the damage sustained by property during the night; even the state of the main street, its dry and solid tracks a danger to man, horse and vehicle. A birthday party at the Marshall ranch renewed Richard's interest and he took mental note of the girl's name, Virginia, and the fact that apart from the Sheriff not one of the guests at the celebrations was known to the occupants of the barber's shop. He was aware as he left the chair that there was a lot of hair around his feet, reminding him how long it had been since he spent any time in civilisation, even a small town. He had, though, made a point of keeping his hair long, otherwise he would stand out in a crowd long before opening his mouth.

Richard headed along the main street and, catching sight of the provision stores across from him, he decided to start restocking in preparation for his departure the next day. His saddle bags were almost depleted of the necessary items required to survive long days and nights in the open.

He started to cross the street almost opposite the store, which gave him a perfect view of what was about to unfold in front of him. Although it all happened so quickly, it was as though each moment was highlighted in a kind of slow motion, it was so crystal clear.

The blonde youngster came out of the store, arms full of packages and groceries. Head held high behind the parcels he could never have seen the spurred boot come from behind the door, tripping him and sending him head-first down the steps and onto the street. Packages flew everywhere and hit the ground around the prone youngster, who was dazed and bruised. Richard's quick temper flared momentarily as he mounted the sidewalk to confront the owner of the boot. The stupid grin on an otherwise undistinguished face was too much for Richard, who hit him hard in the stomach and, as the man's head came forward, he crashed his fist into that inane look of surprise which had replaced the grin. The man went down on the sidewalk holding his broken and bloody nose. Warning bells sounded in Richard's brain as he swung around to face the stricken man's two accomplices. Hands were moving down to their sides and Richard drew his own guns, instantly bringing into play the training of those long months.

(In that instant too, came back to him the recurring horror, never far from the surface, of the one occasion when he had to shoot to kill. He would never forget the realisation that the drunk, all caution discarded with the empty bottles, was going to use his gun. The shock of seeing the look of surprise on the dying face and the lifeless form which was once a human being at his feet, and the knowledge that he was responsible, deputising for God, had remained with him. He was fortunate that the man was not a local, but a drifter like himself. Bystanders had borne witness to the fact that the act was solely in self defence.)

The two men now froze in amazement, hands hovering over holsters, giving a strange scarecrow effect. The boy by now was recovering and being assisted to his feet. Richard motioned to the three men to pick up the fallen packages and assist the lad in placing them in a cart drawn up nearby. Still with his guns in his hands, he followed them onto the street. They glowered at him, evil intentions nakedly evident on their faces, but slowly tossed each item aboard until the task was completed. Richard replaced his guns and dismissed the men, who shuffled across the street and away, followed by laughter, taunts and a trail of blood. The boy was by now looking less shocked. Richard enquired of him if any bones were broken, but could see that the main hurt was to his young pride.

Richard became aware of the presence of the Sheriff, a mature, pleasant looking man, rather out of character for a Sheriff in Richard's experience.

"I don't like guns out of holsters in my town," he drawled, and then curtly ordered, "Come with me."

Richard certainly could not resist such a charming invitation, but before he left the scene he established that the boy, who still had purchases to make, would wait for him. He assured the lad that he would ride with him out of town, thus giving Valiant his day's exercise.

As he followed the Sheriff across the street, Richard wondered if he had over-reacted somewhat. At the time his action had seemed justified. He also had an eerie sensation that he was simply enacting some predestined and prepared scenario The Sheriff held out his hand as his guest entered the office.

"John Champion, Sheriff of Randolph," he said proudly, as if he was announcing himself as President.

"Richard Shaw, Sheriff."

"Yep, heard you was in town." As they shook hands he waved Richard into a chair across the desk from himself. Richard was invited to relate the event as he saw it. This he did, remembering each detail with clarity. The Sheriff listened attentively, then summed up the whole occurrence as being a misunderstanding. It was his opinion that the thing would soon blow over.

"These Marshall boys are a bit high spirited at times," he added.

"Do you have much trouble with them?" asked Richard.

"No," was the response, "Dan Marshall keeps a pretty tight rein on his boys. I'm out at his place tomorrow night, I'll drop a word in his ear," the Sheriff concluded.

"You sound like good friends Sheriff," Richard went on.

"Call me John, son," invited the Sheriff, then added in response to Richard's query, "Dan and I are friends, yes, of many years, and if he didn't pay my wages the town would have no Sheriff. My visit tomorrow is as a guest, leastways, Beth and me is guests - at Virginia's birthday shindig."

"Yes, I've heard about the birthday party." Then in response to the Sheriff's raised eyebrow Richard went on, "At the barber's shop."

The lawman nodded in understanding. Richard stood and, thanking the Sheriff for his time, headed for the doorway.

"By the way," he said turning, "Where is the boy's home?"

"The Mack homestead, you must have passed close by it when you rode in," returned the Sheriff. "'Bout an hour out of town," he shouted at Richard's back as he left the office.

The little cart was now loaded and a tarpaulin had been pulled over its contents. The youngster was not in sight, so Richard entered the store, finding the lad with the proprietor and his wife, both, he judged, in their sixties. They welcomed him warmly and Richard immediately took to them. They were not slow to applaud his action in coming to the boy's defence. He knew their name was Bennett, for 'E & J Bennett' was printed in large letters above the shop front.

"I'm Joshua Bennett." A large gnarled hand was thrust in Richard's direction. "And this is my wife, Edith." He cocked his head in the direction of the counter.

"Pleased to meet you ma'am," Richard swept off his hat, returning her smile.

"I am Josh's Godfather," Joshua Bennett went on proudly. "He don't usually get mixed up in any trouble."

"It wasn't of his making. I'm Richard Shaw by the way, just passing through."

"Knew you was in town," Joshua replied, grinning at the Englishman's look of surprise. "No stranger gits in town without bein' noticed. We kinda hoped you'd be in for grub and tackle afore hittin' the trail." His wife nodded her confirmation as Richard dug into a pocket and produced a list of requirements. Edith took it from him.

"Do you think the danger has passed now, Mr. Shaw?" Her accent was noticeably different from that of her husband.

"I am not sure, Mrs. Bennett."

"You really gonna ride out with the boy?" Joshua asked hopefully.

"Sure thing." Richard confirmed in a more positive manner. They all studied the youngster, who had been listening to the conversation attentively, his blonde head bobbing in the direction of each speaker. He lowered his head in mild embarrassment.

"So, young man, you are Josh eh?" Richard made an attempt to put the boy at ease.

"Yessir, Josh Mack," the boy replied respectfully, "I've never seen anyone as fast as you ..." His excited voice trailed off as he became aware of the amusement on the faces of the three adults facing him. Richard was impressed by Josh's clipped and cultured American which was delivered with a confidence borne of good breeding and a more than basic education. One came upon such a youngster rarely in this country, or indeed in England.

"I'll get my horse and be back," Richard eventually said to Josh. The old couple nodded approvingly as he left, heading for the stable.

Josh led the way back out of town to the West and soon Richard was in the foothills again, not aimlessly as the day before, but now on an errand. He kept close behind the cart as it bounced and clattered on the hard and uneven track. They soon turned off at a fork, leaving the trail on which he had ridden in the day before and the hills off to the left, following the valley, not climbing as he'd anticipated they would. He was surprised at how comparatively green and pleasant this valley was and there was a glint of water somewhere up ahead. How refreshing it was to see trees, not as healthy or grand perhaps as they were at home, but very welcome in this setting. He halted Valiant in order to admire the sweep of the valley. It was then that he knew they were being followed. He told Josh to drive on, hoping to catch up with him.

Richard turned his horse in time to see a dozen or so riders taking the fork in his direction. He held Valiant steady, taking the rifle from its saddle housing. Minutes later the riders came into the clearing and bore down on him.

Chapter 3

Richard, in that minute they took to reach him, analysed the situation, assessing the facts as they presented themselves. There were fourteen riders (not very good odds, he thought wryly); the one in the centre of the pack stood out from the rest in bearing and quality of horse and attire. Two of the men with whom he had clashed earlier outside the store were both in the group to his left. Their friend, obviously nursing a broken nose, was not present. They fanned out right and left and Richard kept the rifle steady on the big man at the head.

"That's far enough!" Richard barked, as a warning to those attempting to move behind him. Each horse stopped and for a moment there was no activity save the snorts of the horses as they whirled in confusion, taking a breather. The riders looked to their leader for guidance and a sign which would commence the action.

It was Richard, however, who fired the opening verbal salvo. "Rather a show of force to follow a youngster." The reply came in a voice of granite, clear and authoritative.

"Curious to know your intentions and involvement. I'm Dan Marshall and I don't take kindly to strangers beating up my boys."

Richard replied hotly, "Your boys, as you call them, are bullies, Mr. Marshall. I've seen their like up and down the land and people like yourself who pay them!"

"Boss, why don't we just ..." The coarse shout to Richard's left was silenced by Marshall's raised, gloved hand.

"Was it just to see fair play that you cut in?" The granite voice asked, with no trace of taking offence.

"Just passing through," Richard explained. "The boy needed help. I intend to see him back to the homestead."

"Of course, of course," the rancher said quickly, then after a short silence he dismissed his men. "You boys ride back to the ranch, I'll ride a ways with the stranger here."

They departed, but not without dissent and some audible misgivings about the wisdom of such a move. Richard and Marshall watched as they rode away, silent until the horses were out of sight. Richard replaced his rifle in its long holster and surveyed the man next to him. He was a deal taller even than Richard's six feet, and handsome in a rugged kind of way. His athletic frame belied his fifty or so years. Richard could not help but be impressed by this man of wealth and character.

They moved off in the direction the cart had taken some minutes before.

"That was a bit foolhardy, your heroics back there," the big man said with the trace of a smile invading the natural severity of his features, "One gun against so many - and a dude at that." Richard ignored the final remark. "I can use it," was all he said.

"Sure you can," was the sceptical reply. The horses momentarily separated as each rider negotiated the hazardous trail, both needing to concentrate to stay in the saddle. "This is a good land, with good people," the strong voice continued eventually, with more warmth in the tone. After a pause Marshall added; "My spread originally didn't come within miles of this valley." He took in the whole scene with a wave. "I've acquired more land over the years and now I find that I have fences in common with the Mack place." They rode in silence for some time, then the rancher continued, "Old Joe Mack settled here long before I arrived, then his son Austin took over when the old fella died." He pointed ahead. "See that tiny river down there?" He talked on, not waiting for a response. "That's the only water for miles and it runs through Marshall territory and the Mack spread." As he paused again, Richard found his voice with the inevitable question, "What is the problem then?"

The rancher sighed, "Since the ranch has developed so much and with my cattle grazing over many more square miles, I need more points of access to the water. I'm driving cattle a mighty long way just to water them." Richard nodded in understanding at the rancher's questioning gaze.

"What does the Mack fella say to opening up a few watering places?" Richard's question was greeted with the impatient reply,

"Austin Mack died mysteriously some two years ago and his widow will not even discuss the matter."

The cart was now in view and Richard, nodding towards it, spoke his mind; "There is no need to take it out on the youngster, whatever your feelings are."

"Some of the boys take things too far," he said apologetically, "I'll put it right with the lad now." They both approached the stationary cart and the rancher, to his credit, spoke to the boy and expressed the hope that he was not hurt. Josh politely confirmed that he was not.

Marshall looked across the cart at Richard, "Say, why don't you come out and join the celebrations tomorrow night? My daughter will be eighteen and hopes to travel. She would be mighty pleased to meet you." Richard thanked the rancher and promised to give the invitation some thought. The two horses moved together and Marshall leaned forward shaking Richard's hand with a firm grip, full of character.

"You're new around here, but if you can find a partner from the town to accompany you it will help the dancin'," he said jovially. Richard smiled and the rancher spurred his horse and was soon out of sight. They had parted on terms inconceivable an hour earlier.

"Thought I would wait a bit, see if you were O.K." Josh cut through his thoughts. Richard smiled again.

"Appreciate that," he said as he looked into the boy's earnest face. Josh was much more at ease now with the man who had come to his aid. "C'mon, my place is 'round the next bend," the boy encouraged. Before they could get in motion, a single rider came around that same bend. Josh yelled excitedly, "There's Ma!"

She rode towards them, erect and proud in the saddle, wearing a shirt and riding skirt which highlighted her fine figure. Her hat was pulled forward revealing, as she drew nearer, dark brown hair gathered at the back and held with a white ribbon. That first impression as she approached, cool and fresh in the high midday sun, would, Richard knew, be a lasting one. At close quarters Richard was taken by her tanned smooth complexion, and he was absorbed by her elegance and bearing, evident even in the saddle. Josh again interrupted his thoughts, "Ma, you must meet Mr. er, er, er," Richard again came to Josh's aid, verbally on this occasion.

"Richard Shaw, ma'am," he said, removing his hat and feeling the heat.

"Kate Mack," she breathed, her long slim fingers nervously toying with the reins. "I was getting worried about young Josh." His musical ear appreciated the tone and contrast in her voice, at the same time soothing and strong, even in her concern.

"I fear that I am to blame for your son's delay," Richard explained lamely. "Now that he is safely home I will bid you goodbye."

"No!" Josh cried out. He was standing in the cart, and now a little embarrassed by his outburst. He went on more evenly, "You must come and see our spread." He looked at his mother for support and continued, "Just 'round the bend." Her clear brown eyes surveyed Richard calmly.

"Well of course, if Mr. Shaw wishes to," she said with a

smile. The smile, he decided later, was the deciding factor in his opting to accompany them. He nodded his assent and they moved off.

Richard rode behind the cart, leaving mother and son in animated conversation. Kate shot an occasional glance back in his direction as Josh's undoubtedly embellished account of the incident unfolded.

The homestead suddenly came into view as the trail rounded a clump of rocks. It was a traditional building with outhouses and barns all within a short distance of it. They pulled up in the wide paddock which ranged before the veranda and front gate. Richard dismounted and assisted the lady from the saddle. Her hands gripped his firmly as she jumped to the ground. The close proximity filled his nostrils with a clean, fresh smell, tinged with a musky fragrance he quickly identified as lavender.

"Josh is full of your praises, Mr. Shaw," she said, "the least I can do is show my gratitude by asking you to join us for a meal."

"You are very kind ma'am," Richard responded, "Let Josh and me see to the horses then." She smiled again in agreement and walked into the house with a distinctive gait. Richard considered that she moved with the grace and dignity of a queen. (He had actually been in the presence of Queen Victoria when she had honoured his university with a visit) He studied the bearing of this woman he had just met and thought it compared favourably with that of his queen.

Man and boy were left behind to unhitch the cart and lead the horses into the barn.

Josh was very talkative with his new friend and hero and during the next half hour or so, Richard learned much about this youngster who was so obviously missing a father. He was happy to have won the lad's confidence, responding easily to the stream of chatter and occasionally ruffling the boy's blonde head. Josh could ride; Josh could shoot; Josh could shoe a horse. So it went on, as Josh was eager to make an impression. His tutor in all these skills had been his father and the lad's eyes moistened when he recalled that "Pa taught me."

On the subject of schooling, Josh was not too forthcoming. His mother had apparently been a teacher in the town, but, confined to the homestead by her duties and the death of her husband, had decided to give her children instruction at home rather than send them off each morning. Josh had obviously benefited from the personal tuition.

Engrossed in their work and conversation, they were unaware of the presence of the little girl until she spoke.

"Ma says you got to come in now." she said. Josh and Richard turned simultaneously.

"This is my sister Samantha," said Josh without enthusiasm. Richard was immediately staggered by the likeness of mother and daughter. Never before had he seen such an amazing reproduction of the original where the human race was concerned.

"I don't like Samantha, you know that," she stormed at Josh. Ignoring her brother's mischievous grin, she turned to Richard with her mother's smile and said, "Call me Sam, Mr. Shaw, I'll show you where to get washed up, Ma is waiting."

He followed her obediently, Josh at his heel raising his eyebrows in light-hearted apology. They all moved towards the house.

Chapter 4

The Mack house was a single-storey wooden affair of generous proportions, with a porch or veranda on all sides. The approach, Richard reflected, was typical of the lady of the house. It was neat, with a low, wooden picket fence and gate. The path to the front porch steps was bordered by flowers, planted methodically. A rough-cut lawn ranged behind the flower beds on both sides of the path. A tree on each side of the house completed the balanced and impressive appearance.

Another path led off to the left towards the rear of the property. He found the latrine at the end of this well worn track, with its three-quarter door allowing necessary ventilation. Returning to the house after his ablutions, Richard took note of a chicken coop with a dozen or so occupants, and a small cow-shed containing the equipment required for milking. Other sundry outbuildings appeared to be storerooms for equipment, wood and provisions. A washroom was conveniently situated between latrine and the house. Forking off again was yet another path which led to the horse barn on the other side of the dwelling. A well stood in a central position in the paddock beside the barn and in front of the house.

The property must have looked quite attractive when the white paint had first been applied. Now, some years later, the sun and the elements had dried and cracked much of it. The roof resembled a patchwork quilt, where repairs had been made to it over the years. These were Richard's first impressions of the physical details of the house and its environs. When it came to the home, these moved into perspective and became very much a secondary consideration.

The warmth of that family circle was evident from the moment he set foot in the house. Richard was introduced to

'Old Jeb', the fourth and last member of the household. Jeb was in no way related, but had served the family for many years and had now been integrated into it. The meal was a formal yet genial affair, comprised of cold meat, vegetables and chunks of bread which were 'Ma made', as Sam put it.

Richard discouraged Josh's attempts at drawing him into retelling the morning's events. Instead, he enquired about the house and the extent of their land. In turn, he answered the inevitable questions about his homeland and its customs. Jeb, much to the chagrin of the youngsters, filled him in with a brief history of the district since he'd first ridden in, a stranger like Richard, some fifty years before. Kate, Richard observed, had lost some of the tension evident at their meeting and was now humming a tune to herself in a relaxed manner.

After lunch (they called it dinner), Richard amazed all present by offering to help with the dishes. His offer was declined, and instead it was proposed that they take him on a tour of the property to travel the fences. Their enthusiasm persuaded him to agree and all five of them, Jeb at the reins, were soon leaving the homestead and heading up the valley in the buggy. Richard sat beside Jeb and there was a constant flow of information coming from behind him. Even little Sam was chatty as certain features passed by, some known only to the little girl, and she urgently brought them to Richard's attention.

The extent of the land was impressive. Less so was the condition of the fences and the general maintenance. Jeb explained that it was the task of Josh and himself to keep the fences in good shape, but his tone suggested that they had been unable to cope with it. The few cattle they encountered looked reasonably healthy to Richard's inexperienced eye, but Jeb was not too sure which were Mack stock and which were the Marshall brand that had wandered into the greener pasture beside the river.

At the end of a delightful afternoon, with the homestead coming back into sight, the family questioned Richard as to his plans.

"I should ride out tomorrow," he answered, "but I'm kind of curious enough to accept Dan Marshall's invitation - so probably the day after," he concluded. The silence that followed told him that his intentions did not meet with their approval.

Later, after tea had been served, Richard spent an even more delightful evening with his new-found friends. He discovered an old piano in the parlour, covered with drapes and completely out of tune. He smiled to himself as he hammered out the 'honky tonk' sound so typical of that country. He was happy to be playing again and the family sang with great gusto. Kate, he observed, possessed a particularly fine voice, a talent not passed on to her son. Josh was totally tone-deaf but produced more volume than any of them.

Time flew, and as light faded lamps were lit around the room, enhancing the mellow atmosphere.

"Where are you staying in town, at the hotel?" Kate asked.

"Yes, it's quite comfortable really," Richard replied.

"You must have seen Auntie Jackie," cut in Sam with enthusiasm.

"Yes, she brought my breakfast this morning," he said, raising a questioning eyebrow to Kate.

"She has been my best friend for many years," she informed him, "the children love her." Kate looked up again from her darning. "Talking of children, it's time you were both in bed," she said. Glancing at Richard, she added, "I let them stay up because of our special guest, they have never met anyone from across the Atlantic before." Richard made appreciative noises and bade the pair goodnight.

The two men were left together and Jeb offered Richard some tobacco, which he declined, never having been a smoker.

"It's done 'em all the world of good you bein' around," he remarked to Richard. "We don't get much company."

Richard smiled and after a short interval observed, "Kate seems to be coping very well."

"Hell-ofa-gal is Kate. Just wish I wus more use nowadays. Needs a mighty lot o' lookin' arter this spread do." Jeb spoke in short statements, each punctuated by an inhalation or exhalation of his pipe. Richard found this mannerism strangely fascinating and was completely absorbed as the old man continued, "Been like my own gal, she 'as. Raised in town she wus, 'ad no folks same us me. Came out 'ere a courtin' and moved in when she got 'itched up to young Austin Mack. Some time back along that wus." Jeb was thoughtful for a moment, pipe suspended in mid-air. "Yep, some sixteen year ago that wus." Richard listened with much interest to this glimpse into Kate's background delivered in Jeb's staccato style. He took advantage of a brief silence to bring the story up-to-date as Jeb sucked on his pipe contentedly.

"What do you think of the Marshall situation Jeb?"

The septuagenarian blew a sweet smelling cloud in Richard's direction as he considered the question. "No harm in talkin' seems to me," he said briefly. Richard nodded thoughtfully as Kate returned from the next room where she and the children slept.

"The kids want you to stay tonight," she announced. "I could make you up a blanket in here," she said, pointing to a corner.

"The barn will do fine, but thanks," he said, "I can ride into town at sun up, check out of the hotel and pick up my gear." Kate busied herself about the room, tidying up after the day's activities.

She straightened up and said to Richard, "Josh tells me that you are invited to the Marshall party."

"I appreciated it, being a stranger," he replied.

Jeb, having finished his smoke, climbed out of his rocker. "I'll leave you two young 'uns, up with the rooster in the mornin', 'night." Their responding 'goodnight' came in unison as he headed for the small room at the rear of the house.

"Jeb's getting frail now," Kate said as the door closed. "Good to have around, Jeb is. Do you know he still gets up at five, for no real reason? He says it gives him time to 'come to'. She chuckled delightfully.

"Has he any family?" Richard enquired, smiling.

"None," she replied, "We have been his family." Kate waved Richard into the rocking chair Jeb had vacated and sat herself down wearily, pushing strands of hair away from her face.

The house was quiet. There was no noise save the gentle creaking of the rocker as Richard swung to and fro, and the steady ticking of a huge clock somewhere in the room. Kate sat facing him, the massive stove between them. The lamp behind her made her hair shine and created a mellow glow around them, fading at the centre of the room so that the far wall was invisible. It was as though they were spot-lighted, ready to enact the next scene of life.

"You look at home in that chair," she ventured, "you could sleep in that tonight."

"I feel at home, but my gear is in the barn," responded Richard, "I shall sleep well tonight, believe me, it has been an eventful day."

Kate continued reflectively, "It doesn't seem possible that you only arrived in the house this morning. I know a little about you but what are doing so far from home, Richard?" It was the first time that she had used his first name and he liked the way she said it. He looked at her for a moment in the silence, then said softly, "Are you sure you're not too tired to talk?"

"Quite sure," she said with a smile that was evident even though her face was in shadow. "Tell me, please." Richard cleared his throat, Jeb's tobacco lingered in the air. He spoke quietly and easily for an hour, pausing only to gauge the reaction of his lovely companion. He told her of his childhood and his youth as heir to the manor in which he was brought up; his education at university and his invitation to America given by his good friend Dave. He related the horrors of the passage across the Atlantic and to her fascination quoted relevant extracts from 'The Rime of the Ancient Mariner', using Coleridge-Taylor's immortal words to portray his feelings about the voyage. He described the training and tuition his friend had given him to adapt him to life here, explaining the reason for his tight schedule on his return trip East and of his rendezvous on the coast very soon. Kate listened as though he were narrating a story or reading from a book. Her eyes never left his face.

Through the silence she said eventually, "And now this young man of title and wealth is staying in a poor homestead with poor people, miles from civilisation."

"It has been a privilege indeed, Kate," he said sincerely, "You have something in your home that I have never known, a warmth within your family." She became, to his surprise, mildly embarrassed, changing the subject quickly.

"I understand that you had words with Dan Marshall on the trail," she said inquisitively.

"He seems a decent guy," began Richard, then, seeing her hostility went on; "I called him and his gang bullies. Now most people in his position would have tried to blow my head off. He can't be that bad."

"The man is arrogant and insufferable," Kate burst out, "He thinks he owns everybody and everything." she concluded. There followed an uncomfortable silence, during which they looked warily at each other across the gloom. Gradually each countenance softened and, responding to Richard's smile Kate said apologetically, "My Austin could tolerate him, as man to man, but since his death it has been difficult to communicate with anyone." Richard's face showed his concern and he said tentatively, "Marshall is your neighbour, Kate, he only wants to talk to you. He has his problems too and his proposals could be beneficial."

"I know what he wants," she said, "He wants to buy me out and it's not as easy as that. This place may be run down but it holds memories." Her voice trailed away and even in the poor light he could detect her emotions. Richard waited, motionless now in the rocker. The silence was almost tangible. "Austin worked hard on this place," she eventually continued, "as did his father before him. When the old man died and it became ours we were proud. Proud to be owners. We worked at it together." She studied Richard closely to see if she should go on, for she was not used to talking this way. He leaned forward and whispered; "Kate, tell me about Austin, Josh must take after his Pa." She was encouraged to continue and brightened visibly as she recalled her late husband.

"Austin was blonde yes, and a good husband and father." Kate stared at the invisible roof and went on slowly, "He was out repairing the fences with Jeb. The old man tells me that Austin collapsed. He could see no reason, just fell to the ground, covered in blood. Jeb rode in to fetch me and we found him just where he had fallen, the blood drying around his mouth and nose. He was dead."

The stillness was marked. Even the clock seemed to tick with less insistence. Neither of them moved. Richard felt compassion as never before and was tempted to go to her, but afraid, in that moment, to break the quietness. She came to his rescue, "Well, my teaching came to an end," she said resolutely, "and here I am, trying to make a living and feeling very sorry for myself. Let me walk you to the barn, I could do with some air," she said, jumping up.

Richard stood, accepting the lamp she offered him. They left the house and moved together towards the barn. At the door they stopped and Richard admired her face, illuminated in the lamplight.

"Kate," he said, "would you do me the honour of accompanying me to the party tomorrow night?" She hesitated, staring at him in the lamplight, unsure of herself.

"What, me go to the party! Are you not riding out tomorrow then?"

"Guess not," he said briefly.

"I vowed never to set foot in that place," she whispered without rancour. "Would you really like me to go with you, Richard? There are many girls in town who-" He placed a finger over her lips.

"You will make me a proud man, Mrs. Mack," he said smiling.

"And you are not patronising me, or feeling sorry for ..." He replaced his finger, cutting off her protest. They both laughed together.

"I will not go alone, Kate," he answered with resolve. She placed a hand on his forearm.

"Ask me again at breakfast," she said, opening the barn door.

"You will think about it?" Richard asked urgently, moving away from her.

"I promise," she called over her shoulder, and was gone into the darkness.

The barn was cosy, with the silence broken only by the occasional snort or hoof on wood as the horses were slow to settle. Valiant was appreciative of Richard's presence and was already quiet. Richard had always found this atmosphere, dominated by the smell of hay, conducive to sleep. He should sleep well tonight, he reflected.

The day had been eventful, starting with a routine shopping expedition, with the aim of obtaining a few provisions. (Was it really only that morning?) He had then been manipulated by events and now found himself in a strange yet somehow comfortable environment. His eyes closed. He resolved to stay for another day, that would not jeopardize his carefully calculated schedule. He hoped that Kate would ride out to the party with him. His thoughts became more and more fragmented as sleep claimed him. The vision of Kate's smile was the last thing to disappear from his mind's eye.

Chapter 5

Richard slept late into the morning, for the sun was already streaming across the barn door and spilling onto the far wall. There were sounds of equine impatience inside the barn and of human preparations and activity outside. He stepped into the sunlight, momentarily dazzled. He never could get used to the brightness and the strength of the light in this country, and standing there without his hat caused him to squint.

Richard washed and shaved at the well and took a bucket filled with water into the house, a habit he had observed among the Mack household.

"Morning," he said cheerfully.

"Morning," came the response in unison from the quartet at the table. Kate had obviously told them of the party invitation and the children were as excited as if they too were going.

"Mother says she cannot go with you," announced Josh sternly, "I think that's a pity." he went on in his role as man of the house.

"But you simply must go Ma!" declared Sam jumping up and down. Kate was silent, filling the table with edibles and pouring coffee into each mug. She smiled at Richard warmly, then sat down and they ate after Jeb had said grace. The old timer went through the day's routine and allocated each a duty. Sam the chickens, Josh the cows. He took responsibility for horses and, farther afield, the cattle. There was to be no fence maintenance that day, the livestock had to take priority. Eventually Kate and Richard were alone, facing each other across the table. Kate threw up her hands despairingly.

"How can I go with you, Richard? It is going to be a grand affair and I have worn nothing grand for years. I don't even get to the Saturday dance at the hotel." Richard wanted to assure her that she would look good and grand in anything, but instead relayed an inspiration that had just that moment come to him.

"Kate, let's ride into town then, Edith would fix you up." Kate was still frowning, but gradually her face lit up and fleetingly Richard detected an element of excitement in her voice.

"Richard, we need so much about the place, it is just so - well, indulgent." He smiled at her attempt at morality.

"A present then, for coming with me." She did not respond immediately and as he studied her face he saw the uncertainty of the situation registered there.

"But why should you spend money on me, Richard, it wouldn't be right."

"And why, Mrs. Mack, did you take me in and feed me as though I were one of the family? That was very wrong!" he chided kindly.

She shook her head. "You assisted Josh and ..."

"And I am asking you to reciprocate by assisting me tonight. I need a partner, a companion for the evening. Here I am facing probably the most beautiful women I have met in my twenty-five years of existence. I shall not give up easily."

Kate lowered her head, her hands clasped tightly on the table top. There was not a word spoken for a full minute. Eventually her head came up and she fixed Richard with a gaze full of tenderness and acquiescence.

"Thank you, Richard, I will be delighted to be that companion."

"Bless you, Kate." His smile revealed his genuine pleasure at her decision. Richard retained his smile as Kate left the room to inform the family of her intentions. Did he also detect a lightness of step?

Within the hour they were sitting in the buggy waving to

Sam, Josh and Jeb, all of whom had left their respective tasks and assembled at the gate. The children, of course, had wanted to accompany their mother. They had been persuaded to stay with Jeb only by means of a bribe in the form of a present from town.

Richard kept Valiant at a walk as they moved through the valley. His horse was never happy in harness and much preferred being ridden. Richard judged that Valiant needed the work-out and had decided to use him with the buggy. Kate and he chatted easily and by the time the town came into view, each had learned much about the other. Kate had been curious about England, and he about her upbringing in the neighbourhood.

They bounced up the familiar curve into town, which looked different to Richard in the morning sun, with the shadows leaning towards them. As always, curious and idle eyes followed their passage along the street until they arrived at the store, Richard securing the horse and buggy.

Kate entered Bennett's store as Richard was attending to Valiant. He could hear the whoops of delight as the proprietors received their unexpected but welcome visitor. Richard mused on the contrast between his arrival in town that day and the day before. As he mounted the sidewalk he could recall so clearly the action which had taken place just twenty-four hours previously.

On joining Kate he was warmly greeted and Edith, winking at him, drew Kate away to look through the stock of dresses. Joshua took Richard's arm and ushered him into the back of the store. Taking a bottle from the shelf, he waved it at Richard.

"Have a drop of this my boy," he said, and proceeded to fill two glasses with a good brand of whisky. They settled back in their chairs and Joshua took out some tobacco. After offering Richard a smoke, he made himself a crude cigarette. "Tell me everything," he requested, "They'll not be through for quite a spell." He cocked his head towards the door. Richard immediately recognised the sweet aroma now invading him from Joshua's direction. So this is where Jeb buys his tobacco!

Richard sipped his drink and felt the warmth of both the whisky and his companion.

"Well, as you know," he began, "it all started right here on your steps ..." They talked, the whisky relaxing them and providing a feeling of well-being. Joshua finally summed up the situation with an emphatic, "It will do her a power of good to get out," referring to Kate and the party. As if on cue, the door opened and Edith slipped inside smiling broadly.

"You're a lucky man, Mr. Richard," she said, beckoning Kate to enter the room.

Men of two generations stood, glasses in hands, mouths agape and rooted to the spot. Kate stood before them, radiant in a dress that could have been made for her. Edith had obviously made adjustments and had even taken the trouble to arrange Kate's hair. It was down over her shoulders, caressing the top of the dress, the dark brown merging uncannily with the cleverly chosen material of a similar hue. She was a revelation.

Joshua was first to find his voice, "Beautiful, Kate." Richard nodded his approval as he moved towards Kate and held her at arm's length.

"Edith," he said, "you are right, I shall indeed be the envy of every male guest."

* * *

It was noon when they settled the account and said goodbye to Edith and Joshua. In addition to the dress, Richard had bought several other items which caught Kate's eye, either

30

as accessories or for her general use. They also selected a doll, brightly dressed and smiling sweetly. For Josh they chose a shirt which they were sure he would like. For Jeb, more sweet-smelling tobacco. They carefully loaded the buggy with their purchases and climbed in. Kate indicated that she would like to see Jackie while she was in town, so they moved along the main street to the hotel and once more secured horse and buggy, Richard pulling a sheet over the items they had bought. Jackie had heard of their presence in town and came bouncing down the steps to meet them. The two women embraced, obviously delighted to meet up again.

"Will you stay for a bite?" invited Jackie." Dinner can be ready within the hour." Kate glanced at Richard enquiringly.

He nodded his confirmation. "You girls go and talk, I'll go and see my friend the Sheriff and join you later. My gear is still in my room." The girls went into the hotel and as he strolled along the sidewalk, he could hear their excited chatter behind him.

"Hi John," he greeted the Sheriff who was sitting behind his desk and studying the back wall.

"Richard, heard you had ridden out," said the lawman, straightening up in his chair.

"Nope," said Richard, throwing his hat in the chair, "got a date at a party tonight."

"The Marshall girl?" the Sheriff was surprised.

"Bumped into Marshall in the trail yesterday, he said to bring a partner so I'm taking Kate Mack with me," Richard said proudly.

"Well I'll be damned!" exploded the Sheriff, "you sure as hell don't waste time, do you?" Then, more jovially, "Beth and me gonna use the mail coach, her dressin' up and that." Then, after scratching his head and pondering for a moment, "Say, why don't we call at the Mack place and take you two

31

along?" Richard tried to imagine Kate riding in the buggy in that dress.

"Done," he said impetuously, "When shall we expect you?"

"Just be ready about an hour 'fore sunset, we can make it before dark then." advised the Sheriff.

Richard expressed his appreciation, then returning to his hotel room took his baggage down to the buggy. He followed the direction of the laughter, recognising the voices of Kate and Jackie. They were in the dining-room reclining in comfortable chairs. Jackie waved him into a seat at the table.

"You two have been moving apace," she said as he ate. "I hope that you won't lead my friend astray," she went on, winking at Richard.

"Jackie's coming out to look after the family tonight," announced Kate, "Can we wait another hour or so and take her back with us?"

"Sure," he confirmed, "Thanks Jackie, it will put Kate's mind at rest."

"I shan't achieve that," laughed Jackie. Richard remembered Valiant and excused himself, thanking Jackie for the meal.

"I'll be in the saloon when you are ready." he said, departing. Valiant whinnied gently as Richard descended the steps and spoke to the horse. He fed it some hay from a supply in the buggy, slapped its rump and ambled the few yards along the street.

The Emperors Delight was quiet at that hour. Just the occasional drinker here and there, leaning on the bar, or sitting at tables, gazes fixed on the glasses in front of them. As always, Richard's accent turned heads. The barman passed his beer across the counter.

"Welcome, Mr Shaw," he said affably, "how long you stayin' in town?"

"Just a few days," replied Richard as he picked up his glass and his change. He settled into a chair and sampled the tepid beer. He was immediately aware of the toothless grin two tables away. Try as he might, he could not ignore the idiot, who was one of three men at the table.

"I'm just stayin' for a few days," the man with the grin said with mock precision. Richard felt his colour rising and again tried to ignore the taunts. With the loud guffaws of the man's companions, this was difficult. To his utter relief, Kate, Jackie and the Sheriff came into the bar at that moment.

"What's this about going to the party in a coach?" chided Jackie. They all laughed and Richard called their drink orders across to the barman, who nodded his response.

"I'll have a glass of milk, please barman," the idiot mimicked, looking even more stupid.

"Shut up, Barrett." the Sheriff cut in and for a moment there was silent obedience. But the mimicking soon started again and to Kate's horror, Richard stood up and ambled over to the source of the banter.

"Listen friend," he said in his best English, "if you were to come to my country, we would welcome you and treat you kindly." He went on, breaking into the hush of the bar. "We might even fit you up with some teeth!" The laughter of all around served only to confuse the man. He stood up, swaying a little. Richard quickly took his hand and shook it. "Can I buy you a drink?" he asked. "Barman, take orders from these gentlemen." The barman, showing signs of relief, did so immediately. The grin was now gone, leaving a rather vacant expression tinged with surprise and non-comprehension. Richard returned to his table.

"We had better be going ladies," he said, "we did say to the youngsters only a few hours." He shook his head playfully at Kate. "Besides, the Sheriff here has got to wash that coach!"

They left the lawman talking at the bar and went into the

street. As they climbed into the buggy, Kate said imploringly, "Richard, please may we show you the school where we taught?" It occurred to him that in fact he only knew half the town. He had never ventured past the stores.

"Of course," he said pleasantly, although he was concerned at the length of time they had been away from the homestead. Turning the buggy into the wide street he urged Valiant towards the school.

It stood next to the church and back from the general line of the street, and was the very last building at that end of town. It was skirted by the traditional wooden picket fence. The school, a single room, one-storey building was being vacated by the children. Whooping and shouting in their freedom, they crowded past the buggy. Some of the older ones waved at Kate and Jackie, and the two ex-teachers responded energetically.

Suddenly, with the children gone, it was quiet and Richard manoeuvred the buggy around the church. He didn't even cast a glance at the trail leaving the town in an easterly direction, nor did it occur to him that his schedule dictated that he ride out in that direction today. With the two ladies as companions, it was hardly surprising, he later reflected, that leaving was not on his mind. He skirted the town at Jackie's direction and eventually picked up the main trail out of town with the hills ahead of them.

The ride homewards was a pleasant one, with Jackie in lively form, bringing out the best in Kate. Richard learned that Jackie had never married, preferring to look after her brother. Now that the business was theirs, she had no time, she emphasized strongly, to worry about men. Jackie had taught at the school with Kate, way back.

"The pay was lousy," she said, "And anyway, who in their right mind wants to spend every day with a hundred children?"

Richard took to Jackie; he suspected that there was more to this woman than her bright and carefree exterior might suggest. They travelled at a canter now and were soon back in the valley, passing the spot where Richard had met Marshall and his boys, and of course, had first seen Kate.

"You were pretty impressive back there." Jackie cut through his thoughts and he was aware of Kate's hand on his arm, as if to confirm Jackie's sentiments.

"Better than using a gun," he replied lightly still conscious of Kate's touch.

They turned into the paddock and the reception was tumultuous. Josh and Sam caught Jackie as she jumped down from the cart on Richard's arm. Kate alighted next and, for a fraction of a second, dallied as he took her hands in his. Parcels were shared out among them and the happy party made for the gate, anxious to be in the house, where a complete update of the day's events was demanded and given.

Chapter 6

Tea was a wonderful affair at which even Jeb was in high spirits. The tobacco they bought for him in town no doubt contributed towards this. There was no question of the children's presents not being well received. Josh was soon in his shirt, tucking items into his breast pocket as, he informed them, his other shirts had no pockets. Sam had her doll propped up in front of her and was holding a lengthy conversation with it, trying to ascertain what it wished to eat. Everyone was happy and appreciating the company of those around them. Richard could recall Christmas dinners at home more solemn than this.

Gradually, very gradually, a feeling of anticipation crept into the proceedings. No member of that household would say that they were conscious of it, but it became a real and present element as the evening wore on. Eventually the tension reached its climax and came rapidly to the surface when Kate rose to her feet. She declared her intention to prepare for the night's adventure; now at last they would see her in the party dress and make-up. Jackie disappeared with Kate into the bedroom. They admitted Sam only after much pleading by the excited youngster.

Suddenly Richard experienced a powerful feeling of humility, having been accepted into the bosom of this simple but wonderful family. He was proud to be associating with such fine people. He could not help but compare them with many of his arrogant and affected friends at home. It also now hit him that he was to be Kate's escort for the night, a prospect which brought with it a measure of excitement. Richard was anxious not to let her down and with this in mind, headed for the barn to make his own preparations. He decided, as he crossed the paddock, to wear his alternative outfit. This consisted of a check shirt, brown jacket and light trousers. He was pleased that he'd thought of changing, as his black garb would hardly be suitable for this occasion.

He first of all washed and shaved at the well, then walked Valiant around the paddock, muttering to the horse in a confidential manner; he was sure that the animal responded with a wink of collaboration.

Richard returned to the house in time to hear the roar of approval and the clapping of little hands. Kate stood there just as he had seen her earlier at the store. Somehow she was now more real, more natural in that setting. As he entered the room, he looked with some amusement from face to face and saw delight registered on each. Sam wore a look of sheer adoration as she stood beside her mother; it was incredible how much more alike they were now that Kate's hair was on her shoulders, as Sam's was.

Jeb broke up the happy family by announcing, and having to shout at the top of his voice, that the transport had arrived.

John Champion, Sheriff of Randolph, drove the mail-coach up to the gate, halting his team of four with a flourish, and receiving a round of applause from his audience who had gathered admiringly on the porch.

"Never seen the likes of a coach here before," muttered Jeb to no-one in particular.

Mrs. Champion was sitting next to her husband, and Richard quickly went down the steps to help her alight. "You must be Richard," she boomed, accepting his arm.

"Pleased to meet you, ma'am," he replied. She patted his arm as if to say that they would resume the conversation at some future opportunity. Richard did not doubt that indeed they would. She left him and lifted her arms to heaven.

"My, my," she boomed again, "just look at Kate!" The

party followed her into the house and engaged in the exchange of news or rather, listened as Beth Champion imparted her latest tit-bits of gossip, scandal and opinion. John shot a sideways glance at Richard.

"She's happy now," he whispered, "Knows all the town's business long 'fore I get it. Not nosey, you understand, just likes to be involved. Told me you wuz in town long afore I set eyes on yer." They chuckled, taking the drinks offered to them by Josh as the bulletin came to an end. Richard considered her a real character, sharing her husband's homely disposition.

The coach eventually moved away from the homestead, with the Sheriff encouraging the team into action. The group at the gate, waving frantically, were soon lost to sight. Richard sat up front with John and the ladies were inside the coach, thus protecting their finery from the dust of the road.

"Four horses, John?" said Richard with a smile. "Very impressive."

"You should've seen the faces in town." John replied with a laugh.

They swung down the trail which Richard now knew well, heading along the valley towards the fork. At this junction the Sheriff turned the horses towards the hills and away from the town, soon branching off to the left again, and Richard realised that he was again on new ground.

Cattle abounded and in the main continued grazing with complete indifference, just the odd one or two looking up, chewing mechanically, and following the progress of the coach with doleful eyes. The fences here were immaculate and Richard admitted to a secret admiration for the owner of this property.

Just as the sun dropped from the horizon, accentuating the outline of the hills, they approached the precincts of the house, the dwelling itself still hidden. A man on horseback sat each side of an arched gateway, motioning the coach on.

"Sheriff," they acknowledged as the coach passed them. The lawman touched his hat in response.

"Hi boys."

The house came suddenly into view as they rounded the trimmed hedgerows. Even from that distance it was magnificent. A two-storey wooden edifice of some age, Richard guessed, but of immense character. He glanced down behind him at Kate's face as she peered out of the coach window. He was pleased and relieved to see that she was also impressed and looking happy. He marvelled at the fact that, after living in this part of the world all her life, this was all new to her.

At the front of the house there was great activity. Marshall must have drafted all his men in that night. Some were helping arrivals down from saddles, others were leading horses away or driving carts and buggies to the back of the house. Arrivals were making their way to the entrance which was festooned with lamps, the glass frames of which had been coloured. Tastefully arranged bunting ran from lamp to lamp and picket to picket, the whole scene was a blaze of light and gaiety. Richard heard Kate gasp behind him, "All these people!" He gave her a smile of reassurance.

"Where are the guests coming from?" Richard asked the Sheriff.

"Other ranches in the territory, some from town, mostly old school friends and the like, I guess, it's much the same crowd every year." He paused as they drew up, enjoying the attention the coach was receiving. "Some cattle dealers from the rail-head comin' too, I hear tell. The night will see a lot of business talk no doubt."

They jumped to the ground and assisted their respective partners down from the high coach. Richard noticed the interest shown in Kate by the men standing by.

"Must be a thousand lamps in there," murmured the

Sheriff to himself. They approached the entrance and Richard beckoned to Beth and John to go ahead of them.

"Enjoy yourselves, you two," said Beth as she propelled her husband past them. Richard placed Kate's arm inside his and followed.

A queue had accumulated in the corridor as guests who had preceded them waited to be summoned into the vast ballroom.

"Don't leave me," whispered Kate in Richard's ear.

"With you looking like that?" he breathed, trying to sound matter of fact.

"Sheriff John Champion and Beth Champion," the over-dressed master of ceremonies announced with clarity.

"Oh, God!" panicked Kate as they waited. Richard prompted the over-dressed man, who made a great show of recording their details. It seemed an eternity they waited as Kate fidgeted and Richard squeezed her arm in support. When the over-dressed man slipped from view, they knew their moment was near.

"Mrs Kate Mack and Mr Richard Shaw," the clarion voice rang out as they moved forward.

There was a distinct lull in the buzz of conversation as Kate and Richard entered the massive, brightly-lit room. To people used to hearing the same familiar names at all public events, the unlikely combination just announced was sure to create interest and curiosity, particularly as they were not even on the official guest list. All eyes followed them to the centre of the room where their host was standing with his daughter.

"Kate, Richard, delighted that you have come." Dan Marshall said with unjustified familiarity. "My daughter, Virginia," he went on proudly. They shook hands and Richard said that Kate and he hoped she was having a happy day. Richard was struck by the girl's beauty and bearing. Her father's daughter indeed.

"I claim a dance later," she laughingly demanded of Richard, flicking her shining black hair from her face, "You really must tell me all about England," she concluded, with the emphasis on the 'must'. Richard answered in the affirmative on both counts and led Kate away as the next guests claimed the attention of their hostess. He caught sight of the bar ranging along one wall and steered Kate towards it. He filled two glasses with punch and they stood together, for the moment not recognising anyone, isolated in that crowded room.

"There is one man too few in this room," hissed Kate, her eyes on Virginia who was enjoying her role as centre of attraction.

Richard shot her a disapproving look, "I could not refuse, could I?" he asked her. Richard was aware of the interested glances Kate was receiving from the male guests, and the rather more suspicious looks from their female companions.

Musicians were assembling on a small platform erected for the occasion and there was an air of expectation prevalent.

"Are you feeling better now?" Richard asked Kate softly. She nodded, sipping her punch, "But don't leave me for a moment." she repeated, but with rather less fervour than she'd said it some minutes earlier. Richard waited for Kate to drain her glass and went to refill hers and his own with the refreshing liquid. He turned with hands full to see Kate talking to four men. As he rejoined her they smiled, nodded respectfully and withdrew.

"What was all that about?" Richard asked, handing her a glass.

"I've been booked for four dances," she replied with disbelief in her tone. They heard a voice behind them.

"And you are booked for one too, Mr Richard." They turned to see who had spoken, half knowing before seeing the face. Beth continued, "You will have John requesting a dance

Kate, that is if he stays sober long enough and gets away from Dan Marshall."

"What happened to Mrs Marshall?" Richard enquired, suddenly curious and ignoring the request for a dance.

"Never was one," said Beth, "One of the few mysteries I've been unable to solve." They laughed and began to relax.

The musicians tuned their instruments, piano, fiddles, banjo and drums, then commenced playing a waltz of early European vintage Richard took Kate in his arms, demanding the first dance, surprised that he felt annoyed at the claims of the other men. They moved easily around the floor. Other couples were smiling at them now and their tension evaporated. Richard felt then that he had known Kate all his life, not just for two days.

Kate was whisked away for the second dance, so Richard sought out Beth. In the course of that one dance he was instructed on each guest's connections and credentials concerning their eligibility for invitation to the celebrations.

Virginia sailed across the floor during a lapse in the music and drew Richard to one side. He scanned the room for Kate, but in vain.

"I must see the world," Virginia was saying, "When are you going back to your country, Richard?"

"I'm due to sail in a couple of months," he replied "But I am not sure." They moved onto the floor as the music struck up again. For some reason, Richard thought of Dave waiting for him. He would certainly have approved of Richard's female partners that evening.

Virginia was a superb dancer, showing up his own comparative awkwardness. She looked up into his face. "How would I get to England, Richard? There would be a lot of riding between here and the coast, I take it?" He explained that the rail-road covered a very small part of the journey, and advised her to wait a year or so, as the track was being laid at a phenomenal rate. "Will you let me travel with you, Richard? Daddy would agree to that, I know," she implored. Her directness took him completely by surprise and he froze inwardly, unable to frame a reply. She tightened her grip on his arm as they moved around the floor. He looked down at her lovely young face which was up-turned, searching his for an answer. He forced a smile. "I will have to think about that." he mumbled inadequately. His conscience reprimanded him. How could he consider it? What would Dave say when he arrived with her? She would never tolerate the privations of weeks on the trail! How could he travel with a young girl? What would Kate's reaction be?

He suddenly and unaccountably calculated that the seven years Virginia was his junior was exactly the number of years Kate was his senior.

The music stopped and his obligation came to an end. He escorted Virginia back to the centre of the room, handing her over to one of several young men anticipating a dance with her that evening.

"Promise to think about it," were her parting words, and he nodded, smiling.

People moved in all directions as the musicians took a break. Kate was nowhere in sight and Richard suddenly felt an overwhelming sense of being a visitor in a foreign country. He thought fleetingly of Caroline back in London, and his family. He went to the bar in an attempt to drown his confusion.

Chapter 7

Later that evening guests were invited to entertain each other, usually by reciting poetry or singing. Richard was able to hear two items as he stood at the end of the bar. The first was a thin, reedy rendering of a song unknown to him, performed by a tiny and very nervous woman, bird-like in her mannerisms. The second was a good bass voice singing a robust interpretation of a battle hymn which had obviously begun life in the recent war.

Before he could hear another contribution, he felt a hand on his arm. The over-dressed man with the clarion voice was at his elbow, requesting that Richard follow him. They crossed the floor and left the room, turning again at the end of the corridor into the study.

Already present and seated was, to his amazement, Kate. Richard observed a stranger to her right, then Dan Marshall and the Sheriff with his back to the door. Marshall stood, indicating to Richard the seat opposite him and to Kate's left. The stranger also got to his feet and Marshall introduced him.

"You two haven't met, I believe. Richard, this is Luke Chadwick, Luke, Richard Shaw." The two men eyed each other, and Richard disliked what he saw, the shifty look avoiding direct eye contact. "Luke is the president of the Cattleman's Association," Marshall continued, "who just happens to be here tonight." He laughed but his attempt at levity was entirely lost on those around the table. The silence was broken only by muffled applause coming from the ballroom.

All those around the table studied Marshall for a moment, looking for some opening statement as to why they had been pulled away from the party. A song got under way along the corridor, but was drowned out by Marshall's powerful introduction.

"Seeing as we are all here tonight," he began carefully, "I thought it would be an idea to have a chat. I won't keep you long," he added quickly, "we must get back to the party soon." Richard was surprised at the rancher's nervousness. Marshall continued, "Before we start the serious drinking and have ourselves a real good time, as I say, I thought we could talk a spell." He beamed at those around him and received hollow laughs from the Sheriff and the Association man, who had obviously already embarked upon their serious drinking. There was another uncomfortable pause as the five surveyed each other. Marshall addressed Richard across the table. "Kate will not talk without you being present Richard, nothing wrong with that of course," he hastened to add. "Glad to have you with us." Richard glanced to his right at Kate and a smile passed between them.

Chadwick was fidgeting at Kate's side all through Marshall's laboured preamble, and took the opportunity of a lull in the proceedings to open his account. "Look you here, Mrs Mack," he said, glaring at Kate from his close proximity, "you really cannot hold up progress any longer. It's a big business we are in and you cannot sit on a piece of land because it's yours and ignore the world around you. Access must be allowed to cattle to drink at that river."

"Must?" Richard cut in hotly, "Must, did I hear you say? Mr Chadwick you have entirely the wrong approach, I should leave the negotiating to Mr Marshall if I were you," concluded Richard, congratulating himself for disliking the man.

"And what do you know about cattle rights, sir?" sneered Chadwick.

"More than you know about the law, that is certain," countered Richard with a glance at the Sheriff. The lawman drained the glass at his elbow, turning the matter over in his befuddled mind. In the background, applause broke out and John Champion took his cue.

"Negotiation ish the way forward," he slurred, "You jush can't drive cattle over private land." This pronouncement was the last the Sheriff would make that night, as he soon lost contact with consciousness. Richard continued as the applause in the ballroom subsided.

"What are you asking Kate to provide, Mr Marshall?" The big man considered the question, holding up a restraining hand to Chadwick, who would have answered.

"Where the foothills touch the valley and Kate's land," he explained, "I need to water the cattle at that end of the range." Richard waited for Kate to take up the questioning, but her look told him to continue.

"So what is your proposition?" he asked. Chadwick was first to respond.

"What the hell are you talkin' to this dude for, Dan? He don't know a steer's arse from its ..." Marshall again raised his hand and silenced him. Richard responded quickly.

"If we are going to talk seriously, then you'll have to get rid of this idiot!" he said to Marshall, cocking his thumb at Chadwick. The Association man was changing colour rapidly and Richard realised that Kate was hating every moment of this exchange. He wondered how she had been persuaded to join the group. Marshall spoke evenly.

"Luke, go and get yourself a drink while we finish up here." Such was the authority of this man that Chadwick rose obediently and stormed out of the room.

"How does a man like that get elected?" enquired Richard as the door slammed.

"He speaks up while others are still thinking," Marshall replied simply. To Richard's relief, Kate found her voice, no longer intimidated by the Association man's presence.

"What do you suggest?" she asked of Marshall. "Access for hundreds of steers across my land?"

"Something like that," said Marshall uncertainly.

"What if Kate sold you enough land to afford you constant watering?" Richard proposed.

"Great," returned Marshall, looking at Kate hopefully. She responded by looking from one to the other, a frown on her face as she considered the implications.

Richard left his seat and occupied the chair vacated by Chadwick at Kate's side. The movement inspired the Sheriff to stagger from the room. Richard leaned towards Kate and explained softly; "You can dictate your own terms, Kate. You'll earn some money to spend on the children and the house. You can live peaceably with your neighbours. You can insist that Marshall maintains the fencing. Will you really miss that strip of land up there?"

Marshall, elbows on the table and hands clasped, looked on expectantly. Kate nodded slowly and somewhat sadly. Richard, mistaking her mood, pressed on with the practical details.

"Kate will consider selling off that section on three conditions, Dan."

"Name them," responded Marshall with enthusiasm.

"One," said Richard carefully, "the price must be right. Two, you install and maintain the fences along the strip. Three, there must be no possibility of fouling the water as it flows into Kate's patch."

"Done," exploded the rancher, jumping up. "I'll pay twice the going rate for the land and observe the fencing clause. Any infected cattle will be kept at this end of the range."

The two men waited for Kate's reaction and confirmation that the terms were acceptable to her. She nodded. "I agree," she whispered. Marshall shook Kate's hand and thanked them both. As they moved back into the atmosphere of celebration, Marshall promised to be in touch within days. They parted company once back in the ballroom, and Kate and Richard were met immediately by Beth.

"Just coming to fetch you two," she boomed for the benefit of all present. "Hear tell you're a musician, Richard." Her booming voice now reached fortissimo. "Got you down for a turn later," she added, rushing off to organise some other unsuspecting soul.

The over-dressed man was using his talent to good effect. He announced; "Mr Dan Marshall, ladies and gentlemen." There was polite applause as the rancher cleared his throat vigorously, and held aloft his hands in mock modesty.

"I am very pleased to welcome you all to Virginia's birthday celebrations. She tells me that the little girl I once had has now become a woman. Looking at her tonight, I think she may be right." Muttered confirmation from predominantly male throats ensued. Virginia reacted with feigned embarrassment. "I don't know how long I shall keep her - she has this hankering after foreign lands - I just hope that she finishes up right back here when she's done roamin'." He paused, continuing thoughtfully, "I am proud tonight. You will not know, any of you, that Virginia's mother died giving birth to her." He looked away, a frown fleetingly crossing his face, and there was complete stillness in that room. Richard found Beth's face as she nodded knowingly. "My wife would have been mighty proud to see her little girl tonight." Virginia was genuinely moved, obviously knowing nothing of her mother. The big man recovered. "Anyways, most of you have visited this house on many occasions and I'm real pleased to see you all again." He smiled at the assembled company who responded appropriately. "Tonight is unusual," he went on, "in that there are two guests who have never set foot in my house before and I want you to welcome them. Kate Mack, a long-standing neighbour of mine, welcome Kate! Beside her stands a young man who has travelled many miles to be here with us tonight, Richard Shaw from England, welcome Richard!" The guests caught the humour of the moment and put their hands together happily as Kate and Richard acknowledged the warm reception. "Now," Marshall shouted when he could be heard, "I must say on behalf of Virginia that she is now ready and happy to receive the gifts you have so kindly brought. Enjoy yourselves folks!" His arms went high in the air again as applause broke out from the guests. Kate, recovering from the embarrassment of the last few minutes and fearing more, nudged Richard.

"We haven't got a present, how could I have forgotten that?" she gasped. Richard delved into his pocket and pulled a coin from it. He placed it in the palm of Kate's hand.

"What is this?" she whispered.

"An English sovereign," he answered, "valuable at home."

She beamed, "What a good idea," and moved forward to present the gift on their behalf.

Richard was discussing American and English wars with a group of men when he was extracted from its midst by Beth.

"It's your turn now," she said, and led him away through the crowd. Kate was talking with a former pupil and Richard caught her eye, shrugging his shoulders and opening his palms in resignation as he approached the platform at Beth's heels.

Richard had noticed earlier that the players had left. The tiny dais was now empty apart from the piano. He lifted the cover, surveying the keys, then turned to address the guests. "I would like to say a word of thanks to Dan Marshall for his warm welcome to Kate and me. We have been delighted to share this happy time with you and, of course, Virginia. For my part I have drifted into many towns during recent months, but have not found in any of them such warm and friendly people as in Randolph and its surrounding district. You good folk will remain in my memory. Thank you." Hushed acceptance of his compliments followed, and the audience anticipated his playing. Richard's repertoire of pieces committed to memory was very limited. He thought for a moment then gently introduced the opening semiquavers of 'Fur Elise,' and he became immersed as the music unfolded. He was pleasantly surprised at the quality of tone and tuning the instrument possessed. The subdued and rather abrupt final chord was followed by enthusiastic applause. Beth was informing those around her that she thought it was Mozart! Richard unwittingly put the matter right by announcing that his second item was also by Beethoven; one of his German dances. This offering received an even warmer response, its rhythmic majesty appealing to all. Richard then remembered the sing-song at the homestead and Kate's tuneful and pleasing voice. "For my final contribution, I am asking Kate to join me." he said, eyeing the sheet of music on the piano stand. He dared not look at Kate as she was propelled onto the platform.

"Can you sing this?" he pointed to the music.

"Abide with me? Not here. Not now!" she protested.

"Just imagine that you're singing at home." he encouraged. Richard played a few introductory bars and the room fell silent.

Kate sang, gaining confidence with each verse. She resembled, Richard considered, an angel, illuminated as she was in the lamp light. She carefully phrased each line with feeling and conviction, it was a moving experience for those who listened. The hush which followed spoke volumes, and seemed to be eternal. As she sung, Richard's mind oddly associated the sentiments of the hymn with Kate's words; 'don't leave me for a moment'. They left the platform and gradually conversation resumed, Kate and Richard found themselves once again in separate groups.

The happy night wore on. Kate and Richard saw each

51

other only fleetingly, but on these occasions they always restored contact with mutual smiles. He was pleased that she was popular among her neighbours and that she had broken the ice socially. Kate had known many of the guests for some years, mainly through her teaching. Her circumstances had been responsible for the drifting apart of friendships and associations.

Just before dawn, Virginia, her hands sweeping her black hair from her face, mounted the platform. "Thank you, thank you for the lovely presents and for accepting the invitations to be here tonight. I do hope that you have enjoyed yourselves, it has been wonderful to see you all again. If you are still hungry, then please feel free to breakfast on the remains of the food around the room." There was a chorus of approval as she smiled warmly. Virginia raised her hand, calling for silence once more. "Before you leave and head for home, I would like to sing for you, and as Richard played the accompaniment so well, perhaps he would help me too." Richard went very hot. So that was why the music was left on the piano. Enthusiasm encouraged by alcohol led to him being manhandled forward to the platform. Her performance of 'Abide with Me' was a good one. Virginia too looked angelic, perhaps it was the effect of the lamplight. Her voice was pure, but less mature than Kate's. Comparisons were inevitable and Richard wondered if the two most beautiful women present had not been in competition throughout the night, albeit unconsciously. The guests responded with respect as they had after the first performance, although many were amused at the situation and it set tongues wagging anew.

Preparations were being made for the homeward journeys. Some of the guests were staying but most were moving towards the entrance. Farewells could be heard in corridors and out in the morning air. Virginia had time to remind Richard of his promise to consider her as a travelling partner.

He in turn apologised for his stupidity in pre-empting the hymn. She smiled her forgiveness and they parted in good humour. Guests were waiting for carriages and horses to appear from the stables. As they waited, Marshall shook hands with both Kate and Richard, expressing his appreciation of the deal.

The Sheriff was, at Beth's direction, bundled into the inner coach and she joined him. Richard lifted Kate up onto the front bench and jumped up beside her, taking the reins from an attendant. Driving four horses was going to be a new experience for him.

There were, as before, two men on horseback at the arched gateway. This time Richard identified one of them by his damaged nose. There was no greeting, just sullen looks as the coach passed through.

The air was fresh, as the sun appeared announcing the new day. A light breeze had persuaded Kate to wear a warm shawl around her shoulders. She sat close, with her arm through Richard's, appreciating the clear air after a night of the smell and fumes of many lamps. They exchanged experiences of the people they had met and talked to, comparing personalities and the different tastes in dress. It was comfortable, just the two of them on that coach bench. There would be no interruptions or claims made upon them for a while.

"Kate," he said after a lull during which he almost lost control of the horses, "I must ask you, who got you to sit in on those talks?"

"John did," she replied. "He was getting drunk and a bit emotional. He made me promise to talk and in any case, you were dancing with the lovely Virginia!"

"You were in great demand too," he countered, "Don't leave me for a moment," he mimicked, "I had one dance with you and then lost you for most of the night." They laughed together as the team trotted on, nearly clear of the Marshall ranch.

"Richard, I never imagined that I could ever hate you, but when you made me sing - and to sing that hymn, wasn't it awful?" she exclaimed, putting her hands over her mouth. "I could have died on the spot!" Richard looked at her.

"I was very proud of you Kate." He tightened his arm trapping hers, "I did apologise to Virginia." Then after a suitable pause, he continued; "She wants me to take her to England."

"What!" exploded Kate, moving away from him, "that's ridiculous - isn't it?"

"Of course, of course," he said reassuringly. He grinned as she snuggled into him again, whether for warmth or affection he didn't know, but it made him feel good.

They were nearing the valley and on familiar ground, having negotiated the fork.

"Are you leaving today, Richard?" she asked, framing with words the fear in her heart. They jogged along in silence for a while. Richard considered his answer very carefully, aware that she was watching him as if life itself depended on his reply.

"I have to review my situation, Kate." he replied slowly, then deliberately and earnestly he explained, "I have reached, if you like, one of life's crossroads, you must have come across them yourself. For the first time in my life I am not sure of the path I must take. The signs are clear, and each destination is indicated, I am simply incapable of making my mind up, and it's a new experience for me. How do I decide?" She nodded in understanding and he wished that he was somewhere more conducive to making important decisions. Sitting on a bouncing coach being covered in dust from sixteen hooves was far from ideal.

He studied her and at that moment saw beyond her outward attraction and perceived a beauty within. He realised simultaneously that his emotions were taking over. He had been educated against his heart ruling his mind. His training with Dave had reinforced this approach. 'Let your emotions in and you're finished, old son', Dave had warned. Dave would see the way forward, why can't I? thought Richard. His confusion was compounded by the pressure on his arm; Kate seemed to be exerting as much persuasion as she dared.

He considered other major decisions he had made in his life, all executed with clinical assurance. His clear objective of three days ago had deserted him and he was sure that the lady by his side must be responsible for this.

A long silence ensued as the sun climbed and the valley smelled fresh around them. What would this day bring? Richard was nervous and uncertain. He clearly had one of two options: ride out and maintain the schedule he had so meticulously adhered to, or stay with Kate. How could he do either? He had an overwhelming feeling of being trapped.

As the homestead came into view, he said on impulse, but with conviction; "Kate, if I do leave, I will be back." She looked up at him and he kissed her gently.

"Thank you for some very happy hours, Richard," she said, and wept softly beside him.

* * *

The homestead was quiet as the coach arrived. Richard halted the team by the barn so as not to disturb the sleeping family in the house. Kate jumped down into his arms, lingered a moment, then walked into the house without a backward glance.

Richard saddled Valiant and by the time he returned to the coach Jackie was installed on the driving bench. She was looking down at Beth, trying to hold a conversation to the accompaniment of snores from the Sheriff.

They moved off along the valley with Valiant tethered behind. Jackie was her usual vivacious self and full of vigour, even at that hour. She plied Richard with questions about the

55

party, demanding to know who was there and what they wore. She gleaned little from him and he imagined Jackie and Beth getting together over coffee later in the day.

Jackie told Richard that Kate was going to sleep until midday. Richard informed Jackie of Kate's acceptance amongst her neighbours and gave her the details of the transaction that had been made. Jackie was delighted with the first piece of news, but failed to respond at all to the latter.

They reached the town just as it was waking and Jackie dropped into Richard's arms outside the hotel in time for her breakfast duties. Jackie gave him a quizzical look as she left him, which had a disturbing effect.

Richard assisted Beth in getting the Sheriff to bed and was amused by Beth's hope that the bank was not raided that day.

He deposited the coach and horses at the town stables where the bleary-eyed ostler was relieved to see him and, in particular, the coach. He explained that the mail run was due to leave within the hour.

Richard rode back through the town and out towards the valley. His intention was to sleep in the barn for the morning, but he decided that sleep would not come easily. He rode on up the valley, passing the homestead turn-off and kept going along the trail into the Mack lands.

He reached the foothills and dismounted, walking Valiant to the place where the river emerged from the rocky slopes and settled into the comparative level of Kate's meadow, before snaking off towards the homestead. At that time of year the river was a mere trickle in the centre of the bed. He could imagine the rain's effect on the flow; the water would rise several feet and extend to where he stood at that moment.

Richard gave Valiant his freedom and the horse gratefully nuzzled the fresh grass around him and pulled up large quantities with a ripping sound, audible in the stillness. Richard strolled along the riverbank as the sun rose still higher. He was suddenly struck by the peace and tranquillity of the place. There was a beauty rarely found in that hard and rugged land. He guessed that Kate would regret losing this glimpse of heaven on the extremes of her property. It was hard to visualise hundreds of hooves churning up the meadow and the river bed, not only devastating the area but fouling the little water that would be allowed to flow on at this time of the year. Richard experienced a strong feeling of guilt. Kate had trusted his judgement, but somewhere along the line his law training had failed him in that he had not checked every detail before coming to a final decision. Perhaps Chadwick had been right to tell Richard not to meddle in an affair he knew nothing about.

Richard mounted, and ambled Valiant towards the homestead, halting at the place where Austin Mack had died. A little group of stones marked the spot where Kate's happiness had come to an end over two years before. Richard paid silent homage to the father of Sam and Josh, of whom he would surely have been proud had he lived.

The awful truth hit Richard like a hammer blow. This was part of the section Marshall was buying, and Kate must have known it. How could he have been so blind and insensitive, how could he have repaid the kindness the family had shown him by treating them in this way? Impulsively, he spurred Valiant into action, immediately apologising to the horse for his ruthlessness, but nevertheless maintaining a steady run.

Richard left Valiant on the trail, making it to the barn on foot. He packed his gear swiftly and, feeling wretched, made a stealthy retreat to his horse. An encounter with one of the children now would have destroyed him and he was grateful that they were probably preoccupied with their chores at the back of the house. With a long glance at the homestead and a silent prayer, hurried but sincere, he urged Valiant along the valley trail towards the town.

He had intended to skirt the town but decided, on a late impulse, to follow the familiar arc into Randolph. Richard tied his horse to the hotel rail and sought out Jackie, who was now clearing the dining-room of breakfast dishes. She heard him out in silence, which in itself indicated the measure of her distress. "I've failed her" were his last words as he strode from the diner with Jackie staring after him.

Richard deposited some money at the bank in Kate's name. Richard immediately recognised the manager as the over-dressed man with the clarion voice from the previous night. The strong voice welcomed him and its owner agreed to supervise the sale of property between Kate and Marshall in Richard's absence. Richard marvelled at the manager's alertness after a hectic night at the Marshall ranch.

Man and horse walked slowly along the main street, passing the stores of 'E & J Bennett' and the school at which Kate and Jackie had taught. Richard finally passed the church and regretted that he had not had opportunity to attend. The trail East was before him, a new challenge and a fresh start after the mess he had made of the last few days. He jumped up into the saddle and set Valiant at a canter, and in his humiliation Richard did not look back for some time. He came to a rise beyond which the town would be lost to view. He halted and turned his horse, gazing out at Randolph with the now strong sun on his back. It surprised him how out of focus the town had become, until he realised, without shame, that his eyes were moist. Other towns he had already forgotten. This town and its people he would never forget. His eyes would not clear so he swung Valiant around, took a last backward glance and rode off into the sun.

Chapter 8

Richard rode hard for the next three days, stopping only to pick up provisions, eat and sleep. Valiant was proving his worth but Richard had to be fair to the grey and the duration of the stops was dictated more by the horse's needs than his own. He set himself targets; a bluff, a solitary tree or the crest of a hill to be reached or even passed before he would consider taking a break.

He tried desperately to push recent events from his mind but was having no success. In his wretched and frustrated mood he did not trust himself amongst people and shunned human contact as much as possible.

Gradually he slowed his pace, knowing that he had made up the lost day and was now back on his original schedule, but the knowledge gave him little satisfaction. Gradually, the thought of riding in this fashion for another six weeks or so had filled him with dread, the excitement of the venture having evaporated. He was now going through the motions in order to reach his destination.

Richard considered joining a coach going East to break the monotony; he had seen many whilst travelling principal trails. He discarded that idea as Valiant would have to run tethered in its wake. The rail-road was the only alternative. Richard warmed to this method of covering the miles and decided to investigate this possibility at the next sign of civilisation.

He realised that any habitation could be days away, as the trail was leading him into desert country, which was going to prove pretty inhospitable. There would certainly be much time to reflect, for better or, he suspected, for worse.

The homestead, now miles behind him, was always prominent in his mind, as was Kate. Each member of that close family featured in his thoughts. Mannerisms, odd bits of conversation and locations would appear in his mind's eye, not immediately identified, but eventually associated always with Kate or her children. Her beauty, gentleness and goodness were virtues on which he dwelt. Other characters came to mind as he rode, good people who had accepted him and made him welcome. Even the less attractive residents of the neighbourhood, some of whom he had clashed with, adopted a more affable nature as his recollections flowed. One question insisted on staying close to the surface of his thoughts: why was he leaving all this behind?

Richard ran into a drifter travelling West. He gleaned from him, over a coffee pot, that a rail-road ran from a settlement just a day's ride from where they'd camped. It involved a minor deviation from the direction he was following but, as the man explained, the overall time saved would more than compensate for that. Richard's companion was interested in his accent and origin. He himself was an ex-lawman whose services had been dispensed with by his town when financing the post had become impossible.

The two drifters talked into the night and took to their blankets only when the stock of wood needed replenishing and the fire spluttered its last. At daylight, his fifth morning out of Randolph, Richard wished his companion well and the two set off in opposite directions.

It was surprising to him that there had not been more conversations on the trail. Those riders he had encountered tended to move on by with a brief, albeit friendly 'Howdee' or pass the time of day with a nod or touch of their hats. Richard had also expected more traffic on the main routes between the towns he passed through, perhaps comparing them with the highways at home, where travellers would frequently meet a coach or four-wheeled vehicle of some kind.

His riding routine reverted to its normal pattern. This consisted of walking Valiant in the main, with an odd canter, but on occasion, and where the terrain encouraged it, giving the grey full reign and getting a 'full head of steam' (to quote a contemporary locomotive term). At other times he would dismount and walk the stiffness out of his limbs, leading Valiant or letting the horse meander around him, particularly where the grass was lush. Richard loved his horse and accepted the undoubted intelligence of the animal. Those big dark eyes registered, he was certain, understanding and complete loyalty.

The one aspect of months in the saddle that Richard disliked was the lack of sanitary arrangements. There were adequate opportunities to perform natural bodily functions on those lonely trails, but the rudimentary nature of the process jarred on his background and upbringing making it somewhat offensive. When a stream was available, as was now the case, then he was considerably happier. Richard smiled to himself as he dangled his hands in the swiftly moving water. He stared into its shallow depths at the green strips of weed constantly tugged by the swift flow. As his mind's eye focused on that other waterway he had left behind him, Richard wondered if he was not resisting, like the greenery below him, the inevitable flow, the tide of events that had engulfed him. He shrugged off his reverie and whistled to Valiant.

Late in the day Richard was attracted by the glint of metal which proved to be the track for which he was searching. He followed as it curled away to the North and into a mis-match of buildings, obviously assembled hastily on the arrival of the permanent way a couple of years before. Pens and corrals were in abundance, suggesting that this was a major location for the transporting of cattle and other livestock.

Richard learned that a train heading East was due to leave mid-morning the next day. He was advised by a cowhand who

61

travelled regularly on the train that he would have to disembark the same night at the track's terminus, where construction was still underway. He decided to clean up and remove his five-day beard. He found adequate accommodation for Valiant, but rather spartan lodgings for himself in the Rail-road Hotel.

Richard ate in the hotel and later retired to the lounge, carrying his beer across to a corner seat. The increasing affluence of ranchers in the vicinity was apparent, by their spending power and the fine clothes of both the men and women.

He resisted his habitual urge to write in his diary, feeling little enthusiasm for the task and choosing instead to retire early in an endeavour to catch up on sleep lost the previous night around the camp fire. Richard stretched out on the lumpy and springless bed, knowing that sleep would come only as his mind wearied of its regular retrospective pattern, involving his stupidity and flight.

It was nearer noon when the train arrived the next day and an impatient Richard boarded the carriage nearest the horse-coach. He supervised Valiant's installation and security, and that of his saddle-bags. He would visit the horse at regular intervals, he decided, and with this in mind sought a seat in the adjacent coach. He chose a window position and stared out at the bustle on the low platform. Smoke eddied around the station so that people were one moment visible and the next obliterated. An official had informed him that the train would be pulling out 'directly' which, Richard reflected, could mean anything in this land. However, he had to admit to an element of anticipation regarding his first journey on the rail-road system.

Sitting with his leather case on his lap, fingers idly playing with the straps, he thought again of his diary with its comprehensive record up until a week ago. He slipped it out of the case and glanced through its leaves. There were three pages on which no entry had been made. How could he possibly bring the record up to date? Where would he start? The easy option was to discontinue updating it and terminate its existence. He considered the hours he would have to spend on the train, a copy of Dickens' 'David Copperfield' his only distraction from the noisy, lurching environment. He took up his pencil and began writing, suddenly lost in the events of recent days.

Richard was so preoccupied that he had failed to observe another passenger taking the seat opposite him. Only when he paused to stare into space, deep in thought, did he notice her.

"I do beg your pardon," he said, rising, "I was far away."

"No matter," she said, "don't let me disturb you, honey." Richard took his seat and continued with his writing, while his travelling companion busied herself with superficial toiletries. He put the diary down, running out of space and resolving to resume at a later opportunity on a sheet of paper which could be attached to the appropriate pages.

"Haven't seen you on this run before," said the lady, dabbing her nose with an excess of powder and giving him an exaggerated smile. Richard shook his head, and she went on: "I know most of the passengers who travel regularly - you English?"

"Yes, I am, Richard Shaw is the name."

"I'm Katherine, most people call me Kate." Richard stared at her, speechless. He saw the thick make-up on a girl about his own age, the tinted hair and the gaudy pink lipstick which gave her complexion a pallid effect. She mistook his silent attention and slipped off her jacket, revealing a dress Richard guessed had been made for someone half her size. Her breasts seemed to be striving for freedom which, as she leaned towards him, they almost achieved. He was enveloped in the aroma of cheap, sweet perfume. The rise in his temperature was not the result of any erotic spectacle before him, but of his annoyance with it. To be approached in this way and to be confronted with the name he respected more than any other was just too much.

"I think you had better find another seat, young lady," Richard said evenly, "I'm sure that some of your regulars will be on board," he added spitefully. She straightened and looked as though she would cause a scene, staring at him and puzzled by his aggressive attitude. Without a word, she exposed one complete breast to him in defiance, tucked it away, donned her jacket and flounced off up the coach. The chuckles of two men could be heard from across the aisle. Simultaneously the locomotive screamed and the smoke thickened all around. The coach shuddered, then moved slowly forward to the rhythm of the huge iron beast at its head.

Richard spent the day reading and gazing out of the window, where he saw drastic changes in the landscape occur with regularity. His reading consisted of paragraphs, or at the very most, a page at a time. Then his eyes would be drawn to the window through which the variations in topography were unfolding. Now a barren plain; then a range of hills; next a river snaking away and narrowing towards the horizon; then human activity introducing a township and perhaps a station at which the train either eased to a halt or screamed defiance. His fascination with this land could not suppress the nagging feeling of regret that possessed him. With each mile the feeling grew and his question remained unanswered: why was he increasing the distance between himself and, he had to admit it, Kate?

The afternoon heat in the coach became insufferable and Richard spent a great deal of time in the more open and airy stable coach. In his present mood, he much preferred the company of his horse to that of loud human beings, who seemed to form a majority on that particular train. Richard could confide in his equine friend and whispered into the large, flicking ear that Valiant should take this opportunity to rest as much as possible because that night would see them on the trail again.

They left the train at the rail-head amidst much activity. The track was to extend eastwards and men and beasts laboured and toiled in the cool of the evening. Temporary shacks and stables were scattered everywhere with no semblance of order or planning. Richard was keen to get clear of this mayhem before darkness fell.

Later that night he made camp, letting Valiant wander and choose the choicest grass available in a tiny gully where water ran in the wet season. It was now dry but afforded some shelter from the night breeze which carried just a hint of chill. His experiences of the day had been interesting but how glad he had been to lead Valiant down from the train and ride off into the privacy of the trail. He suspected that he was becoming anti-social, uncharacteristic of someone for whom company had always meant a lot.

As Richard lit a fire he recalled Dave's exasperation at his first attempts. Successful on this occasion, the only sounds were in fact the crackling of the fire and the hiss of boiling water spilling onto the flames. Occasionally he would recognise the sound of grass being pulled as Valiant munched somewhere in the darkness. He drank the hot coffee and indulged in a small whisky. He decided not to eat, the inactivity of the day not having given him an appetite.

Richard calculated that the day had saved him over a week's riding, and that Dave's home must be only three weeks away. He calculated too that he would soon join the trail he'd used on his outward journey, familiarity would assist his progress on his way to the coast. He was anxious to reach it without delay.

Richard lay back on his saddle and thought briefly of home and his family. He wondered if his father's health had in fact deteriorated as predicted by his physician. Mother would, no doubt, be organising the family home, appointing and dismissing servants and gardeners with monotonous regularity. Caroline came into his mind's vision, and he missed her at that moment. He was sure that she would find another suitor in his absence. He considered his own career in law, for which he had trained. Could he really settle to the routine of office and courtroom that his father had planned for him? He knew that William Shaw's ambition was to make his son the third partner in the firm, with himself and George Steady playing the senior roles. As Richard lay under the stars his life in London seemed a million miles away. He watched the rising moon and wondered if it was shedding its glow simultaneously over his manor home and here over the camp fire.

He regretted his loss of resolve and clear cut objectives of two weeks ago, knowing deep within him that he would never possess such incentives again. Perhaps he was belatedly growing up and was experiencing the development from youth to maturity. Whatever the reason for his uncertainty, he knew its source. That minor incident on the steps of Bennett's store had not only altered the planned course of events but, even more worrying, his attitudes and ambitions. He resolved to pursue his present aim of reaching the coast where he would have time to take stock of the situation.

The next couple of weeks were uneventful. Richard, now on familiar territory, bought supplies from store proprietors he had seen on his outward journey, many of whom gave him a nod of recognition.

The last week on that trail was a miserable one due to the deterioration in the weather. It was now getting late in the year and the climate had changed literally overnight. He awoke one morning long before sun up needing an extra blanket. Midway through the next day it became wet, and from that moment on he rode hunched into his long coat, hat pulled forward to fend off the battering and stinging rain.

Richard cursed his luck. After months of fine and dry weather here he was, days from the coast, with winter descending. Dave and he had discussed the fact that his return voyage would again be a winter one, but both had accepted the inevitability of it. Richard had arrived during the winter so knew what to expect, dreading the return across the Atlantic nevertheless.

He spent that last night at a stage post and slept soundly in the knowledge that only a few miles now separated him from a welcome reunion.

Chapter 9

There were four members of the Holland household. Nat was a shipping agent whose involvement with the ocean, its ships and cargoes, was total. A dapper little man whose lithe, five feet high frame exuded boundless energy. His dark curls leapt about his head, suggesting an absent-minded and erratic nature. Such an assessment would have been a long way from the truth. Nat was shrewd in business and utterly reliable. His wife, Sarah, of the same height but of a stockier build, was the epitome of fastidiousness. Her dark thick hair was kept in an immaculate bun with not a strand out of place. She bustled where her husband darted, but she was never far behind him when she was needed. Sarah ran the home and played hostess to Nat's business associates with an efficiency and commitment born of a love for her husband. Her warm hospitality was legendary among those involved in the east coast trading.

Their son, David was well built and muscular carrying very little excess weight and matching, if not exceeding, Richard's height of six feet. David's fair wavy hair had, on many occasions, come in for parental criticism as it became unmanageable. His general dress sense left a lot to be desired, but he was a man of action and these things concerned him little. There was another son, Philip, whose passion was the sea. He was seldom spoken of and never seen. On being questioned about his brother, Dave would throw out a hand in the direction of the ocean muttering; 'out there somewhere.'

Dave now had his place back in the family agency having returned from England and the university he had attended with Richard. His duties took him up and down the coast, either accompanying Nat, or independently taking on assignments such as New York itself, knowing how much Nat hated the place.

The Holland home stood on a high promontory, affording a superb view of the bay and distant shipping. The bay was far enough down the coast from New York to enjoy solitude, and had a beauty of its own. At the same time it was close enough to the huge conurbation, just an hours ride away, to provide an ideal haven for people such as the Hollands whose activities often took them into the city.

Richard approached the familiar landmark with relief, fatigue nullifying his delight at having reached his immediate goal. He had pushed both himself and his mount in an attempt to prove to Dave his resourcefulness and ability. Both man and horse were lean, the disciplines of two years evident in their appearance. He was arriving days before the arranged rendezvous having traversed the major part of the country.

Richard had spent the last night at a stage post in the vicinity, wishing to arrive in a presentable condition. He hoped that his early appearance was not going to catch Dave away from home, as he could not wait to see the look on that mischievous face as Dave's prophecy, Richard's safe arrival, was fulfilled.

At the gate Richard dismounted wearily, securing Valiant to the rail. He made his way up the long path towards the front porch. The house had an unusually quiet air about it, with curtains not fully drawn back, and he wondered if the family could be on vacation. As he rounded the house a movement attracted his attention. Someone was bending over a flower bed and he made his way towards the figure, assuming it was a gardener. It turned in surprised, hearing Richard's footfall on the gravel, and he immediately recognised the face of Sarah Holland. She straightened, clutching her back as she did so. Richard could not recall her being in bad physical shape, quiet the contrary.

Sarah gasped; "Richard, oh Richard." He was taken aback by the intensity of her welcome. She clung to him as if a mother and son were being reunited. She was weeping and whispering in Richard's ear, but he could not catch the words. He held her away from him, searching her face for a clue as to her distress. Sarah Holland was not subject to such extremes and she had always impressed Richard by her strength and stability. Her present state was giving him a cause for anxiety, he was eager to establish the reason for her erratic behaviour.

"What is wrong, Sarah?" He asked, holding her shoulders.

"We lost David." She sobbed. Richard by reason of fatigue or stupidity did not take in the implications of this statement.

"Sorry, what was that?" He stammered, confused.

"We lost David." She repeated, "he was killed last month." Richard stared at her, incapable of speech. He took her into his arms again, as much for his own comfort as hers. He gazed over her shoulder at the far horizon where the blue of the morning sky was reflected in the ocean. Its beauty eluded him. After the initial reaction of disbelief, an overwhelming feeling of despair and hopelessness pervaded his being. His devastation was complete.

Sarah led him into the house and he followed blindly. No word had passed between them for minutes and it was she who made an attempt at conversation. "Nat will be home for his meal later, you will stay, won't you Richard?" He nodded confirmation, his eyes roaming around the living room they had just entered. Richard recalled the many hours that he had spent there with Dave. After long days pursuing their outdoor activities they had relaxed and passed evenings in this lovely room. They had read, and discussed a multitude of topics ranging from current developments in prophesying the weather, to a light-hearted comparison of girls on each side of the Atlantic. This had been the routine for six months and a strong sense of brotherhood had established itself between them. Sarah Holland brought him back to stark reality.

"Please sit down, Richard". He did as requested as she went into the kitchen, soon to reappear with two mugs of steaming coffee. "We had no way of knowing where you were Richard. We did telegraph some of the larger towns but no one had seen or heard of you." He cursed himself inwardly for not having kept to the original route Dave had planned out for him. But then, if he had, Randolph and its associates would have been unknown to him. Why had he deviated to discover that town? His mind was not clear enough to answer such a question.

Sarah was searching his face and Richard realised that he was expected to comment on her remarks concerning his whereabouts.

"I took the rail-road, went off course a bit." He said, and she nodded, accepting the half truth. Sarah handed Richard his coffee and occupied the chair next to him, hands gripping the mug. Richard sipped the liquid testily. "Do you want to talk about it, Sarah?" he asked, sufficiently recovered to be inquisitive as to how such an indestructible character such as Dave could lose his life.

"Four weeks ago," she began, staring at her coffee, "four weeks ago David went on a business trip which was to last for several days. There is a rail-head, just, um, just north-west of here. Nat wanted to investigate the possibility of moving goods inland that way rather than through New York. He understood that the track was due for completion next year." She paused, looking up at Richard. "He never came back. Days later we heard that his body had been dumped on the track. Our local sheriff arranged for David's body to be brought to the house, taking the view that he had died the night he left here." She paused again, struggling with her emotions. "Richard," she sobbed, "the body was in an awful state. The sheriff reckoned that a whole herd must have run over him."

Richard listened, his horror turning rapidly to anger. "How did he die, Sarah, not trampled to death?" He asked gently.

"No, no. He had been shot."

Richard turned this fact over in his mind. From behind? In his sleep? Was he outnumbered? "He was shot in the back," Sarah added, confirming his suspicions.

Midday meal was a sombre affair that day. Nathaniel Holland had taken his son's death very much to heart. 'Murder', he raged, 'by some yellow skunk who could not even face him.' Richard shared his bitterness as they talked together, the three of them, for the rest of the afternoon. Before darkness fell they took Richard to the little graveyard overlooking the harbour. A simple stone bore the fact that David Nathaniel Holland lay there. Date of death was not inscribed, but his age of twenty-six years was. Richard was overcome by emotion as they stood there, heads bowed, and a stiff breeze tugging at their coats. How he wished, in that desperate moment, that Kate could also be at his side.

* * *

Early next morning, soon after sun-up, Richard said farewell to the Hollands and, assuring them of his caution, set Valiant purposefully toward the north-west. He had decided on this course of action after a sleepless night during which his mind had been in turmoil. Something had to be done, he had to investigate at the very least, for he owed that much to Dave who, after all, had equipped him for the task. Preparations had begun long before daylight as Nat and Richard had wordlessly oiled and greased Richard's guns. They ensured that his holsters were smooth and would afford rapid release of their deadly contents should the need arise. Sarah took no part in this operation at all. She maintained that it was the local sheriff who should be looking into the matter, not Richard. Admitting that there was no activity in that quarter she conceded, but only after declaring she could not live with losing Richard as well.

Richard had no difficulty at all in finding the trail. Sometimes at a walk, then at a canter, Valiant was guided along the well-worn track, around which there was much evidence of its use. Jettisoned and abandoned rubbish was strewn along the verges, deposited in ditches and even tossed into overhanging branches. A broken chair; an old blanket; and a shattered cart wheel found in the space of a few yards.

The rail-head was reached around midday and Richard was utterly dismayed at the scene before him. There was an atmosphere of chaos about it. The clamour of metal on metal, cattle in pens, and the shouts and laughter on the streets combined to produce a cacophony, evident long before Richard gained the hilltop and the rail-head came into view.

Richard's first consideration, a habit of many months, was the safety of Valiant. He found a reasonable stable on the south periphery of that expanding complex. His saddle bags were empty, and the sum total of his possessions were his horse, guns, and a limited but sufficient amount of money. The stable man surprised Richard by his sober integrity (Richard of necessity had become, in those many months, a good judge of character at first meeting) and he wondered how the man found himself in such a place. Richard explained to him that his exit could be a hasty one and the Ostler nodded knowingly, affording Richard access to the stable at all times. He even agreed to saddle Valiant at night-fall should an emergency occur.

Richard braced himself as, keeping to the centre of the street, he ambled down into the crowds which thronged it, having no idea when he would be retracing his steps. Such was the confidence in the quality of his training that failure did not enter his mind, nor did he countenance the thought that he might not return. He forgot, momentarily, that his tutor had not.

As he walked, Richard could not stifle a wry smile as the staff of Shaw and Steady, London solicitors, came into his thoughts. How bizarre the antics of the senior partner's son would seem to them. His smile evaporated as, forced onto the side-walk by congestion on the street, the seriousness of his mission claimed full attention.

He observed around him immigrant workers from many parts of the world. Those with local dialects were mainly business men or traders, selling their wares or, no doubt, assessing the viability of using the rail-head to their advantage in the future. This had been the reason for Dave's visit a month or so before.

There was much drunkenness even at that hour. As he passed them two young girls invited Richard to buy them a drink and get friendly. The saloons, many of them temporary structures, teemed with customers, the clink of coins and bottles added to the general hubbub. Tinkers and drifters plied their wares in every conceivable nook. Acrobats, jugglers, and animal trainers performed where they could. Richard was saddened by the sight of men teasing a bear, the animal obviously uncomfortable in the heat, and away from its natural home much further north.

A man dressed in black warned the populace that it was streaming into hell, repentance its only salvation. Richard had to agree that hell must be something akin to this.

Ducking into the entrance of one of the more mature saloons, Richard wordlessly chose a drink and carried it to a wall seat, dropping his hat beside it on the table. Sooner or later he would have to ask questions, attracting attention to his accent. For the moment he was happy to make his drink last and observe the scene around him, aware of the fact that he needed a plan.

The answer to his predicament came in the form of a young girl. She caught Richard's eye as he watched her move around the saloon. She invited him to buy her a drink and, forgetting his gentlemanly instincts, he pushed a coin across the table in her direction. The girl left for the bar, returning and occupying the vacant chair at Richard's table. She entertained him with small-talk which ran off her tongue with an ease gained by experience. Her fingers traced the rim of his hat as she spoke. Richard recognised the potential here in his search for information. There could not be a bar or saloon in town that she would not be familiar with.

Richard stood, and, inviting her to follow him, pulled back her chair. She nodded her appreciation and they left the saloon. She led him to a small, shabby hotel, which was, no doubt, occupied throughout by the girls. The room they entered was basic in size and furniture. A rough single bed the only, albeit essential, item of substance.

Richard surprised the girl by expressing his desire to talk, not make love. At first she was suspicious and reticent, becoming more co-operative as he placed money on the bed beside her. He quickly discovered that her name was Rebbeca, and that she had recollections of shootings in the recent weeks. Richard described Dave to her and she listened attentively. She promised to talk to the girls and, discreetly, to some of the men who were regulars.

Rebecca was, Richard found, a cut above the average girl in her situation. She was dressed attractively but her clothes bore no resemblance to the gaudy flamboyance of her colleagues. Her hair was short and evenly trimmed, forming the neat frame for her round, girlish face. She smiled frequently revealing dimples, which, with her sparkling eyes, gave her a mischievous look. She had an open manner which appealed to Richard, her eyes engaging his as they talked. He was tempted to pry into her background to learn something of her story. He wished to leave that place as swiftly as possible, however, and decided to keep to the task at hand.

They sat together on the bed, backs to the wall, deciding upon a strategy. Richard was grateful to have an ally, particularly one with local knowledge and a good ear for gossip. How useful Beth Champion would have been in this situation, he mused, his memories side-tracking him for a moment.

They left the room late in the afternoon. Rebecca to her rounds, and Richard to return to his seat in the bar of the main saloon. For two hours he studied those around him, learning nothing of any consequence save how volatile each moment could be. Eventually lamps were lit. Men left their tasks, coming in from the gathering darkness to slake thirsts, pushing into the already crowded bar area. Richard left the saloon, having to push his way to the door. He had to keep his appointment with Rebecca in her room, hoping for a morsel of information to set him in the right direction.

Richard climbed the stairs and turned into the room, surprised that the door was open. His eyes were not adjusted to the gloom of the room after the saloon's glare, so he never knew what hit him. He was aware only of a loud crack against his scull, and the bright lights that accompanied the pain. Then a deep darkness claimed him.

Chapter 10

Richard was conscious initially only of the pain. It coursed throughout the length and breadth of his body which was, he soon noticed, naked under the blanket. Without moving a muscle he looked questioningly at the girl dabbing his head.

"You've been kicked all over," she said, "but I reckon you'll live." Rebecca came into the lamp-light and took the bowl from the girl who had spoken to him, dismissing her with a nod.

"Welcome back Mr Shaw," she bantered, "I don't suppose you saw who did it?" Richard wanted to shake his head but decided against such drastic action.

"No," he replied huskily.

"Nasty crack on the head and a rib or two gone, I'd say." He winced as she tested the tightness of a strip of sheet tied around his rib cage.

"I must be getting careless," he said, trying to smile but finding it too much effort.

During the course of the next hour, Richard was encouraged to eat a broth Rebecca had prepared for him, and with the assistance of both girls managed to dress very gingerly. His head and ribs were aching, but he was relieved to find that his limbs were comparatively free from damage. Rebecca guided Richard back to the bed, making him as comfortable as possible, patting a pillow vigorously and easing his head down onto it.

"I have some news," she said, sitting on the bed beside him. " I think the guys who did this must have overheard my enquiries - you weren't robbed were you?" Richard shook his head as much as he dared. "No," she continued, "it was to frighten you off. Your friend was shot in the Golden Nugget.

Seems he took a shine to a girl who was spoken for. He was challenged by two guys and a gun-fight followed. The other girls remembered it too when I spoke to them about it."

"What happened?" Richard urged impatiently.

"The two guys were killed, then, as your friend was packin' away his guns, a shot from the sidewalk killed him, leaving all three in a heap." Silence followed, broken only by the spitting of the defective lamp somewhere in the room.

"Can you bring the girl here, do you think?" Richard's distress was not helping his condition.

"She's left, gone nobody knows where, but there were plenty of people in that bar, leave it to me, I'll be back soon as I can." She kissed his cheek and left him, Richard mumbling his thanks as she crossed the room to the door. He heard her clumping down the stairs and was left in the stillness of the room. He lay there trying not to move a muscle.

Later Richard got to his feet with great difficulty, needing to answer the call of nature. He rummaged around until he found the pot used for the purpose. He now established that his only injuries were to his head and ribs and he guessed that they must have hit him with something very hard, a gun butt probably, then kicked him around the room. He checked his guns, fastening the belt around him and dropping the two revolvers into the holsters. Not since he'd first put on a gun belt two years ago had he been so aware of their weight. It pulled on his damaged rib-cage. He practised several draws which had him sweating with agony, and he fancied that the pain had slowed him down.

He remained in that pose with hands poised above his guns as footsteps approached the door from the stairs. He recognised Rebecca's clump again and sure enough it was she who slid inside the door. She looked disapprovingly at his gun-belt, undoing the buckle and letting it fall to the floor with a thud. She made him comfortable once more on the bed. "The man you want runs a freight business down by the track. The two your friend killed were his boys, so were the two who gave you a warm reception tonight." Rebecca put her arms gently around Richard. "Be careful, this Radford feller's got a lot of friends, which is why it was all kept quiet."

"I do appreciate the trouble you're taking Rebecca, and all your kindness." Richard said.

"You paid for it," she answered brightly. "You don't want my body, just my nursin'. Guess it makes a change," she concluded frankly and not without humour. Richard hugged her as much as his injuries would allow.

"Show me this Radford's place, will you?" He rose from the bed and picked up his hat.

You're the boss." she said, raising her palms to heaven in a gesture of hopelessness, then turning to extinguish the lamp.

It was getting late and the noise level, rather than abating, was in fact reaching a crescendo which would peak at some point in the night ahead. They crossed the main street, dodging examples of lurching, staggering and fighting humanity. Richard reached for Rebecca's arm, slowing her down, seeking support as he felt nausea overcome him. They leaned on the sidewalk for a few minutes then continued their slow progress towards the many shacks and offices beside the track. Rebecca pointed to a door marked 'despatch office' and they halted. The office was lit, the occupant obviously still working inside.

They stood together in the darkness and Richard held her shoulders.

"Do you want to ride out with me?" he whispered.

"The girls need me here," she replied, almost too quickly, "I sort of mother them. I'll stick around for a while." She kissed him and was gone into the shadows of a hundred shacks and the clamour of another night.

Richard was anxious to confirm in some way the information brought to him by Rebecca. He decided to visit the scene of the crime.

The Golden Nugget saloon was a dreadful place. Even with the confidence Richard possessed, he hesitated before entering. The small one-storey creation was divided into two areas, basically a bar and a gaming room. Smoke swirled, strata upon strata curling upwards and hovering above head level. Nostrils were abused by the odour of sweat, stale beer and the smoke itself. Richard for safety's sake again sought out a wall table which was occupied by a lone drinker. He wasted no time and in response to the man's nod asked;

"D'you recall a shoot-out here a few weeks back?" The man surveyed the quality of Richard's clothes and armoury and, of course, took in the accent.

"What if I do?" he said, with a belligerence to which Richard was becoming accustomed.

"Tell me about it," Richard coaxed, laying notes on the table before him. The man, who could have been handsome but for his rotten teeth, picked up the money, motioning to Richard to bend nearer.

"Fancy guy, like you," he drawled, his stale breath causing Richard to wince, reminding him of his injury. "Tried to take on the whole outfit I reckon."

"Which outfit?" Richard asked quickly. The man indicated towards the bar.

"The two drinkin' at the end of the bar run a team which operates between here and the West, workin' with the rail-road."

"Thanks," said Richard, rising. He moved towards the two men at the bar, convinced by their reactions that they were responsible for his condition.

I want some goods moved," Richard said, watching them

closely. One pushed himself away from the bar and eyed Richard suspiciously.

"Better come to the office," the man said, finishing his drink and trying to appear nonchalant.

He left his colleague at the bar and led Richard through the swing doors onto the sidewalk. They threaded their way through the crowd in the street. Richard was not surprised when they made for the shack with the door marked 'dispatch office'. The man swung open the door and they went inside.

"Got a customer boss," he said to the only occupant sitting at a desk. The hulk of a man made no move to acknowledge any other presence in the room. Richard was in no mood for courtesies and, annoyed by his reception, or lack of it, thumped on the desk, jarring his ribs. The hulk's bearded face came up, scowling.

"Who th' hell d'you think you are?" he barked.

"Don't you know?" snapped Richard, feeling suddenly weak.

"Get outa my office!" the hulk bawled. Richard knew that he had to get this over quickly so he launched in at the deep end.

"You met a friend of mine, few weeks back in the Golden Nugget saloon. He had his back to you I believe!" Richard felt the adrenalin flowing and picked up the lamp from the table as he backed against the door, keeping both men in view.

"I want some answers to my questions," he rapped, "or I'll smash this lamp on the wall." Richard knew that the timber structure would burn in minutes and his adversaries were aware of that too.

The hulk was recovering from Richard's challenge and was uncertain as to what action he should take in response.

"You Radford?" Richard asked tersely, lifting the lamp to encourage a reply.

What if I am?" the hulk sneered. Richard knew hate for the first time in his life, an alarming experience.

"You remember David Holland then, the friend of mine you shot from behind." Richard spat the words out with all the venom he could muster, hoping that his true physical weakness was not evident.

"He had it comin' to him," the man to Richard's right interposed, "Took a girl that wasn't his to take, shot two of the boys."

"In self-defence," Richard interrupted.

Radford saw his opportunity. Richard was facing the man who had spoken and was holding the lamp in his left hand. Richard's eye caught the movement as the big man went for his gun, obviously kept in a desk drawer. The action which followed once again happened as if in slow motion, every move indelible upon his mind. The gun came up from behind the desk in the huge hand about to level on him. Richard's bullet passed between Radford's eyes, drilling a hole that rapidly became a jet of blood, covering the look of disbelief and astonishment frozen on the bearded face. The massive frame rose from the chair then toppled, crashing to the floor. Richard stood over the body like an avenging angel, he felt suddenly dizzy. The gun in his right hand was now pointing at the man standing behind the desk, who was still in a state of shock.

"That was Radford, I hope." said Richard with a nervous smile, immediately ashamed of his black humour. The man nodded in the affirmative. "It was he who pulled the trigger that night, yes?" The man nodded again.

Richard replaced the lamp and slipped his gun back into the holster, remembering his injuries.

"I owe you for roughing me up," he said, holding his ribs.

"He gave the orders," replied the man nervously, pointing

to the body. Richard was weary and feeling very unsteady, he decided that enough was enough.

"Don't leave for two minutes," he instructed. The man nodded his understanding, relief clearly showing on his face.

Richard slipped through the door, feeling his way in the darkness. He quickly found his bearings and headed south up the slope and away from the rumpus around him. He was bathed in sweat when he reached the stables and his head was thumping with a sickly, regular beat. He was relieved indeed to see that the ostler had been as good as his word and Valiant was saddled and ready. Richard doubted whether he could have performed the task in his present state. He pulled him himself up into the saddle, patting the grey's neck.

Each movement of the horse jarred his body and the pain seemed to spread from his head and ribs and envelope his whole being. Richard held Valiant at a steady walk to minimise his discomfort. He felt no elation at a mission accomplished, on the contrary it worried him that he felt no remorse or conscience at killing a man. His recurring nightmare regarding the drunk he'd shot no longer troubled him either.

With Dave gone and Kate lost, his life was now aimless. His arrival in that country had been so full of promise. Richard overwhelmingly felt the urge to seek the comfort of his homeland.

Chapter 11

Richard had booked his passage but could not sail for three days. He spent those days with Sarah and Nat Holland. They appreciated his presence which filled the gap in their lives to an extent. Their other son Philip was still at sea and as far as they knew, unaware of his brother's death.

Sarah had tended Richard's wounds and obtained an opinion from her doctor, who, when he called, rather made light of Richard's condition, muttering that he had more important calls on his time. However, he assured Sarah that the ribs would mend in due course and Richard's head would clear after resting for a day or so.

"He's a good man really," Sarah said as he left, she always saw the best in everyone.

Life in that household was just as Richard remembered it when Dave was alive. There was much coming and going as Nat's associates called for an ad hoc meeting, a business lunch or dinner. Occasionally one of them would stay the night, particularly in the winter months.

The Sheriff arrived at the house and, as always, timed his visit to share the midday meal. His mission was to clear up some details regarding the sudden death of a Captain Radford. Richard and Nat had already established in their own minds that Dave's death must be in some way connected with Nat's recent condemnation of Radford's business methods. Nat had apparently uncovered deals that were anything but legitimate.

The Sheriff's version was that Dave had become involved with a girl in controversial circumstances. This Richard could well believe, as Dave's conquests regarding the opposite sex were as far flung as London and the west coast of America.

The three men were still unsure as to the link between Dave's indiscretion and Nat's adverse report on Radford. There was no motive to justify a killing.

Richard admitted that he was the Englishman last seen with Captain Radford and made a statement claiming self-defence. The Sheriff departed, requesting that Richard always be available if needed. The Hollands kept quiet about his imminent departure and Richard was grateful for that.

On the day Richard was due to join the ship homeward bound, a telegram arrived from London. It read: 'Father ill. Please return. Mother.' It was a perfect example of Mary Shaw's brevity and contained no suggestion of affection or maternal instinct. Richard wondered whether the message was an understatement or a wild exaggeration of the truth. His mother was capable of both.

Richard was to leave for the harbour late in the day, and spent most of it in preparation. He was encouraged by the Hollands to store his clothes and equipment in Dave's room. This was appropriate in that it was Dave who had supervised their purchase. He changed into the conventional clothes in which he had arrived, that of an English gentleman, and in which he now felt uncomfortable. His gold watch and chain appeared garish as he adjusted the time and wound the watch for the first time in almost a year.

The moment he had dreaded for many weeks now arrived. Richard had to say farewell to his horse, Valiant. He could not contemplate the grey having any other master, so he paid the owner handsomely to feed and exercise him for a year. Nat promised to keep an eye on the stable from time to time.

Richard visited the horse as they passed the stables in the buggy on the way to the big city and its harbour. He clung to the grey's neck and wept unashamedly. For two years there had been a partnership between man and beast and on many an occasion Richard had preferred the company of his horse to that of humans.

Nat and Sarah made the journey to the docks with him and he hated parting company with them. Richard was surprised to see Nat throw back his curls as he tried to hide a tear. Sarah was not so inhibited and clung to him, the love they bore for each other plainly evident. "God go with you," she breathed finally. They waved as the ship steamed away from its moorings and Richard underwent an acute feeling of depression as they were lost to view. He stood by the rail for an hour as, one by one, the landmarks faded and the coastline disappeared. All the experiences and events of those two years suddenly and oddly seemed not to have any substance. They had ceased to be realities, just figments in the memory or imagination. He shivered and went below, taking with him to his cabin a full bottle of whiskey. He later passed out, weeping uncontrollably.

* * *

That voyage seemed to last an eternity but in actual fact was only one day longer than his outward journey. Then he had had the excitement and anticipation of a new adventure, the prospect of spending two years in the unknown. He reflected that on his arrival, those six months with Dave were probably the happiest of his life, even though business had taken Dave away for periods. For the same reason Dave had been unable to tour with him, hence the importance of the planned reunion back on the coast. All those plans had been cruelly dashed. Now Richard was returning and the two crossings could not present a greater contrast.

As the days dragged on Richard found that even the passengers were uninteresting. He was beginning to wish that he had arranged to escort Virginia after all. Each day his thoughts covered the same ground, the valley, the people and the town. Kate riding towards him on that first occasion, the dance they had at the party and little Sam's look of joy as she beheld her mother. Those were some of the happy moments that it was a pleasure to recall. There were those things of which he was not proud however. The deaths of two men now haunted him. Incidents which had seemed to be justified at the time but now weighed heavily on his conscience. Then the overriding feeling of guilt when he reflected on how he'd bullied Kate into selling her land, betraying her trust in him. A thousand times he had longed to know how she felt about him now.

"Excuse me sir, is this seat taken?" Richard, still deep in thought, stared blankly at the man standing before him.

"I'm sorry," he replied at last, "No, it's free, I believe."

"Thank you." The newcomer dropped into the chair and unrolled a newspaper.

The afternoon was pleasant and they were about half way across the Atlantic, Richard judged. He had decided to sit on deck, opting for the leeward side in common with most passengers. He was watching the ocean being tossed aside as the ship penetrated the unusually calm and smooth waters, creating a frothy, seething wash which settled beside and behind the vessel as it progressed, eventually resuming its former placid swell, as if no ship had ever passed.

Other travellers were sitting as he was along the rail, or leaning against it smoking, talking or reading. It was predictable that as the weather improved, so the occupants of the ship came up onto the deck, grateful to breathe fresh air for a while.

The man in the next seat suddenly put his paper down and sniffed into the wind. "What a pleasant change from yesterday," he said, stretching his arms.

"Still chilly though." offered Richard, rubbing his hands descriptively.

"One feels the cold after the heat of the summer." the

man went on, pulling his coat around him. One does indeed, echoed Richard to himself, marvelling at the standard of conversation. "With a tan like yours you must have been enjoying life in the open," the man said, eyeing Richard.

"Almost two years on the trail." Richard offered. The man nodded knowingly.

"You'll feel the pinch at home," the man continued, "they are predicting a hard winter". There was a break in their exchange as he folded his newspaper again and donned his gloves.

"What line are you in?" Richard enquired, feeling that he should make some contribution to a sterile conversation, and growing curious about this neat, middle-aged traveller.

"Oh, shipping," he replied, "and what about yourself?"

"I'm to go into law," said Richard unenthusiastically, "but I shall be keeping my options open."

The man nodded with the trace of a smile. "Rather travel, eh?" Richard let that ride and took up the subject of shipping.

"Do you happen to know Nathaniel Holland? He's in your line of business on the East coast."

"Yes, of course," the man answered, looking up. "A very good friend and colleague of many years, how do you know him?"

"I was at university with his son David, who invited me to visit America," explained Richard.

"Good Heavens," the man said incredulously, "what an amazing coincidence! I operate between Liverpool and agents like Nat along the coast."

"Do you cross the Atlantic often?" enquired Richard with awe.

"Quite often, but it beats being confined to an office, what? However, we must have a drink together later and discuss our mutual friend." With that he rose and hurried away, walking quickly with the ease and expertise of a seasoned passenger. The abruptness of his departure reminded Richard of the closing of negotiations once terms had been agreed. Richard returned to his thoughts and study of the ocean.

The shipper was not in sight at dinner, but as Richard leaned on the bar afterwards, he was at his side offering to buy the round. It was at that bar that Richard learned an amazing fact about the Hollands.

Sarah Holland is not David's mother," he was saying, "She married Nat a decade ago when his first wife, David's mother, died. There was great controversy when it happened." He paused, ordering the drinks. "When Nat and Sarah got together, she was already married to a sea captain called Radford, who at the time was serving a sentence for smuggling. Sarah left him and married Nat." With that the shipper emptied his glass, wished Richard goodnight and, as on the previous occasion, hurried away.

Richard, now alone at the bar stared at the multi-coloured bottles secured behind it. He roused himself and took his glass to a quiet corner seat, struggling to assemble the facts he had just been told and make some logical sense of them. Dave had never given any hint of the situation regarding his parents in all the time he had known him. Richard had killed Sarah's former husband, a fact both Hollands had kept secret. David had been killed by Philip's father! As these horrific facts tumbled through his brain Richard became utterly bewildered. This was far too much to absorb. Richard swallowed the remaining half glass of whiskey, feeling the liquid burn his throat and kindle a glow inside him, diverting his attention for a consolatory moment. Soon his mind was incapable of analysis and he pushed the problems of the present into temporary abeyance. His final thoughts for that particular evening were that he had set out for America with an uncomplicated agenda and now, with his schedule in tatters and his mind in turmoil, he was going home, probably to take on his father's business.

The gentleman in shipping became part of his routine for the rest of the crossing. They discussed every conceivable subject during those last days on the ship, but never again did Nathaniel Holland come up in conversation. There was always the same abrupt conclusion to each and every meeting. Richard reflected on the fact that neither man knew the other's name.

At last the day arrived when the English coast came in to view. The wind was fierce and Richard drew his coat around him. He gazed across the white foaming ocean, realising that he should be elated at his homecoming. He turned, his eyes sweeping the empty horizon from which they had come. Beyond it were people who had touched him deeply. If it had been possible he would have swung the vessel around there and then, but instead he would be treading home soil within an hour or two.

He did not see the shipper again and wondered at his story concerning the Hollands. Richard began to doubt the man's credibility.

There was no lightness of step as Richard descended the gangway. There was no impatience as he was kept waiting for his baggage. There was no sense of anticipation as he was driven to the railway terminus where normally his fascination with the huge, dirty locomotives would have brought him some satisfaction. He booked a seat in the first-class carriage of the next departure for London. He had three hours to kill so, depositing his luggage, he took a stroll into the city. Richard found the enormousness of Liverpool completely overpowering after the wide-open spaces which he'd grown used to. The prospect of London and city life filled him with apprehension. He was amazed at his reactions and recalled that two years had almost altered his personality beyond recognition; the fun-loving city dweller had been transformed into an anti-social, introverted day-dreamer.

How cold it was on that railway station! When the three hours had passed, he found his train and climbed into the carriage in order to derive a little warmth. Richard was unable to grasp the fact that he was home. He tried to doze, for only then did his thoughts cease to trouble him. But he was unsuccessful in achieving even temporary oblivion.

Chapter 12

The train left Liverpool on that dark and cold night an hour behind schedule. Richard's carriage was full but he discouraged conversation by not engaging the looks cast in his direction by those around him. He recalled the last time he was on a train, in the coach with Kate, the lady of pleasure. The very thought of that name sent him once more down memory lane to the events which had taken place some three thousand miles away.

It was midnight when he emerged from the station in London. Snow was falling and the cold was intense. Richard wished that he had immediate access to his wardrobe, where more suitable clothes awaited him. What he was wearing at present was totally inadequate.

Richard had neglected to inform his mother of his arrival, had he done so the family coach would have been at his disposal. As it was, he had to stand in a queue with people stamping their feet and blowing on cold hands. As Richard reached the head of the ever increasing line and the next carriage arrived, he noticed the woman immediately behind him. Her clothing was even less appropriate than his own and lines of weariness were etched on her not unattractive face. He invited her to share the carriage. The cabby was sure that it would take just a minor deviation from Richard's route to drop her where she lived. Richard had no knowledge of the address, but took the cabby at his word and was pleased to accommodate the extra passenger for part of the way.

His travelling companion looked absolutely frozen, so much so that Richard was led to take off his coat and place it around her shoulders.

"Gawd bless yer sir, yer a real gent," she said smiling,

and Richard smiled too on being reintroduced to the cockney accent. "I bin t'see me fam'ly what live up country. Shan't see 'em agin 'til arter Chris'mus. Should've bin 'ome long ago - missed the early train ar did."

"Yes, the festive season will soon be upon us," Richard replied, reminding himself as much as responding to her words. "Has it been snowing long?"

"Started t'night, just arter dark, 'least where I was," she replied. Richard had not been aware of the snow until he had reached London and wondered why he had not noticed it earlier in his journey. Perhaps he had been sleeping. He pulled at his watch chain trying to establish the time as the watch dangled before him.

The carriage came to a halt and the cabby was yelling instructions above them. Richard opened the door, letting in an icy blast, and jumped down onto the snow. The woman stepped down, accepting his assistance with a smile.

"Ta," she said, and disappeared into the gloom. Richard could just discern the outline of the drab tenement block with an occasional lit window. He shivered as he visualised a night behind those cold, curtainless panes.

Very soon Richard began to recognise familiar landmarks, all of which would soon achieve a white anonymity if the snow continued to fall at its present rate. An hour later he was passing through the gates of his home, the carriage negotiating the circular drive before stopping in front of the house. He paid the cabby and the carriage left, leaving him alone with his baggage at his feet. It was then that he missed his coat, realising immediately that the women had left the carriage with it still around her shoulders.

He put that problem behind him as he tried to make something of his present predicament. He would freeze if he stayed out in the cold much longer, so he made his way to the back of the house where he hoped to gain entrance through the servants' quarters. Richard wondered if Bates was still the butler, or if he'd been replaced in one of his mother's purges.

Richard felt his way in the darkness, his tired mind desperately trying to recall the layout of the gardens. He found a fence and went sprawling in the snow, cursing under his breath. The snow was still falling and the stillness around him magnified every sound and movement he made.

Eventually he turned the corner at the rear of the house and followed what he remembered to be a path leading to the huge summer house and rose garden. He found the gate, but could not swing it open for the weight of snow behind it. In desperation he jumped the low fence and once again hit the snow, feeling a twinge from his rib injury.

Richard pulled himself up and, standing at the door, peered at the bells before him. There were four, obviously designed to summon each member of the staff. He judged that the top bell would be for the butler and pulled vigorously. There was no sound, no clang inside the door as of old. He pulled the second, then the third, and in frustration the fourth, marked 'cook'.

The snow was still falling silently as Richard stood in disbelief. He moved along the rear wall and found the window of the butler's room, thankfully on the ground floor. He tapped lightly on the glass pane, repeating the act with more urgency on receiving no response. He hit the pane again, much harder, thinking that he must surely awaken the whole house.

He sighed with relief as a lamp was lit inside the room, and he was pleased to see the robed figure of Bates illuminated in its glow. Bates held the lamp up to the window to determine the source of the disturbance. Richard thought how ghastly and ghostly he must look at that moment, covered in snow from head to foot and with his long hair in complete disarray.

Bates held aloft his free hand in recognition and the room became dark again as the butler moved into the corridor beyond.

"Master Richard!" Bates whispered, genuinely pleased to see him.

"Good to see you, Bates," Richard responded. "Sorry to wake you at this hour."

"I'm glad that you did Master Richard - but where are your bags?" Bates followed Richard to the front of the house and assisted him in unlatching the bulky door with as little noise as possible. Richard's baggage had all but disappeared as the snow deepened perceptibly. Bates lit another lamp for Richard and the two of them climbed the stairs to Richard's first floor room. They wished each other a good night, what was left of it, and Richard surveyed his room in the lamplight. How strange it was, that room he had actually been sorry to leave, that room in which he had slept, played and lived for twenty-three years. He suddenly realised how exhausted he was and, shedding his outer clothes, damp with snow, slipped into bed, finding sleep almost immediately.

* * *

Richard knew that he would not see his mother until the breakfast gong sounded. He took time in shaving and carefully selected well-worn, albeit now unfamiliar clothes. He studied himself in the wardrobe mirror. His tan seemed incongruous with the snow still drifting past the window. He had a longing for the heat of that land he had just left, immediately realising his stupidity. It would be winter there too.

He hoped that Kate and her family were warm at the homestead. He wished that he ... Richard admonished himself for his recurring day-dream, knowing that the mental torture would go on.

The gong summoned the two members of the Shaw household to breakfast.

"Master Richard, Ma'am," announced Bates in the time honoured manner.

"Darling, how lovely to see you, why did you not cable me?" Mrs. Shaw stood up, placing her napkin on the table. Richard considered her slight frame and thought that she had aged somewhat, but her natural elegance was still present.

"Sorry mother, it was difficult at that hour," explained her son, kissing her outstretched hand. "How are you? How is father?"

"I am fine dear, but your poor father ... you must go and see him this morning Richard!" Mrs Shaw was now restored to her role as dominant mother in addition to that of mistress of the house.

"What ails father, is it serious?" Richard asked.

"Of course it's serious, and he has missed you," she said in dramatic tones. "It's his mind, he's breaking up Richard." Richard ate slowly and chose his words as deliberately.

"Am I still expected to become a partner, mother?"

"Of course, of course, what else will you do?" she boomed.

"I don't know yet," he mumbled.

"What! What did you say? I cannot hear you if you talk into your breakfast, Richard!"

"I'll talk it over with father and Mr Steady, mother," Richard said, ignoring her sarcasm.

"What is there to discuss? Your father has prepared the papers and they're waiting in the vaults for your signature. Really, Richard, you can be so infuriating."

"I need time, mother, time to ..."

"There will not be much time if your father deteriorates at his present rate," she cut in. "And where did you get that awful sunburn Richard, you must be glad to be away from that horrid country." Richard struggled with himself, not wishing to clash with his mother at this early stage. He sidestepped the affront.

"David was killed three months ago," he said soberly, wondering what his mother would have made of his night of vengeance in that living hell.

"Playing with guns, no doubt. Sarah must be simply devastated. Oh, the worries children bring to their parents." She got to her feet, declaring that she had to visit the servants for the day's briefing. Richard also stood and watched her go in disbelief and a growing feeling of despair.

Richard left the house later that morning, having selected his warmest clothes. The snow had stopped falling for the moment, but the sky was threatening an imminent resumption. The family coachman was not known to Richard and they exchanged mere nods as he climbed into the coach. He remembered his coat and gave the driver instructions to take, in the reverse direction, the route he had followed the night before. He jumped out at the tenement block, intending to cover the short distance into the city on foot.

The coat itself did not worry Richard overmuch, but a rather good wallet was in the pocket and it contained his rail ticket and some small change. The former was now invalid and the latter insignificant, but the wallet had been a present, given to him by Caroline when he'd left the country. He wondered, fleetingly, how she was, no doubt he would soon find out.

Residents were engaged in shovelling the snow from the main steps. Richard had nothing to go on by way of a name or flat number, so he approached a man leaning on his broom, taking a breather.

"I'm looking for a lady who arrived home in the early hours," he said. "Has family connections in the midlands, I believe."

"That'll be Mrs Forest, top floor," said a female voice, and Richard observed the source of the information some yards away.

"Thank you," he shouted, touching his hat, and moved towards the steps.

"Number two-one-five," she shouted after him and Richard acknowledged with a wave of his hand.

He knocked and waited. The sounds of activity within the flat did not result in the door opening. He knocked again. Richard was contemplating his next move when the door flew open, and sheer aggression in the form of a large human male lunged at him, catching him completely unawares. The aggressor hit Richard a glancing blow to the temple which would have pole-axed him had not he turned his head. Another huge fist hit Richard in the chest, but now he had regained his defensive skills and was riding the punches. The huge bulk of the man had pinned him against the wall, over which he could see the road some sixty feet below. Richard's fury erupted and he hit the frame holding him down with rapid punches, bruising punches aimed at vulnerable targets. The weight on him lessened and moved away. Richard saw the big right-hand fist coming and took timely evasive action. He heard the knuckle smash against the brickwork. The man yelped in pain and then grunted as Richard hit him hard in the stomach with all the force he could muster. He was about to hit that face on which pain was registered when he remembered the broken nose he'd administered those few months ago. He held back, preferring to hold the man in a vice-like grip. The struggles ceased as any movement the man made would have broken his arm.

"I told e' what'd 'appen if 'e came back," the man said breathlessly.

"I haven't been here before," snapped Richard, sensing the situation.

"I knowed they'd send another 'un," he went on as Richard eased the pressure on his arm.

"I don't want money." Richard explained, "I am here on another errand entirely."

"What d'you want then?" the man enquired suspiciously.

"My coat," Richard replied, getting straight to the point and letting the man pull his arm free. The face gradually registered some understanding and Richard could almost detect the brain assembling the facts and signalling to the vocal chords.

"Ar, I got it, you're the gent who took pity on my missus last night."

"That is correct," said Richard, "I would now like to take my coat and leave you."

"She pawned it only an hour ago guv, we needed the money see, for oil and food." He went on to qualify his predicament; "My cart don't bring in much see guv, people don't want to ride in a cart these days."

"What about the wallet?" Richard asked.

"Didn't see no wallet, guv," the man answered unconvincingly

"I do your wife a favour and you steal my wallet." Richard was indignant.

"Sorry guv." The man reached into his back pocket and produced the wallet. Richard took it from him, shaking his head at the man, who looked on sheepishly.

"Did you say that you owned a cart?"

"Can I take 'e somewhere guv?"

"To Central London please," Richard replied urgently.

* * *

Richard rewarded the man, Henry Forest, well for dropping him at the hospital. As the cart departed Mr Forest shouted after Richard; "What about the coat, guv?"

"Keep it." Forest touched his cap and was gone.

The scuffle was forgotten, but Richard was reminded of it by the nurse on reception who insisted on cleaning his head wound before directing him to his father's ward.

William Shaw had changed so much in two years that Richard would have passed his room had he not seen Mr Steady just leaving it. They shook hands and agreed to meet the next day.

Richard approached the bed and took his father's hand. "Hello father," he said inadequately.

"Sorry I missed you yesterday, son, I had an important meeting, you know how it is." Richard was overwhelmed with compassion. His father and he had been close right from the early days. Richard had always taken priority where his father was concerned and this had been reciprocated. "You been in a war?" his father continued, inspecting his son's minor injury, and emitting a cackle of laughter that was almost inhuman. "Damned snow, it makes my head ache," he concluded, staring out of the window.

William Shaw was still gazing out at the snow, wrapped up in his own fantasy world and oblivious to Richard's presence. He squeezed his father's hand but got no response. He sat for some time stroking the lifeless fingers, then laid the hand lovingly on the blanket and left the room, miserable and confused. The situation was now clear. His father was no longer his strength and inspiration, no longer the dominant lawyer respected in the city, no longer master at Shaw Manor, his lovely country home.

The snow was falling heavily again as Richard left the hospital grounds. The silent streets seemed to echo to the crunch of snow under his feet. He ate alone at a nearby inn, then wandered the streets again, stopping outside a church now brightly lit in the dusk of the evening. The bitter cold and the sound of music drove him inside and he joined a smattering of people in the pews who were listening to a recital on the organ.

The exciting last minutes of a Bach Prelude and Fugue lifted his spirits. Richard remained in his pew for an hour after the echo of the final chords had subsided. He prayed silently for his father. His intercession widened in scope to include his friends over the water.

"Keep them safe," he prayed aloud in the now empty church.

* * *

Richard halted the carriage at the tenement block. Bottle in hand, he lurched up the steps, negotiating each one with care. Henry Forest opened the door, his wife standing behind him. They clung on to Richard as he fell across the threshold, Henry skilfully catching the almost full bottle of whiskey.

"Thought thish would keep you warm," slurred Richard. Three mugs were produced and clinked in a toast to friends.

Richard collapsed into a chair and was covered by his own coat.

Chapter 13

George Steady was everything his name suggested he should be. (It had been Richard's father's delight to advertise their services in those early days as 'Shaw and Steady - the reliable ones', hoping that the general public would appreciate the word association.) William Shaw's partner was a man in his mid-fifties with not a hint of grey to be seen in a head of black hair combed straight back and greased down, giving the appearance of always being wet. He was neat in appearance and meticulous in business.

Mr Steady had never been known to give advice or guidance that was anything but absolute truth and the letter of the law. This service was never dispensed without reference having been made to the appropriate chapter and verse, all of which lined the walls of his room. The volumes came in various shapes, sizes and conditions, filed chronologically and recorded in an index of enormous proportions. Each and every judgement, precedent and change in legislation was promptly added or amended in the relevant section or Act.

The condition of Richard's father was a source of genuine distress to Mr Steady, and he expressed alarm at his partner's rapid decline. He was a man for whom Richard had the greatest respect, and he faced him now across the polished desk as they discussed the future of the firm and Richard's role within it.

It was assumed that Richard would occupy his father's office which was adjacent to Mr Steady's. They agreed that Richard should commence his duties on the following Monday morning, giving him time to settle in before the Christmas break.

Each wrung the other's hand warmly over the desk and Richard left to check the office next door. His father's taste in wall covering was vastly at odds with his partner's. A Van

Gogh took pride of place behind the desk, flanked by the works of local artists, many of whom had received commissions from William Shaw. Richard noticed a picture his mother had painted some years before, of the rose garden with the manor providing the backcloth. Her signature, 'Mary Shaw', was unmistakeably inscribed at the foot of it.

The desk was immense. It was constructed of heavy oak and was six feet square. Pulling the heavy drawers open was a task in itself. The outstanding feature of the desk was the green leather top which was the pride of the caretaker and cleaning staff as they diligently maintained its sheen. This had been one of William Shaw's more expensive purchases at the local auction rooms. Richard installed himself behind the desk hoping to get the feel of his new role, but he had never felt so unnatural in his life and an uncharacteristic sense of panic set in. He looked down at the items on the desk before him; a pristine blotter, ink and writing implements, stationery and a few oddities his father had accumulated over many years. One of these was a brass statuette of a naked male, also acquired no doubt at some auction. His mother had consistently complained of its presence on her rare visits to her husband's place of work.

Richard had a sudden urge to write a letter. He knew to whom he must send it, and had a good idea of its contents. He took a sheet of paper bearing the firm's name and began to write, carried away with fresh enthusiasm. 'Darling Kate,' he wrote, substituting it for 'Dear Kate', then compromising with 'Dearest Kate'. That resolved, he wrote swiftly and with a flow that surprised him.

When the letter was completed, he leaned back and read it through to himself, knowing immediately that he could not reveal his inmost feelings in such a manner. Nat Holland would telegraph his letter to Randolph, saving the six-week overland journey. What would Nat and the recipient at the hotel make of his letter as it stood? He screwed the sheet into a ball and aimed it at the waste basket, missing hopelessly. Richard retrieved the missile and put it into his pocket, its contents were too personal to leave around the office.

He started the letter again, writing now rather more deliberately and considering each word. This time the finished letter met with his approval, but he hesitated at the foot of the page, uncertain about how to sign off. Richard would have liked to indicate that he would see her soon, but how could he say that with any honesty? The traditional endings were all far too formal and he cogitated for some time on suitable alternatives.

Two words came to him and immediately became fixed in his mind as he repeated them. Richard considered them fully appropriate and wrote them above his signature.

He held the letter out in front of him, arms on the desk, and it occurred to him that in two months or so Kate would actually hold that very sheet on which he had written, and which he was now holding. Richard prepared the envelope and pushed the letter inside, immediately withdrawing it to read aloud for the last time:

Shaw & Steady
Leopard Chambers
Leopard Buildings
London.

3 December 1869

Dearest Kate,
I must tell you straight away of the hope I cling to, that you have forgiven me for my foolishness, immaturity and impetuosity. I cannot live with the knowledge that you bear me a grudge.

You are constantly in my thoughts and prayers. You Kate, Josh and Sam, and of course Jeb. May Christmas at the homestead be a happy one, how I would love to share it with you. Kindly pass on my regards to Jackie and thank her for interceding regarding this letter. Also remember me to John and Beth, Edith and Joshua and if you should see Dan Marshall please extend to him my best wishes.

My arrival at the coast was traumatic. David had been killed just a few weeks before and my conduct in that connection as I sought revenge does not make me proud. I have lost my best friend and the prospect of losing your respect also fills me with dread. I do not deserve your consideration but any communication from you would make me most happy. Just tell me how you feel, please?

The money enclosed should, on arrival, purchase a belated Christmas gift for each of you from 'E & J Bennett'. I shall think of the four of you, particularly on Christmas Day, in the hope that you will have received this letter via Nat and the telegraph.

Keep warm this winter, ever yours,
Richard.

Richard sealed the envelope addressed to Nat, with instructions enclosed for its relay to Randolph, and subsequent dispatch overland. Nat would at that stage enclose the money from funds left with him. The clerk in the firm's post room was most helpful and dealt with the stamp requirements, promising Richard to include his letter with the day's outgoing mail.

When Richard stepped light-heartedly onto the street it was snowing again. The family coach was waiting as arranged and he jumped inside, grateful of the isolation which afforded him time to mull over the day's events. Instead he imagined the wind blowing down the wide main street of Randolph, carrying before it debris and brush, much as it had on that first night he had spent in the town. He could not visualise snow there, for he had not seen any during the whole of last winter, just a bitter wind and driving rain. Old Jeb had told him that it could snow in the valley and that he remembered times when the livestock had been threatened by its depth. In his mind's eye Richard saw the mail coach on which Kate and he had spent those last moments together. That same coach would deposit his letter to Kate at the hotel. He wondered when it would reach there and recalled with a wry smile that the weather conditions in the Atlantic were always a deciding factor in estimating the duration of a crossing. Richard had regretted the bulky nature of his letter, which was rather lengthy for the signalling process.

The appearance of the familiar tenement flats brought Richard back to reality. He enquired of the driver (another new face, as his mother was never satisfied with any driver she employed) as to why he had taken this indirect route. He was informed that the main thoroughfare was blocked with snow and stranded vehicles. Richard requested that he be allowed to alight, assuring the driver of the brevity of the stop.

Mrs Forest opened the door and invited him in, her thin ginger hair falling down over both ears despite her attempts to restore its respectability with the palms of her hands. Her mumbled apologies for everything in general were lost on him as she disappeared into the flat, beckoning him to follow. The layout of the flat was now well-known to him with its poor furniture arranged tidily and decor in need of fresh paint and ideas.

"'E's out with 'is carriage, like a kid wiv a new toy," she said as they occupied the only two chairs. "You'll never be sorry yer set 'im up, 'e'll go straight nar 'e's earnin', you see if

109

I ain't right!" Her hair almost obliterated her face as she made an emphatic gesture.

"I'm so pleased." Richard got to his feet. "If he comes anywhere near Shaw Manor, tell him to call on me." He placed an envelope on the dresser. It contained a greeting and bank notes.

"I'll tell 'im," she promised, following Richard to the door.

"Goodbye Mrs Forest, thank you for understanding the situation last night," Richard said gratefully.

"Any time luv," she answered laughing, and reached up to kiss his cheek. "It's us should be thankin' yer."

"Happy Christmas."

"'Appy Chris'mus," she echoed. Richard waved at the top of the steps, descending gingerly on the icy surface, cleared of snow but freezing. He was pleased at the outcome of that morning's exchange of Forest's old cart for an almost new carriage on which Forest's name would be emblazoned. The agreement assured Richard of a regular income, but he doubted that any money would come his way. The look on Henry Forest's face was reward enough.

Richard's carriage eventually deposited him at his front door, and he entered the house with no ceremony, closing the door behind him. His mother was arranging greenery in the hall. "Bates' day off, he's back this evening," she said matter-of-factly, reading his mind. "So glad you're here dear, I have invited the Jeffersons for dinner, it will cheer you up. Richard, do get your hair cut. It looks positively primitive!" Richard was allowed no right of reply as his mother was now ascending the stairs. He had completely forgotten the traditional Friday dinner parties.

Richard wandered into the music room in which he had spent many happy hours. He sat at the piano staring at his reflection in the polished blackness of the grand. Amazingly, Caroline had come into his thoughts very little. The Jeffersons' only daughter had been his first lover some five years before. It had been widely speculated that the pair were destined to marry and society had marked this down as a future event. The Jeffersons had actively encouraged the match and were still full of hope that all was not lost in that direction.

The young couple themselves, however, had realised, despite moments of passion and hours of affinity, that they preferred to remain as they were and had made no progress towards matrimony. Richard momentarily compared Caroline's tenderness to the coldness of the women with whom he had occasionally spent lonely nights on his travels.

He lifted the piano cover and exercised his fingers on the shining keys, sweeping down the chromatic scale and ascending with a flourish. He drifted into 'Fur Elise' and played it for Kate, being rewarded by the vision of her smile. Richard had the morbid temptation to play 'Abide with me' but became confused as two beautiful women merged in his mind, both singing to his accompaniment.

Richard left the piano and crossed the room to where a pile of music was stacked, an accumulation of years, and picked up the top album, a new publication acquired just prior to his leaving. It was Brahms and he flicked through its pages searching for the composition that had delighted him two years ago, finding the page and placing the music on the stand. It was the opus 117 Intermezzi and he caressed the keys, becoming totally involved in the sombre richness and lyrical invention. It came to him anew why this work had so captured his soul, and such was the inspiration of that moment, he vowed that wherever he might roam, this music would accompany him.

Remaining at the piano for most of the evening, he cleansed his mind of all else that tried to dominate it. By the time he had dressed for dinner he was ready to perform the duties of host, almost his old self again.

There had been some doubt as to whether the Jeffersons would get through the snow, but promptly at six the bell clanged and Bates ushered their guests into the hall, where Richard and his mother were waiting. The Jeffersons were, all three, tall and fair. Caroline was wearing her blonde hair rather longer than Richard remembered it and he was struck anew by her beauty. Greetings were exchanged all round and Mrs Shaw took Caroline's parents into the drawing room. Caroline flung her arms around Richard, causing Bates to retreat hastily. They held each other for some time, each gauging the other's reaction and response after such a long separation. Her blonde head nestled into his chest then her face lifted upward in that familiar gesture. Remembering, he kissed her.

Eventually they considered it prudent to join their elders and moved into the drawing room, not having uttered a single word between them, yet having communicated quite effectively.

"You found the roads passable?" Mrs Shaw was saying unnecessarily. "Such a bore this snow."

"My, how handsome your son looks with his tan!" Charlotte Jefferson remarked as the couple entered the room, silencing their hostess for several golden moments. She recovered, predictably.

"Richard, take Caroline into the music room, you must have so much to talk about." The pair took off and gratefully did as instructed.

"Oh Richard, I have missed you," said Caroline in the safety of the music room. No further words were possible as they rediscovered each other.

"Caroline, please!" protested Richard breathlessly.

"You don't love me any more," she chided in mock severity.

"I do love you passionately, darling," he responded playfully, "but we eat in a moment. I can't look too dishevelled."

"Richard," she said urgently, "I must know all about your adventures, right down to the most intimate detail - did you miss me?"

"Yes, yes of course," he lied, wondering why he had not missed her more, but deep within himself knowing the answer.

"You didn't write - not a word," she protested.

"We agreed ..." he started.

"Yes, I know," she cut in apologetically, "Will you promise to tell me everything?"

"Of course." He drew her to him more in defence than from any feeling of desire. Richard considered at what point he should begin to shade the truth regarding his activities. How could he explain to Caroline, or any of his friends, the vastly differing lifestyles, or his acquired expertise with his horse or with a gun, resulting in the extinguishing of two lives?

"Hey, come back to me!" pleaded Caroline, intercepting his stare. "Tell me all about it." Richard smiled at her lovely face with its perfect complexion, her wide blue eyes watching him, searching his face.

The situation was relieved by the gong sounding and calling them to dinner. Caroline hung onto his hand as they reached the dining-room, letting go only as they parted to face each other across the huge table.

Richard found the evening taxing, both emotionally and mentally. He imparted simple tales of everyday life in America and went into detail regarding his routes. He aroused much humour as he described the crossings and the seasickness which abounded, but could see by his mother's face that it was no subject for her dinner table. He answered questions from all points of the table, the most searching of which came from opposite him, and Richard found himself telling Caroline what she wished to hear.

It struck him as he ate - the conversation having momentarily moved away from him - to whom could he divulge every truth? It seemed to him that there was just one soul-mate with whom he could be completely at ease, and she was thousands of miles away.

Much of that evening was spent in the music room, where Caroline and Richard played duets on the piano at the request of their parents. Richard recalled how Caroline always used to annoy him by her carelessness. That evening was no exception, and as their elders chatted quietly the two on the piano stool engaged in mutual frowning and head shaking. The performances ended with smiles however, each happy to be in the other's company.

Arthur Jefferson brought the evening to its conclusion, addressing the hostess; "Mary, it's still snowing and we really should not delay our departure any longer."

The Jeffersons disappeared into the snowy darkness, but not before Richard had promised to take Caroline to the theatre the next evening. The house was quiet and he returned to the music room which was now invaded by Caroline's perfume and presence. He played the Brahms again, restoring sanity to his world.

Later that night, Richard lay in bed wishing that he was sharing the homestead barn with Valiant. He thought that he could smell straw and fell asleep immediately.

Chapter 14

Saturday began with glorious weather. All the heavy snow-laden clouds of the previous weeks had dispersed and the sun shone out of a blue sky. Richard walked in the garden after breakfast on paths cleared of snow but which had frozen during the early hours. He considered it good to be alive on such a morning.

The frozen snow packed onto branches and misshapen hedgerows sparkled as they caught the sun's rays and the sheer whiteness of it dazzled eyes accustomed to the gloom of the winter. Richard's stroll took him round the garden which was hiding under its winter anonymity. He knew the potential that would be realised with the coming of warm sunshine. All the beds, now white with untidy stalks and dead heads, would erupt into a magnificent display of contrasting flowers and colours. Each bed had been carefully planned and supervised by his mother. His stroll finally brought him to the kitchen garden and he halted outside the huge wooden gate beyond which no one, save the gardeners, would dare set foot. Even his parents, on the odd occasion they wished to traverse the inside of those walls, would be accompanied by the head gardener.

Pushing open the gate took all of Richard's weight and strength. He entered the garden for the first time in years and memories flooded back as he stood just inside the gate, surveying again that vast enclosure. It had been an awesome place for a small boy, walled in as it was. He had fantasised over the existence there of 'little people' and a variety of other imaginary beings. The stories his mother read to him were re-enacted behind what were, to a youngster, very tall brick walls. He recalled, just a year or so later, walking with his father and the head gardener and disturbing a blackbird, its shrill warning cry echoing around that confinement. Richard had tottered after it, arms outstretched, screaming excitedly, then heart-broken at the realisation that the bird would not come to him. He gradually, too, came to realise the shattering truth that there was no magical world within, only vegetable patches, currant bushes and greenhouses. As he now walked the slippery periphery path in the shadow of the wall, he could still feel that childhood chagrin, even though twenty years had elapsed.

Much later still, his father had presented him to the head gardener. Richard had been instructed as to the prudence of maintaining such a garden, rendering Shaw Manor almost self-sufficient and independent. 'Alus prudent m'lad, alus prudent 'tis.' Richard smiled to himself as he pronounced the word prudent as the head gardener always had, with the emphasis on the second syllable. It had obviously been a word the gardener had picked up from William or Mary Shaw and used proudly in that unique fashion as often as he could. However, old Bert Rakes (or Raker, as he was known) died soon after Richard met him and there had been a succession of head gardeners since then. Richard shook off what seemed a myriad of memories, pulling the heavy gate shut. It felt at that moment as though this very act itself was shutting off his childhood and youth, the walled area a repository for his early life. With an imperceptible shake of the head, he retraced his steps to the house.

Mrs. Shaw had taken the coach into the city to visit her husband and then friends. Richard, aware of his lack of recent exercise, resolved to walk for most of the day. He attired himself appropriately and informed Bates of his intentions.

He left the Manor and at the end of the drive turned his back on the city and its affairs, and set off into the country. Walking was difficult and following the tracks already made was the obvious course, but the frozen base of the ruts made progress hazardous. The alternative was to tread the hard virgin snow, an exhausting process. Richard found that he had little choice in the matter, as attempting to follow the icy track of a cart wheel, he would slip and overbalance; he was happy to place a foot in deep snow to achieve a temporary stability.

About a mile from his home Richard came across a notice set back into the hedgerow and festooned with icicles. He brushed the snow from its face with gloved hand, revealing the fact that there were stables at the end of a narrow track going off at right-angles. He vaguely recalled the presence of horses in the area as riders had passed his home on numerous occasions. Such equestrian activity had been of little interest to him prior to his arrival in America.

He turned down the track, which bore witness of its use by way of horse-shoe impressions in the centre of the lane away from the drifted snow on each side. He found the stables were quite extensive and as he approached, familiar sounds greeted him. A whinny and snort from within brought his own horse sharply into focus in his mind's eye. It posed the question: why had he not brought Valiant back to England with him? He would surely have found accommodation at a stable such as this, and as Valiant had been broken to harness and saddle, the grey could conceivably have been used with the coach.

Richard was still turning this over in his mind when he noticed a stable-hand walking towards him, clutching a broom and bucket.

"Can I help you sir?" he enquired.

"Er, may I look at the horses, please?" Richard said simply.

"Yes, come with me. Do you wish to ride?" he asked pleasantly. "The conditions aren't favourable for lessons - should improve if this weather keeps up though. Have you worked with horses at all?" The stripling of a lad, whose eyes were on a level with Richard's chest, kept up a stream of questions and facts until they neared the first stable. They wandered through the long sheds, patting the occasional horse curious enough to pop its head over the stable door, no doubt in the hope of receiving some tit-bit or another. Richard saw few horses of the stature of Valiant's sixteen hands.

"Will you be wanting to take a horse out?" the boy enquired, peering up at Richard.

"I certainly will, and I'm quite an experienced rider."

"We have a good reputation in the city sir, and our rates are very competitive." The lad reeled off all the attributes of the stable in a well-rehearsed recital. The tour of inspection over, Richard thanked the hand and promised to return when the weather improved with a view to becoming a member of the local riding club.

"Could I keep a horse of my own here?" Richard asked as the boy took up his bucket and broom.

"You could, yes sir, the private stables are over there. All full at the moment, but there may be vacancies later." Richard thanked him again and headed back up the lane to the main road.

As he resumed his journey cautiously, Richard resolved to bring Valiant over if he could get the grey's owner to sell. He had to face the fact that this might well be impossible, and anyway, how would the horse cope with the crossing?

Richard's progress was punctuated by meetings with neighbours. They were eager to hear of his exploits as they rested for a moment before going on their way screaming happily and slipping on the ice. His destination was an inn he thought was just within walking distance in the conditions. His doubts regarding its accessibility were allayed as the village where the inn was situated came into view as he rounded a bend. Two years away had clouded his memory of such places and he stepped inside the inn with an unfamiliarity that surprised him.

For an inn as popular as this one, there were very few customers. A handful of regulars had braved the conditions and were standing in a semi-circle facing a huge open log fire. Richard joined them and entered into the cheerful banter. His mind strayed back to the sparsely populated bar at the Emperor's Delight in Randolph. He absurdly imagined the toothless one making an entrance here and being ridiculed for his American drawl. Richard smiled to himself at the parallel. He listened to the desultory conversation around him, feeling the fire's warmth. As he sipped his beer he watched the flames devour the logs around which they flickered. He had been told as a child of the pictures one could detect in a fire, and as an adult had seen many images unfold in his camp fires.

He snapped out of his reverie as the grandfather clock in the lounge captured his attention by striking three. He was suddenly aware of the gathering gloom, emphasised by the prominence of the fire's glow. He pulled on his coat and left the cosy atmosphere of the inn, the icy wind biting into his face. After an hour the light faded and black night clouds began to fill the sky. His progress became even more difficult as the shadows hid the treachery of the ice and the sharpening frost solidified the ruts.

There was little activity on this road now that darkness had fallen. Richard had the impression that he was its lone occupant, grateful in a way for his privacy, feeling ridiculous as he scrambled his way painfully along the shining surface. He stood stock still for a moment to regain his breath. There was utter silence, just the pounding of his heart from the exertion. The chill wind penetrated his clothing as if it did not exist and his breath clouded before him. His ribs reminded him of their recent fracture as he inhaled the frozen air deeply.

Remembering his evening appointment with Caroline, he pushed himself forward again, determined to master the conditions just as he had on so many occasions during the past two years.

The light was now so bad that without the reflected snow he could not have maintained any direction at all. The tracks were just discernable against its whiteness, giving him a visibility of some two or three yards. He was somewhat disorientated but staggered on.

Shaw Manor was a welcome sight as it suddenly appeared out of the darkness with its familiar contours and lighted windows. Richard was greeted by an anxious Bates, who informed him that his mother had sent the coach back from the city for his use. She would be returning late and would have an alternative conveyance.

Richard washed, shaved and changed into evening dress, surprising cook and the maid by appearing in the kitchen. They prepared a hot meal for him and giggled as he took it. Both about Richard's age, they had never before seen a member of the Shaw family in the kitchen unless it was to issue orders or complain. Richard thanked them both, and hurried to the dining room where he quickly devoured his meal, then jumped into the waiting carriage.

He knew that Caroline would be dressed for the occasion and the new production of 'Hamlet' they were to see was an occasion indeed. He was not disappointed. She was waiting for him as the coach arrived at her front door and was looking delightful. At close range she was even more wonderful, filling the coach with her fragrance and holding her head up to him in that manner of hers. He kissed her lightly. As they headed for the city he related his day's adventure to her, she reciprocating by describing her Christmas shopping spree. They felt comfortable together as they always had in times past.

The performance was one of the most moving Richard

had seen, an opinion corroborated by Caroline as they wined and dined in an adjacent restaurant afterwards. As always, she was perfect company and Richard had relaxed his guard sufficiently for her to glean certain details of his travels. When, after several glasses of wine, he confided in her that he had killed in a gun duel, she burst into uncontrollable laughter, mistaking his severity for humour. Disappointed, he made no further attempt at opening up his heart.

Caroline was, without doubt, the most intelligent of his friends and acquaintances and that included many of his old university colleagues. She would expound on Shakespeare, Bunyan and Nietzche as if they were personally known to her. She was an expert on theatre life and its productions, and would recite line after line of famous works as a party piece, imparting a drama and pathos into her interpretation that had her audiences spellbound.

As a musician Caroline was acceptable but as a conversationalist she was brilliant. She was also an accomplished manager of all things domestic. The Jefferson home on the city's periphery was run by Caroline while her parents were away on business for long periods. Her predominant achievement, however, was her knowledge of literature, whether foreign translations or works written in her own language, and her expertise on the subject had always been a source of pride to Richard, who had very often been at her side as she impressed scholar and layman alike.

The Jeffersons were jewellers in the city and Caroline's father was also very active politically, seeking nomination as a candidate at the next parliamentary elections and fiercely opposed to Gladstone's government. The Jeffersons were also avid theatre goers. Arthur Jefferson often made generous contributions to the theatre at which they had just spent the evening. As patron, he was able to obtain priority bookings and the best seats in the house. Richard and Caroline benefited frequently from this advantage, tonight's premiere being no exception.

Caroline assisted in the family business - she used to say that it was a way of meeting people. Her father was obviously proud to have her by his side and maintained that her looks and personality attracted custom, her very presence in the shop being good for business. Richard wholeheartedly agreed with this theory, as it was whilst he was in the shop delving through trays of various items of jewellery that he first set eyes on Caroline. The reason for his visit and the would-be recipient of the purchase had long escaped him, but he remembered to this day the way he had been consumed with undying love for the blonde assistant in the city jewellers.

A year Richard's junior, she had been slow to respond to his advances, allowing him to escort her home from a university concert only after much persuasion. That evening had been the start of it all. He had eventually won her heart on the piano stool as they shared the keyboard on musical evenings sponsored by the families who were brought together by this liaison.

Richard's mind drifted back to when Caroline had contracted a mystery illness, baffling her family doctors. One had diagnosed consumption, a second considered that she'd had a breakdown of some kind. A third opinion actually suspected an attack of scarlet fever. Whatever the complaint, it was responsible for reducing her to a mere skeleton weighing no more than a child.

Caroline had been admitted to a country hospital in the west of England, some two hours from Shaw Manor. Richard had visited her each Sunday afternoon that he had been home from university. The family coach had always been at his disposal and he left regularly after lunch, returning the same evening. He could visualise her now, that spare frame waiting at the window, looking for his coach with its unmistakable markings. Over the months Richard had perceived a steady improvement taking place in her, until that unforgettable day when she had been sent home, virtually cured. There had been great rejoicing in the two households on that occasion. Richard had been convinced that she had suffered a nervous breakdown as she had been, and still was, very highly strung, tending to live on her nerves. They had become very close during those days at the sanatorium, drifting apart somewhat as his visit to America loomed. Richard had thought of her from time to time on those endless trails, but she had not featured much in his mind after he had ridden into Randolph.

They emerged from the restaurant at midnight, and a carriage driver responded to Richard's wave and took them to Caroline's home. Richard asked the cabby to return in two hours and they entered the house, which was completely in darkness.

"Mummy and Daddy are away this weekend," she said wickedly as they stood in the hallway, "and the servants are in bed."

They climbed the stairs together, a lamp between them. Once inside her room Richard placed the lamp on the bedside table. The same aroma lingered, it was Caroline's aroma which she left wherever she went and which was still mildly discernible in his own music room. The decor in her room had not altered and the furniture was as he remembered it too. Had he really been away?

"Time is not on our side, Richard," she implored. "Are you sure you have to return tonight?" He nodded as she came towards him, head tilted upwards (dramatically, he thought) and this time the kiss was not one of politeness but an indication of his desire.

Through their eventual nakedness they regained all the familiarity accumulated on past occasions. He again marvelled at her gentleness and ultimate passion. His own culmination seemed to free him of his frustrations and anxieties.

Later, she whispered in his ear as they clung to each other. "Should we not be married, Richard? It's expected of us." He lay watching the shadows move around the ceiling.

"Do you love me then?" he asked, turning his head and looking into her eyes. She was silent for a while, staring at him.

"I love being with you," she replied, "is that not the same thing?" Richard was not prepared to discuss love intellectually and, having no answer to her question, kissed her deeply.

There was no more discussion or sound of any kind, save that of their movement and heavy breathing. Richard was caught up in the sensual world of which he rarely partook, and was happy to enjoy its transient delights.

* * *

Bates was alert to the fact that the master of the house had not yet returned home and was in attendance as Richard's carriage reached the front of the house.

"Thought I would save you searching for the back door, Master Richard," he said in the hall, raising one eyebrow just a fraction in wry humour that had been known to surface from time to time, although Richard doubted that his mother would have been aware of it.

Richard expressed his gratitude to Bates and wished him a good night, what remained of it. Bates, thought Richard, must be the perfect butler, particularly as he'd survived Mrs.

Shaw's scrutiny all these years. Perfection, he concluded, was a necessary requirement for survival at Shaw Manor.

* * *

The coach arrived at the front door on that Sunday morning as it had for as long as Richard could remember. He assisted his mother into the vehicle and climbed up beside her. He missed his father acutely at that moment, the family's incompleteness suddenly striking him.

The drive to the local parish church had taken place in all weathers. Richard recalled an occasion when the roads had been flooded after heavy rains. The cabby had expressed grave misgivings at the wisdom of making the journey, but had reached the church and navigated the return home. The driver had been replaced the very next day.

The church was full that morning which rather surprised Richard, travelling conditions being as they were. He nodded at several acquaintances in the congregation, receiving nods or smiles in return. The Reverend in the pulpit, who was unknown to Richard, was in great form. Encouraged by the good attendance he launched into a series of Advent thoughts and quotations, punctuating them with relevant hymns. Richard wondered if Kate was in her pew at Randolph that day. In his confusion, he could not calculate the time difference.

The text chosen as a basis for the sermon was 'Where your treasure is, there will your heart be also', given a seasonal slant. The text affected Richard deeply, and he concluded that this Jesus Christ must have been an astute man. Richard's prayer as the service came to its 'Amen' was for guidance. A prayer from the heart, as he had a glimpse of where his treasure lay.

Chapter 15

The family conveyance was waiting for Richard long before sunrise was due on that Monday morning. He had eaten breakfast alone and apart from his greeting to Bates had not spoken a word before getting into the coach.

At this hour the cold was penetrating. Even inside the coach Richard was obliged to pull his coat tightly around him and huddle into a corner for warmth. His apprehension regarding the day ahead did nothing to stop his uncontrollable shivering. He had intended, during the journey, to flip through papers relevant to his first appointment, but was discouraged from doing so by the cold and the meagre light coming from an external coach lamp.

By the time the driver had negotiated the traffic and they had reached Leopard Chambers, the grey dawn had arrived and city lamps were being extinguished.

Richard occupied his father's desk on which flowers (he had no idea where they could have been obtained at that time of year) had been placed in one of William Shaw's antique vases. The staff were very understanding of his situation and ready to assist in every way they could. Richard found his position frustrating in the extreme as he struggled to recall his training and make some practical use of it.

As the week progressed the routine became more familiar. Richard felt that he was at last of some benefit to Mr Steady, who nevertheless kept an eagle eye on him, praising or correcting his efforts as appropriate.

So, inevitably and without deviation, Richard's weekly programme became established. From Monday until Friday he was in the city, in and around the offices and courts of Leopard Chambers. On Friday evenings he played host to whoever his mother chose to invite to Shaw Manor. On Saturday he walked to the stables and rode his favourite bay along the lanes and bridle paths near to his home, and afterwards the evening was devoted to Caroline. The traditional drive to church on Sunday was followed by an afternoon with friends or spent alone in the music room. He visited his father each day at lunchtime, and always left the hospital in a depressed mood.

Christmas provided a welcome variation from this routine. Richard was delighted to accompany his father home for the festive season. It had in fact been decided that William Shaw should be released from hospital permanently as there was little that could be done for him. A male nurse was to be in attendance at all times, a condition his mother had insisted upon before consenting to the arrangement.

The house looked wonderful that Christmas Eve and Richard complemented his mother on this fact, receiving a curt reminder that she had made no special effort, and that the house had looked equally attractive during his absence. Richard's enthusiasm was not to be dampened and he admired the floral and evergreen arrangements placed strategically around the house. He appreciated the aroma of burning wood as log fires had been lit in every room. A huge Christmas tree stood in the drawing room, bearing colourful decorations of all sizes, reflecting the lamp light and giving an effect of constant movement.

A group of carol singers paid their traditional visit to the manor. Family and servants congregated in the drawing room and joined the group in the singing of well-known carols. The tree around which they stood appeared to twinkle with delight as its branches were stripped of brightly-wrapped packages, which were then handed to excited recipients, who in turn presented their own gifts. Richard's thoughts winged across the ocean on many an occasion during the day, making him rather more remote than was natural.

After dinner Richard played the piano for his father. William Shaw had always been the paternal influence behind his music making as in fact behind all his achievements. He knew that his father appreciated the music played for him and selected pieces he had loved in past years. William Shaw, still only fifty, looked very old as Richard studied him over the piano. As he played, his father was taken by sudden sleep and the male nurse gathered him up in his arms like a baby as Mrs Shaw watched imperturbably. The nurse left the room bearing the meagre frame and Richard stared after them, wondering why such a noble character should be smitten with this indignity and dependence.

Christmas Day was to have been spent at the Jeffersons but Mr Shaw's condition had led Richard to object to this arrangement. The invitation was reversed and the two families spent the day at Shaw Manor.

Richard had promised to play the organ at church for the morning service, the regular incumbent of the organ loft being away for Christmas. His mother had decided to stay at home to supervise the preparations she said had been thrust upon her at the last moment, and it was Caroline who accompanied Richard in the coach. She agreed to turn the pages of music for him, a task he always found difficult when having to cope with pedals, stops and manuals.

The couple exchanged greetings with their many friends in the congregation. The question as to the date of their wedding was on many lips, as it was generally assumed that they had entered into an unofficial engagement. Caroline welcomed the assumption, as Richard may have done prior to his visit to America, but he somehow felt the need for caution, though at that stage not knowing exactly why.

As if the delay caused by talking to acquaintances was not enough, Caroline and Richard then made matters worse by taking the coach driver (another new face) into an inn near the church where they mingled with revellers who packed the bars.

"Merry Christmas!" was the cry from well-lubricated throats as the crowd dispersed and the three picked their way over the ice to the coach.

They were in disgrace on arrival at the manor, having delayed lunch by one hour. Forgiveness of this irresponsible behaviour may have been forthcoming were it not for the good humour of the young couple and the complete absence of contrition. As they ate in the strained atmosphere, Richard allowed himself the luxury of casting his mind back to the previous year, when he had spent a miserable Christmas in a cheap hotel at the most distant point of his travels. The only way he'd had of making the situation tolerable and the company acceptable was to drink. And drink he had, losing consciousness for hours and finding later that he had been robbed of every cent in his pockets. He had, at that time of course, been unaware of Kate a hundred miles to the east. Richard's thoughts came back to the present and settled on the homestead and its occupants. Had they received his letter? Would a reply arrive at the office next month? What would it contain - utter rejection or a forgiving tone? His sigh signified his desire to be with that little family he had known for just two days. He was suddenly aware too of the reason for his caution regarding marriage to Caroline and felt guilty as he returned her smile across the table.

* * *

The new year heralded the arrival of a new decade. With it the weather turned milder and the snow and ice, which for so long had been part of the landscape, gradually disappeared. The ice-covered ruts now became open furrows of water rendering the highways just as impassable as they had been before the thaw. These drastic changes in the climatic conditions were not reflected in Richard's life, which deviated very little from its course. He became more secure behind his desk as he gained experience, yet paradoxically, felt an unsettling yearning which he could not clearly define.

One particular day towards the end of January became an eventful one on three counts: a meeting with an old friend, the receipt of a letter and the threat of an impending decline in his fortunes.

Richard was returning from lunch and waiting to cross the busy road near his Chambers. He was idly watching the horse-buses and carriages as they queued, blocking his way. He was aware of a familiar figure perched atop one of the carriages just ahead of him, though somehow he was not sure. His eyes dropped to the gold lettering on the door and his first guess was confirmed. It was indeed Henry Forest. Richard instinctively jumped up beside him, swaying the vehicle and receiving a look of alarm from its owner.

"Mr Richard!" Forest exclaimed, "'Ow good ter see yer." The carriage moved forward as they gripped each other in a strong handshake. "Can I take yer anywhere?"

"No, no thank you," Richard replied. "But how is business?"

"Grand, just grand Mr Richard, wiv' the 'orse buses and trams off the road in the bad wevver I wuz doin' just grand. Workin' day and night I wuz."

"Keeping out of mischief then?" laughed Richard. Forest scratched his ginger head under the cap which Richard had hoped he would have exchanged for more sophisticated head-wear.

"I'm a changed man, Mr Richard, seen the light I 'ave, and the missus too. We joined the mission at Whitechapel."

"Mission! What mission?" Richard was puzzled.

"New Christian Mission. They wuz preachin' in the street. Me and the missus stood in the crowd. We reckon they wuz preachin' just to us. They need a lot o' money for a new 'all in Aldgate. Do a bit to 'elp when we can, like."

"Well, I certainly am impressed, Henry, delighted that you're going straight." Richard found himself caught up in his friend's enthusiasm.

"'Ere, take this money, Mr Richard, I 'aven't forgotten our deal," said Forest, pushing a handful of notes in Richard's direction, then grabbing the reins as they caught up with the vehicle in front.

"Henry, give the money to the mission," Richard said, declining the offer, "Anyone who can make an honest man of Henry Forest deserves it."

"Thank yer, God bless yer Mr Richard," he said gratefully, "The missus and me's movin' into the city next month, a little 'ouse wiv a stable nearby. Better for business bein' in the city. Missus said to invite yer and yer lovely lady to the new 'ouse, I'll leave a message in yer office when we moves and it all 'appens."

Richard had travelled the best part of a mile from his offices and decided that it was time to alight.

"Good to see you, Henry. Regards to Mrs Forest, and let me know when you move." They shook hands again and Richard left the carriage as it lurched forward once more. The sounds from the departing vehicle caused Richard to stop and stare after it in disbelief. Henry Forest, ex thief, was singing at the top of his voice to the city around him, with numerous modulations and mis-pronunciations, but the words rang clear; 'Bless His name, He sets me free,' to a tune Richard had heard in many a bar - 'Champagne Charlie'!

Richard arrived at his office to be informed that a personal letter awaited his collection in the post room. He was late for an appointment and resolved to collect his mail later. It was towards dusk, with the lamps freshly lit, when the letter in question arrived on his desk. He absent-mindedly cast a glance in its direction, then froze as he recognised the hand which had written the envelope.

Richard knew immediately that it was the bold script of Nat Holland in America. He stared at the envelope, trying to decipher whether it was from Nat himself or perhaps from the authorities following up their investigations into Radford's death. He shook as he realised that it could be a telegraph version of Kate's reply from the interior. He slit open the envelope unsteadily, excitement blurring his vision for a moment. There were two sheets folded together, one signed in Nat's hand, and the other a typed 'Kate'. He dropped the former onto the desk and read the letter from Kate, savouring every word. Without hesitation he read it for a second time:

Hilltop Hotel
Randolph

January 1st

Dear Richard,

It was with great joy that I received your letter via Mr Holland. It is most kind of him to assist in this way. I now look forward to your written word.

Josh, Sam and I are well. Jeb is not I fear. He is not able to do much these days. Virginia left some weeks ago headed your way, she will give you all the news in detail. She is a remarkable young lady of whom I am very fond. Her father too has been most kind. Thank you for achieving this reconciliation.

The children talk about you often, as do the townsfolk.

Seth Barratt is always singing your praises (remember him? No teeth!).

I cherish the time spent with you and I cannot believe that it was only two days. Please explain why you feel that you have failed me, in those two days you almost changed my way of living. The children were heartbroken that you did not say goodbye, we do miss you Richard.

When you receive the written letter you will see that the children signed off personally. Sam is nine next week and Josh will be fifteen in May. How time flies!

We are keeping warm despite very low temperatures, cold winds and flurries of snow. Jackie is going to send this to Mr Holland tomorrow.

God bless you, Richard. Please write again.

Kate, Josh and Sam.

The other sheet was a note from Nat warning Richard that the feeling against him was, in some quarters, turning into hostility. The Sheriff who had instructed him to remain available was very unhappy with Richard's departure and had reported the circumstances to higher authority. Nat indicated that he would keep him informed of developments, but still did not come clean as to the family involvement of Radford - if it was in fact true.

Richard left the office and took a seat in a nearby park. He read Kate's letter again, wishing that it was her own writing rather than the impersonal and regular print of a telegram. The prospect of Virginia visiting him soon filled him with elation, for he would indeed learn from her of recent happenings around Randolph.

Folding the sheet carefully he then pushed it into his pocket. He returned to the office and Mr Steady, spending the rest of the afternoon assisting him in preparing a case brought against Henry Forest's Christian Mission, and in particular a Mr William Booth, its founder. The charge was disturbing the peace.

The third event on this day was revealed as Richard returned home that evening. In the drive was a police carriage, a constable at the reins. He indicated that his superior was waiting inside the house. A stern Bates took Richard into the drawing-room where his mother was supplying the policeman with tea.

"This is Sergeant O'Malley Richard. Sergeant, my son Richard."

"Thank you ma'am," said the Sergeant with a delightful Irish accent.

"How can I help you?" Richard asked with some anxiety.

"Would you be good enough to call at the Central Police Station tomorrow sir, about midday if that is convenient."

"Yes, of course," Richard replied, "but for what purpose?"

"I really can't tell at the moment sir, I am just delivering the message. Thank you. Good evening madam, good evening sir." The policeman nodded at Mrs Shaw and Richard and was escorted out by the ever vigilant Bates.

"Richard, what is this all about?" Mrs Shaw asked as the drawing-room door closed.

"I have no idea, mother, I shall no doubt find out tomorrow." He climbed the stairs to prepare for dinner, leaving his mother in the hall, shaking her head despairingly.

Chapter 16

Eventful days have a habit of grouping themselves after an extended period of relative calm and inactivity. This was such an occasion, for after the excitement of receiving Kate's letter and the chance meeting with Henry Forest, followed by the arrival of the police, Richard faced a second day which was to be anything but routine.

He spent two hours at the police station near his office and learned of the situation across the Atlantic, which was much as Nat had indicated in his note. Sergeant O'Malley had that morning been briefed on the case and Richard gave him the whole story regarding Dave's murder and the death of Captain Radford. As he spoke, Richard realised that any listener in Victorian England would be horrified by his execution of the seaman, and by the look on Sergeant O'Malley's face those who questioned him were no exception.

The burly policeman also informed Richard of the intentions of Dave's brother, Philip, at sea during the events in question, to even the score and avenge his father's death. Sergeant O'Malley also confirmed that Dave had been Nat's son by his first marriage and that Philip was Sarah's son by Captain Radford. Richard reflected on how much easier it would have been if Sarah and Nat had confided in him initially. Nat had omitted these facts from his recent note.

The final shattering blow was delivered by the policeman as Richard was preparing to leave the station.

"Mr Shaw, you have been requested not to return to America, for your own safety and that of American citizens."

"I consider the last point to be in bad taste," responded Richard hotly.

"Their words, not mine," added the Sergeant defensively.

"Good day to you," Richard said curtly, turning on his heel and leaving the premises. He dropped by the office and, having no further appointments that day, informed them that he would not be available until the next morning. Rather than wait for the family conveyance, he hailed a carriage and headed for home.

The full impact of the interview came to him as he was flung around his carriage (mentally recording his appreciation of the Shaw coach with its superior suspension). The prospect of never seeing Kate or the valley again was totally unacceptable. Richard had at the very least intended to spend another holiday there. As he stared out across the busy streets thronged with people, his desolation increased. What should he have done, let Radford get away with Dave's murder? What would the authorities over there have done to investigate the matter? He supposed that, having established the facts, he should then have notified the local Sheriff, but Richard concluded that in the course of verifying information given to him by Rebecca, he had been forced to kill in self-defence.

He was in a slightly easier frame of mind as the carriage left him at the front of the house. He was thankful that his mother was not at home. Richard greeted his father in the drawing-room, trying to elicit a warm smile for him but failing dismally. His father would have understood his predicament and given him sound advice, but instead was only able to follow his progress across the room with tired, lifeless eyes.

Richard heard the family coach arrive as it swung around the drive, and fled to the privacy of his room, not wanting a confrontation with his mother but accepting the inevitable fact that he would have to face her at dinner.

Richard remained in his room in contemplation, piecing together the facts. He was struck by the injustice of it all and knew that he had to take some action, but was unsure of the form it should take. He decided to seek advice from the imperturbable Mr Steady, but was not sure that he was ready to impart the whole story to his senior partner.

Dressing for dinner, he seemed to have made no progress and was dreading the inquisition at dinner, with his father a mere spectator.

Fate, however, was to smile favourably upon him as the second occurrence of the day unfolded. Richard heard Bates respond to the clang at the front door, his familiar footsteps crossing the hall followed by muffled voices as the door was opened. Bates then returned to the bottom of the stairs where Mrs Shaw was obviously waiting. By this time Richard's curiosity had got the better of him and he had gone to his door, his excitement mounting as he overheard the butler's announcement.

"There is a young lady to see Master Richard, m'lady," he said, annoying his mistress with the constant and habitual use of 'Master' when referring to Richard.

"Show her into the morning room Bates," she commanded, "I will inform my son."

Richard's heart leapt as he hurried along the passage, meeting his mother at the top of the stairs.

"There is a young lady in the morning room, Richard, all the way from America, probably the farm girl you are expecting. Before you go, what did the authorities want with you yesterday?"

"Some misunderstanding, mother, I hope to sort it out." said Richard managing a smile. His mother threw her hands in the air in despair and Richard descended the stairs, now eager to see Virginia again.

She was standing in the centre of the room studying family portraits and Richard considered her to be a study herself in elegance and beauty. The evening lamplight fell on her jet black hair. She was dressed in black, which exaggerated the paleness of her skin, and as she turned he thought that she looked very tired and drawn. They wordlessly embraced, each glad to see the other.

Richard held her at arm's length, recalling the birthday party and the young hostess.

"Virginia, what a lovely surprise, I didn't expect to see you so soon. Your Pa was right, you certainly are growing up fast."

"Richard, how could I come to England without looking you up?" she asked with mock severity.

"How did you find me?" Richard asked, guiding her to a chair.

"How many Shaws are there with your pedigree?" she laughed, crossing her legs and tossing her hair back. "It was simple really." Richard heard his mother's footfall.

"Mother, do come and meet Miss Virginia Marshall. Virginia, my mother, Mrs Mary Shaw." Virginia rose from the chair and stood beside Richard.

"I am honoured to meet you ma'am," she said in her lovely drawl. Richard was aware of the look of absolute surprise on his mother's face. She recovered quickly.

"You are very beautiful, my dear," she said, taking Virginia's hand. "I am beginning to see why my son spent so much time in your country."

"Not on my account, ma'am, I assure you," Virginia responded, glancing aside at Richard, "We met only the once." Richard decided on the spur of that moment that he loved that drawl and realised how much he had missed it.

"You will stay for dinner, of course," his mother was saying, more as an assumption than a request.

"Well, I booked dinner at the hotel and ..." Virginia was not allowed to finish as his mother took over, her hands dramatically held aloft.

"Nonsense my dear. Richard, tell Miss Marshall that she must dine with us."

"Please do," Richard coaxed, not hiding his smile of resignation.

"Well, if it's no trouble, thank you." Virginia capitulated.

"Come with me my dear, I will show you the guest room." His mother whisked Virgina away and up the stairs. Richard knew that he had to get Virginia to himself, as questions were tumbling through his mind. He needed many answers from her and he probably needed to confide in her. She seemed more mature than at their last meeting, yet only six months had elapsed since then.

The two ladies, who incredibly seemed to be getting along very well, glided down the stairs as the dinner gong resounded through the house. Richard met them at the foot of the stairs and followed as they entered the dining-room.

Virginia kept her hosts entertained with the details of her journey, made by coach and ship. She too had hated the crossing and had arrived at Liverpool late the previous night, reaching her London hotel in the early hours. Mrs Shaw expressed amazement at their visitor travelling to Europe alone. Richard wondered if the hazards of the venture would ever have crossed Virginia's mind. Gradually Mrs Shaw began to dominate the proceedings as she gave her guest an insight into Victorian London and the changes that were taking place in the city.

As the three moved into the drawing room for coffee, Richard brought the subject back to America, preferring to hear from Virginia than experience his mother's prejudiced views of life. Eventually Bates announced that the coach was at their disposal and Virginia took the opportunity to inform the Shaws of her weariness, caused by not sleeping during the passage. She wished to seek her bed as soon as possible.

"Do call and say goodbye before you move on, Virginia," Mrs Shaw said, to Richard's surprise.

"I sure will, and thank you for your hospitality Mrs Shaw." responded Virginia.

As the coach got under way Virginia whispered to Richard, slipping her arm through his, "I wasn't sure of a welcome tonight Richard, I almost stayed away."

"Virginia, you are just what I need, believe me," replied Richard earnestly. "You have certainly grown up, you appear completely different somehow."

"A birthday party is not the best introduction to anyone is it?" she laughed, "But I never forgot you and was determined to find you. Can't shake me off that easily you know. Seriously, you don't have to worry about me," she patted his arm reassuringly, "I'm promised to Richard Chadwick and we intend to marry next year when I've completed my travels."

"That terrible association man," began Richard.

"His son," she interrupted, "he's very different."

"Do you love him?" Richard realised that he was speaking out of turn. She pondered over the question as the coach negotiated a right-angled turn, throwing them together. She made light of it.

"Well, you're not available are you, so I've exchanged one Richard for another."

"Virginia, be serious," Richard implored. "Travelling will change your whole outlook on life. When do you leave England, by the way?"

"On Saturday, I sail to France, then travel by road or rail to Germany, Italy and then back to England. After that, who knows?" she exclaimed happily. "Richard, you haven't asked me about Kate," she concluded more soberly.

"Almost afraid to," he admitted, "Can we talk at the hotel for a while?"

"Sure," she said, her lovely smile cutting through his tension. "Dear Richard, you're still confused by it all, are you not?" Richard watched her flick back her hair, then stared out of the window at the city lights. His mood eased somewhat.

"My early days were influenced almost entirely by males, even at university I was too busy for female company. In recent times my main influences seem to be women and I am still trying to make the adjustment." They laughed together as the coach stopped outside the brightly lit hotel. Richard dismissed the coach and they moved into the hotel lounge, occupying a low two-seater couch.

The to-ings and fro-ings of a busy international hotel were lost on the couple as they were absorbed in conversation.

"I must ask you, Richard. What happened to your flowing locks?" She ran her hand through his relatively short hair.

"You've heard of Samson?" he said, returning her smile.

"Ah, one of your women, I see!" she teased. He placed a hand on her arm.

"Tell me about Kate," he whispered. Virginia hooked her arm inside his and snuggled closer.

"It's quite a story," she said

"I'm listening, as long as you're not too tired."

"Kate is well, so there's no cause for concern there," she began, "We, that is, Kate, Jackie and myself meet twice a week. I collect Kate in the buggy and Jackie has a meal ready for us. We spend the evening talking and sometimes singing, but generally enjoying each other's company. Then each Saturday we go to the dance at the hotel, father and Jackie's brother act as escorts, but we have no shortage of dance partners." She elbowed Richard playfully. "Anyway, our friendship is a direct result of your intervention, so tell me Richard, why did you disappear after telling Jackie that you were a failure?"

"I can't relate to you the feelings of guilt and despair which took hold of me then, Virginia, looking back and attempting to answer your question. It was ridiculous yes, but

I assure you my frustration was such that I had to move on." Richard looked off into the crowd around them. " I have regretted my action ever since." He was momentarily lost in thought. His gaze returned to his beautiful companion. "Does Kate ever mention me?"

"Very rarely. Jackie does and so, of course, do the children, but Kate just listens and keeps her thoughts to herself, which is unusual, I grant, as Kate, when you know her, is very forthcoming. She and Jackie are great company."

"Did they teach you at the local school?" he enquired on impulse.

"No, Pa sent me to a city school. I only came home on rare occasions, but it taught me to be independent, although I did miss home." They were silent for a moment. There were questions regarding Kate and her environment that Richard was impatient to ask. He decided to do so without delay.

"Virginia, what of Kate's water supply, did the river still provide her with an adequate amount at the end of last summer?"

"Of course. Father only keeps a couple of hundred of the most hardy cattle in those foothills. In any case, the ground is so rocky that the river bed is churned up very little."

"And the little shrine?" he asked softly.

"Father fenced it off, at least a quarter of an acre." Richard was relieved but could not resist a sardonic smile. This was good news but it made his retreat of last year even more pointless and absurd.

"Virginia searched Richard's face. "Do you think of those days around Randolph very often?"

"I would never have believed that three days could have had so much effect on me, in fact they have changed my life," he replied honestly, "I find it very difficult to settle. You too will have a problem when you return from your wanderings."

144

"We shall see. I'm for bed," she said, unsuccessfully attempting to stifle a yawn. Richard jumped to his feet and gave her his arm as she struggled out of the low seat.

"I'm sorry to have kept you up, may I see you tomorrow?"

"You'd better!" she responded, "Would you take me to the theatre, I'd simply love that."

"See what I can do," he promised.

"Goodnight, Richard." She kissed him and he held her for a moment.

"You have been a tonic," he said, "I'll pick you up here at six tomorrow. Sleep well!"

"I will so long as the room keeps still," she laughed, mounting the stairs. She turned and waved finally before disappearing at the top. He remained watching for a few minutes in case she should reappear and, realising that he was now alone again, made for the bar. He engaged a couple in conversation and learned that they were sailing the next day to America. Excitement showed on their faces as it was to be their first venture from the coasts of England. Richard kept his own counsel on the subject, not wishing to dampen their mood or ruin the keen anticipation they both felt.

Suddenly he found that he had talked enough, tired of inconsequential chatter and needing to be alone, having much to consider that night.

He left the hotel and made off in a south westerly direction, having decided to walk the whole way to the manor. At a steady pace this would take him two or three hours and he would use the time to consider his position and come to decisions that would give his life direction. Absorbed in his thoughts he plodded steadily on, moving through the well-lit city then, as his shadow lengthened before him, into the darkened suburbs. He did not notice the thin drizzle that floated down, soaking him through to the skin.

Chapter 17

Richard worked very hard that next morning, feeling no ill effects after his arrival home in the early hours. He was anxious to clear his desk by lunchtime and achieved this soon after noon.

Leaving the Chambers, he hurried along the busy city streets thronged with those who travel into town each day and who at this time were heading for habitual lunch venues. In his haste, Richard was not content to move at the pace of the crowd going in his direction. He jumped from pavement to street and, when his safety was at risk, back to the pavement again, avoiding the wheels of a carriage and having gained a few yards as a salve for his impatience.

The City Jewellers was located some fifteen minutes' walk from his office and as he walked, he hoped that Caroline had decided to go into the shop that day. He knew that theatre tickets would be almost impossible to come by at this late hour and that the Jefferson influence was his only hope for that evening. He knew too that he would have to be discreet in introducing the girls to each other, they differed completely in background and personality and were contrastingly beautiful.

Richard nodded at the doorman "Is Miss Caroline in today?"

"I did see 'er smornin' guv," he replied, swinging the door open and touching his cap. Richard entered the shop and spotted her immediately, indicating his understanding as she pointed to the side door. She greeted him warmly as always, there was rarely anything theatrical about her in his presence. Even the characteristic tilting of the head which he had thought dramatic in the past now looked spontaneous as he kissed her.

"I would like to think that you're here because you missed me," said Caroline mischievously.

"It's always good to see you, Caroline," he replied genuinely.

"If you are thinking of buying something for my birthday next month, then let me show you some samples, sir," she went on playfully. Richard accepted the reminder and made a mental note.

"Caroline, do you remember that I told you of a birthday party - the Rancher's daughter?"

"Ah yes, Virginia wasn't it?" she said without hesitation.

"You really are remarkable the way you retain detail." he said, truly amazed.

"Particularly detail of that kind," she responded, poking him in the ribs. "But what of her? She is calling on you I suppose."

"She's here, arrived yesterday and would love to go to the theatre tonight. Can you help?"

"Of course, you bring her to the best theatre in town, I'll get two tickets for you."

"Two, why not three, can you not accompany us?"

"We're entertaining tonight, prominent members of the opposition. I could join you later though, I would like to meet your American. She sounds rather interesting."

"Are you sure you don't mind ..." he began.

"Of course not, just remember to collect me at ten, or as soon as you can."

"You are an angel," he said hugging her.

"I know, but keep it to yourself," she said impishly, "But Richard, on a more serious note, I need to talk to you on a delicate matter. Are we meeting on Saturday?"

"Yes of course, but what is the problem?"

"It's a bit complicated," she said, moving towards the shop, "Leave it until Saturday."

"Right." He put an arm around her, "The tickets will, I take it, be at the box office, and I'll see you around ten."

"Right," she echoed, looking up at him tantalisingly. He kissed her and they entered the shop, now full of lunchtime customers.

"'Bye darling, and thanks," he whispered as she left him already smiling at a prospective purchaser.

* * *

Richard walked to Virginia's hotel from his office, arriving early. He went to the bar ordering himself a drink from the same barman as the night before. From where he was sitting he could see the whole dining area and he watched as residents and guests ambled in. The head waiter seemed to have the seating plan imprinted on his mind as he guided the diners to tables reserved for them.

Promptly at six, Virginia appeared. She was a revelation in a white evening gown which contrasted strikingly with her black hair. His breath was taken away for another reason too, as her hair was piled up behind her head and secured by a white ribbon. This was the style Kate had been wearing the day he'd first met her, and Virginia now had the same air of charm and sophistication.

"I see that I meet with your approval." She smiled at Richard's gaze of wonder as he rose to greet her. All heads turned as she descended the stairs, their attention commanded by the combination of accent and beauty. He was a proud man indeed as he handed her a glass of her favourite wine and they toasted absent friends before being shown to a table.

They were situated in the centre of the huge dining-room and on the table was a display of flowers. Matching tablecloth and napkins blended with the impressive decor, and chandeliers provided light which gave at once an atmosphere of cheerfulness and affluence. They ordered from a comprehensive menu and sipped their drinks, studying each other.

"So, who is Caroline?" Virginia asked, resuming the conversation they'd started in the bar.

"My intended," he replied simply, "or so everybody would tell us." She watched him across the table.

"And will you marry?" Richard was silent, deciding to be frank with this girl now seemingly mature beyond her years. He framed his reply carefully.

"It is possible, Virginia. She is without doubt a delightful and intelligent young lady and we've known each other for almost six years now."

"But?" Virginia was still searching his face in that candid American way.

"But," he paused, reflecting on the truth. "But, Kate." He kept a keen eye on the girl across the table, not wishing to miss any of her reaction.

"Richard," she began slowly, "I must tell you that Kate is seeing someone."

"What do you mean, seeing someone?" he responded fearfully.

"Well, friendly with a man - they meet at the hotel dances and on other occasions too I believe." she explained awkwardly. Richard looked stricken and she regretted having told him at this stage of their evening together.

"Who is he?" the inevitable question came, "Do I know him?"

"Jackie's brother, Matthew," she answered tentatively, "you may have seen him around the hotel."

"How serious are they, Virginia?" he asked after a moment, not able to put a face to Jackie's brother at all. He had to wait for a reply as the waiter came to their table and it was five minutes later that he looked at Virginia for some response to his question.

"Richard, they are both lonely people who enjoy each other's company. It may develop, it may not. He's a fine man and you don't need me to tell you of Kate's attributes. I think Jackie is hoping that they'll get together, that's natural, and some of the townsfolk are for the idea. Beth Champion has them hitched already." Her hollow laugh inspired not a flicker of a smile from Richard. Virginia considered that she had said enough and concentrated on the food which had just arrived, watching him sympathetically.

Richard had never thought this a possibility and immediately saw the arrogance of his assumption. He had known Kate for only two days and had then run off like a spoilt boy for whom everything had not gone his way. How could he expect Kate to pin her faith and future on such instability? Virginia was aware of his inner torment and covered his hand with hers on the table.

"Richard, nothing has happened yet, they may never get any closer. Anyway, you have me to fall back on," she added in an attempt to lighten his mood. He smiled wanly, appreciating her efforts.

"I do need you as a friend, Virginia. There's a lot I must tell you," he said, feeling the comfort of her hand.

"Kate is my best friend I reckon, she thinks the world of you. God knows why, when you charged off like that, but any friend of Kate's is a friend of mine and that sure does include you, Richard." He was moved by her sincerity.

"Bless you," he said, lost for words. They ate in silence for a while, suddenly aware of the hubbub around them as all the tables had become occupied. Virginia said, looking up.

"You have to be honest with friends, Richard."

"I will be, you can be assured of that," he confirmed, realising why Kate thought so much of this girl.

* * *

151

The evening was a happy one during which Virginia was thrilled at the spectacle of London theatre life. Caroline had obtained excellent seats in the stalls for this production, a typical Victorian comedy which used the poverty and immorality of the times as vehicles for humour. Richard saw no justification for scenes where scantily-clad women cavorted wildly around the stage, but glancing around him realised that it was accepted as modern theatre. He fell in with Virginia's excitement at just being there.

As the two of them had sat waiting for the curtain to rise, Richard had told Virginia of the letter he had written and something of its contents. He told her too of the reply he had received which, among other things, informed him of her own impending arrival in England. Virginia responded with information she knew would interest him. Her father had supervised the painting of the homestead, which had been done at his expense. Dan Marshall had also made one of his men available to Kate should she require assistance at any time. Kate had money in the bank as a result of the property sale, and the price paid had been a generous one. Kate now took the children to school each day and was generally more involved in town affairs. Virginia told him that Josh had taken Richard's flight harder than anyone and the lad was convinced of his return, as he had not said goodbye.

Richard was unsure of his ability to cope with all this information. He was still confused mentally, unable to envisage what role he could play in these developments. He recalled a story Caroline had dramatically related to a gathering of friends some years ago. A man was circling a street lamp, just staying within the light it radiated. Round and round he went until challenged by a second man, who had been observing the ritual.

"What are you looking for?" said the newcomer.

"A coin," said the man.

"Are you sure that you lost it here?"

"No, I lost it over there," he replied, pointing into the darkness, "but there's no light over there!"

Richard felt sure that the story had a message and a relevance for him, and that perhaps he was searching in the wrong place. He would not find what he sought in this environment, illuminated as it was by ease and affluence.

* * *

The curtain came down finally and a buzz of appreciation filled the theatre. They hurried out into the night where cabs and carriages were awaiting the mass exit - guaranteed custom. Richard made a cursory search along the row of vehicles, hoping to see Henry Forest, but without success. They climbed into the first available carriage and headed for Caroline's home. It was then that Richard took Virginia into his confidence regarding the events in America and the police follow-up. She listened spellbound, watching him in the flickering light of the carriage lamp. Richard's timing was not good, as they drew up in Caroline's drive just as his story came to an end.

"It will give me time to think about it," she said, responding to his frustration.

The Jeffersons were in the hall to receive their two visitors, having minutes before waved goodbye to their evening guests. Richard introduced Virginia to Arthur, Charlotte and Caroline, thanking them for the ticket arrangements that evening. Virginia, too, expressed her genuine appreciation of their kindness. The two girls cast an approving eye over each other as Richard led them to the waiting carriage.

Caroline and Virginia were instant friends, once again to Richard's surprise. The American seemed to inspire confidence in everyone she met.

The three of them spent the next two hours in a small inn adjacent to the theatre. Not only was it open until very late, but it was also the haunt of actors and actresses and, on occasions, even playwrights. Caroline was able to point out famous faces to Virginia. "That's the man we saw tonight, isn't it Richard? cried Virginia. He followed her eyes across the room. Before he could respond, Caroline had attracted the actor's attention.

"He played the male lead role," she confirmed. The actor was introduced to Virginia and Richard and later brought some of his colleagues over to their table. All were known to Caroline and she and Virginia were in their element talking well into the night.

They escorted Virginia back to her hotel in the early hours. Richard passed on his mother's invitation for her to join them at dinner the next evening, Friday. This she accepted gratefully and thanked Caroline and Richard for a lovely evening.

"What time should I be ready?" she asked, embracing them both.

"Six, right here," Richard said with an American accent which made them smile.

"What a delightful young lady," was Caroline's reaction as they stood by the carriage. "And my, isn't she beautiful, she was turning heads in the theatrical world."

"Your feelings of admiration were reciprocated I'm sure," said Richard, "Come on, let me take you home."

"What a lovely idea," purred Caroline, tugging at his arm and holding her face up to him.

* * *

Later, as they sat close in the carriage, Caroline broached the subject that was worrying her.

"Richard, you may not suspect this, but your mother and my father are seeing a great deal of each other." Richard was thrown by the introduction of this completely new topic and sat frowning at her.

"What are you saying?"

"I am saying that they are having an affair," she stated boldly.

"Caroline, what evidence have you to support that allegation?" In his heart, however, he had wondered about these friends his mother visited so frequently.

"I come home to the house at various times during the day, particularly when we're due to entertain. I hear them about the house."

"Mother says she visits friends," he said defensively but without conviction.

"A friend," she corrected, "Father is always disappearing from the shop - on business trips he says, but often he goes home." Richard was astounded. What of Arthur Jefferson's political aspirations?

"Is there anything to be done about it?" Richard asked, at a loss.

"No, we do nothing," she said firmly. "In any case, it was us who brought them together remember?" Richard could not for the life of him imagine why Arthur Jefferson should wish to exchange his wife, a gentle soul to all who knew her, for his mother, whose only role in life was to dominate.

Both Caroline and Richard agreed, before parting, that nothing should be said at this stage. It did give Richard just a twinge of satisfaction to learn that his mother was not perfect after all.

* * *

Richard spent Friday morning in court and was relieved when the sessions were completed. He arrived at Leopard

Chambers just in time to see Virginia installing herself in the General Office.

"Richard," she burst forth, "I have spent a delightful morning with Caroline in the city. You are a lucky man! Apart from her looks, she is clever and speaks beautifully. Do you know, I became aware of my accent talking to her. Never before have I been ashamed of it, Richard." He smiled at the faces around the office, which were turned in her direction. Virginia was at last showing her eighteen years as she launched into an excited account of her morning of sightseeing and shopping.

"Let's go and eat," he said, taking her arm and guiding her to the door. She was still describing her visit to Parliament in the company of Arthur Jefferson as they arrived at a tiny but select restaurant a stone's throw from the chambers. They squeezed into an alcove away from the crowd. Richard recommended a dish to her and he ordered their requirements, which included a bottle of wine he knew she would appreciate.

"Guess what I have here, Richard?" She dug into her bag, extracting a small leather purse, and placed it before him. He opened it and let the contents drop onto the table. It was a shining sovereign piece. "I carry it with me as a good luck charm," she said, laughing, "Do you remember giving it to me?"

"Of course," he replied, laughing with her. "I do hope it brings you luck. Keep it in case of emergency anyway." Richard listened as she chattered on and was captivated by her zest for life and her appreciation of every minute of it. "So when did you arrange today's schedule?" he asked when the opportunity arose.

With Caroline last night," she replied deviously. "She said that you would be pleased to see me - and I do have to arrange travel insurance and attend to various other things ..." On she went and Richard marvelled at the confidence of youth, forgetting that he was only seven years her senior.

The two hours they spent together flew by, but at the end of it Richard had organised for her currency exchange, insurance and documentation. He escorted her back to the hotel and once again arranged to collect her at six that evening. Only as he hurried back to Leopard Chambers did he realise that they had not discussed his problems, neither of them had raised the subject. He dismissed his initial disappointment with the consolation that it had been good to forget his worries for a few hours.

Chapter 18

Richard could not remember an occasion when so many people were due to arrive at the house on a Friday evening. He had not seen the guest list and his mother had certainly not discussed it. He was surprised, then, to learn that what he had anticipated as dinner with his family and Virginia, was in fact going to be a full table. Richard had the uncharitable thought that his mother was either attempting to impress Virginia, or to show her off to her guests.

It had been arranged that Virginia was to be escorted to the manor by the Jeffersons, so that Richard could perform his duties as host more effectively. He was about to go upstairs and prepare himself for the evening when he saw Bates emerging from the dining-room. Richard enquired of him as to the contents of the guest list.

"There is a list and seating plan, Master Richard, shall I bring it to you?"

"No, no thank you Bates, I'll go and look myself," said Richard, wondering how old he would have to be for Bates to drop the habit of twenty-five years, that of referring to him as Master.

The plan was arranged on a small table just behind the dining-room door. Richard counted twelve places at the rectangular table, the maximum by tradition, (Richard vaguely remembered his paternal grandmother establishing this tradition and the discipline with which she upheld it) although there was room for more. In addition to his mother and himself at each end of the table, (the farthest possible distance away, which suited him) there was Virginia to his right, then the Reverend Peter Farraday and his wife. To their right, not surprisingly, Charlotte and Arthur Jefferson. On Richard's left was Caroline, who was between him and George Steady. Grace Steady on her husband's left had the local Squire Charles Strange and his wife Clarissa on her left. Richard wondered when all this had been arranged, and concluded that it must be for the benefit of the ravishing young American.

He left the dining-room quickly and bolted up the stairs. If he was to be ready to receive the guests then he would have to hurry. He was about to take the final leap onto the landing when the appalling fact hit him. His father had been excluded. He headed for his mother's room and rapped on the door.

"Yes?" mother's voice demanded.

"It's me, mother," Richard shouted back through the door.

"Oh, do come in - but be quick, I have so much to do," she added as he appeared. He got straight to the point.

"Why is father not in his usual place tonight, is he ill?"

"Your father is not joining us, and in his absence, God forbid, you are man of the house."

"Not while my father is alive, I'm not. He has eaten with us every evening and tonight must be no exception." Mrs Shaw swung round to face her son.

"How can your father cope with so many people? Be sensible! He will no doubt fall asleep and disgrace us all," she exclaimed, brandishing her hairbrush. "In any case, the table is full, there are twelve places, or are you unaware of that?"

Richard was fuming "Some consultation would have been helpful," he shouted, "and I tell you now, if father is not restored to his place, then I shall not be present and neither will Virginia, so you can break with tradition and set another place."

"And who will I sit each side of your father?"

"Caroline and me, it will be an honour"

"You're talking nonsense, the two girls are either side of you."

"They will understand, and as for room, move Arthur

Jefferson closer to you, that will delight you both!" Richard knew that he had taken a risk, but Caroline's assessment was obviously correct as his mother turned back to her mirror, speechless. He was relieved that the shouting match was over and the uncomfortable silence was broken as he moved towards the door. "I will instruct Bates to revise the plan," he said, closing the door on his mother, who spoke not a word.

Richard called in at his father's room along the landing. "Be ready in an hour, father, we have many guests tonight for dinner."

"Very well son," his father responded as Richard placed an arm around his shoulder.

"I'll be next to him," Richard explained to Mr Stafford, the male nurse, who nodded in understanding.

Richard spent five minutes with Bates, who was delighted at the change of plan, then bounded upstairs to dress.

Host and hostess stood yards apart as they made their visitors welcome. The Jeffersons and Virginia were first to arrive and Richard explained to the girls the reasoning behind the revised seating arrangements. Richard was now to sit on his father's right with Virginia on his right, and Caroline occupying the chair on his father's left. They both entirely agreed with Richard's logic in the matter.

The Squire and his wife were the next arrivals. He was a portly fellow with a constant breathing problem and an ill-tempered countenance. His partner, in complete contrast, was always smiling, so much so that her sincerity had to be in question. They were taken to the drawing-room to join the Jeffersons and be introduced to Virginia. Richard noticed that Virginia and Caroline were laughing together and deep in conversation as though they were friends of long standing.

Richard recognised the Reverend Farraday as Bates led him into the hall. The churchman announced with a flourish that Mrs Farraday had taken to her bed and was mortified at missing the occasion. Richard silently and inwardly gave thanks to the good Lord for sending his messenger with such good tidings. He wished Mrs Farraday no harm, but the table had now been restored to its twelve places.

George Steady and his wife Grace were welcome guests in all circles, and nowhere more than at Shaw Manor, where the name of Steady had been linked with that of Shaw for so many years. Richard shook his partner's hand and sensed that all was not well. As they strolled towards the drawing-room George Steady whispered to Richard that they must talk on an urgent matter on Monday, first thing. Richard gave it no more thought as he moved from group to group, keeping well clear of his mother's own circle.

Richard, despite his mood of antagonism, had to admit that dinner was a convivial affair that evening. The five courses lasted nigh on three hours and the quality of the food and its presentation won the highest accolade, Caroline's unqualified approval. William Shaw had been his old self in bursts, delighting in the occasion and the company around him. His frequent outbursts of gibberish had been accepted in good part by all present. Richard had deputised for his father by giving a spontaneous after dinner speech. He referred to Virginia and her background, giving a fleeting insight into life in America, finally declaring how proud he was to be on his father's right as of old, and indeed how good it was to see William Shaw, the owner of Shaw Manor, at the head of the table again. These concluding sentiments received warm applause from around the table and for the first time in his life, Richard saw his mother avert her gaze as his eyes moved from face to face.

The ladies made their way into the drawing-room after dinner, leaving the gentlemen to stretch their legs under the table and light up cigars. As the port was passed around and glasses filled, Richard introduced a subject raised at dinner but not elaborated upon.

"So you don't approve of Mr Gladstone's Education Bill?" he said, waving his glass in the direction of the Squire.

"Indeed I do not, we'll be bankrupt in no time at all," wheezed the Squire.

"But I think free education is an admirable idea," the vicar boomed, forgetting that he was not in the pulpit.

"Just another example of this government's incompetence," stated Arthur Jefferson, delighted at having an opportunity to air the views of the opposition.

"How many parents will avail themselves of this facility?" the Reverend boomed again.

"It will be compulsory, I believe," George Steady informed them, and nobody was going to doubt his prognostication.

"Really!" they responded, almost in unison.

"Poppycock!" shouted the Squire, "absolute poppycock this is. Majority of 'em are brats - I pity the teachers."

"You would vote against the Bill would you, Arthur?" Mr Steady glanced in Jefferson's direction.

"Indeed I would, and any other ridiculous scheme they hatch up," he replied confidently. Richard wondered how an intelligent businessman became so illogical and blinkered when it came to politics.

"It is bound to benefit future generations," Richard observed with conviction. The argument flowed from one to the other, becoming heated as the port flowed with it. Richard got to his feet and suggested that it was time to join the ladies. The sounds of laughter greeted them as they approached the drawing-room, changing into a chorus of approval as the men appeared.

Richard was immediately taken to one side by Charlotte

Jefferson. Two things Caroline had inherited from her mother were her colouring and gentleness.

"I understand that my daughter has spoken to you on a delicate matter, Richard, I just want you to know that I have been aware of the situation for some time."

"I'm so sorry, Charlotte," he whispered, aware of Caroline's glance in their direction.

"Don't be. It's something I live with," she said evenly and with resignation.

"But we feel guilty, it was we who introduced them and brought them together." he explained.

"You are wrong to feel guilt," she confided. "Mary first met Arthur in the shop when Caroline was just a girl."

"I see," he nodded, "Let me get you another drink, we'd better join the rest." They moved across the room and Richard took note of the conversations and the participants. Virginia was talking in animated fashion to the Reverend Farraday, whose occasional comments were clearly audible, he obviously was not used to being verbally outdone and he struggled vainly for parity. Caroline was dividing her attention between Richard and her mother on the one hand, and the bulk of the Squire who stood before her, his shoulders heaving in extrovert laughter at some witticism of hers. Inevitably, Mary Shaw was in a group comprising Arthur Jefferson and on this occasion, Grace Steady. Clarissa Strange was beaming at George Steady as he addressed her with a contrastingly serious countenance. William Shaw had retired to his room and would not be seen again that evening.

It was very late when the dinner party eventually broke up. Before Virginia left with the Jeffersons, Richard arranged to be at her hotel at ten the next morning to transport her and a considerable amount of baggage to the station.

"I'll see you tomorrow evening, Caroline," he reminded her as the girls went through the door together.

Host and hostess remained distant as they saw their guests off the premises. Richard was again disturbed by George Steady's unusually dour farewell. Richard turned away from the door as Bates closed it for the last time. His mother had gone. He sought inspiration and solace in the music room, closing the door behind him.

* * *

They sat on the station platform and the noise was deafening. Virginia's beauty was not tarnished even in surroundings such as these. The feeling between them, however, was unusually strained.

"What do you expect me to say?" she argued. "We agreed days ago to be frank with each other and I was being just that." Richard had expected support from her when he raised the subject of his predicament, and had been thrown by her unsympathetic attitude.

"Can we get out of here for a while?" he urged as a screech from a departing locomotive echoed through the huge canopy. Standing, he assisted her to her feet and they moved off the platform and through the vast hall of the station, turning aside into a comparatively quiet corner. The sounds of the terminus were muffled now and Virginia broke the long silence between them.

"God, Richard. It sounds like a horror story!" she exclaimed.

"I'm sure it does," he agreed, "but you surely realise the situations that arise over in your homeland?"

"The guys I know shoot tin cans and rabbits," she said impatiently. "Anyway, what do you intend to do about it?" He was silent, hurt by her flippancy.

"You agree that I should take some action?" he asked, breaking the stillness.

"Sure, but Richard, leave your guns at home." He moved away from her towards the noise of the station.

"Come on," he said curtly. She softened visibly, putting a hand through his arm.

"Of course you must clear your name, Richard. Father will help you, I'm sure."

"Yes, I will need the advocacy of people like him and John Champion."

"Right," agreed Virginia. "I'm sorry for my outburst, I'm a little tired." She squeezed his arm.

"You were a little frank too," he smiled at her, pushing a strand of hair from her temple.

"Who did you say this Philip was?" she asked.

"Dave's brother, or rather, an adopted brother, why?"

She thought for a moment. "Does his ship ever dock in England?"

Richard had not considered that a possibility. "I suppose he must at some time or another." he answered, accepting the implication.

"When we meet again in six weeks' time, we'll devise a plan of action," she said brightly, "By the way, Caroline may accompany me back across the Atlantic, she will tell you tonight, no doubt." Richard, rendered speechless by this news, guided Virginia back into the hall where a group of urchins spotted them and sought financial aid. Richard tried to ignore them and was reproved for doing so by Virginia who began to delve into her purse.

"You'll be mobbed if you give to any of these," he warned.

"But I have never seen such poverty - don't you wish that you could help, Richard?"

"I do what I can," he replied as they reached the platform where her train was waiting. They boarded the train together and Richard found Virginia a window seat, stowing her luggage above and around her.

"I'll get a porter at the other end," she said in response to Richard's concern. He nodded and jumped down onto the platform.

"If you need anything, let me know," he said through the carriage window. "I'll meet your train when you return."

"Goodbye, Richard." She kissed him warmly, "If I'm in trouble I'll surely send for you." Her wicked smile held him as the train negotiated the platform curve and she was lost to sight.

Chapter 19

The departure of Virginia's boat train left Richard with plenty to think about. He strolled back along the now deserted platform, assembling his thoughts into some order of priority. The station hall was still busy and the group of dirty children he had ignored previously accosted him once more. He halted, digging deep into his pockets, taking out all the loose change he had. He gave each of them a coin.

"From Virginia," he explained to each grubby, upturned little face, then he hurried on before the news got around.

The Shaw family coach with the coat of arms boldly emblazoned on its side looked resplendent in the morning sunshine. The return of Spring, or at least the promise of it, set Richard's adrenalin flowing as the warmth of the sun reminded him of America and its associations.

As the coach moved out of the city, Richard reflected on his life and how complicated it had become. His freedom, career and very existence were under threat. Now there was the possibility of Kate, Virginia and Caroline all being in Randolph. This presented itself as an absurdity. However, as he could not return to that distant town himself, what did it matter?

Relations with his mother had completely broken down and they met only at meals, acknowledging each other solely for the benefit of the servants. Bates had obviously read the situation from the start and it distressed the ageing butler visibly. Only Richard's dear father was his natural self, his affliction rendering him impervious to the hostile atmosphere around him.

There were dubious delights awaiting him that evening too. Caroline wanted to see the Victorian comedy that Richard had seen with Virginia during the week. Richard's heart sank, but he acceded to her request, disliking the production even more than at first viewing. The utter farce of the proceedings contrasted starkly with his dire personal situation. The one weakness in his relationship with Caroline was that, despite their closeness and intimacy, neither could confide in the other in any depth.

It was in the little eating house after the show that Caroline informed Richard of her ambitions to travel. This included a visit to Randolph and the Marshall ranch. Richard should have made an effort to explain his predicament to her but let it pass, reproaching himself as a procrastinator of the first order.

Sunday was a peaceful day - the calm before the storm, if Richard but knew it. For the first time since his return he took his father and the nurse to church that morning, his mother pleading a headache. The Reverend Farraday had caught his wife's malady and so a new parson occupied - and a much more cultured voice emanated from - the pulpit. The text around which he developed his message was, to Richard's discomfort, the Commandment 'Thou shalt not kill', and he tried not to squirm in his pew. Richard, there and then, made probably the most important decision of his life. He would return to America. He resolved to consider all the implications during the week ahead.

During that evening Richard retired to his room, eager to write to Kate, to tell her of the arrival of her letter and the visit of Virginia. He commenced writing with the intention of following the agreed procedure involving Nat Holland. Midway through his lengthy epistle, he decided to tell Kate everything, and as a result, to send the letter to her direct. He told her of his feelings toward her and of his involvement with Caroline, whom he adored. He made reference to Matthew Flint, Jackie's brother, and asked her to consider carefully before making an irreversible decision. By way of explanation, he revealed that

170

because of her, he could not commit himself to any permanent liaison with Caroline. Finally, he outlined his situation regarding the death of Radford. He assured her that he intended to clear his name. He included messages for Josh and Sam with a sincere wish that they were all nearer.

The completed letter was bulky and he placed it in his case so that an envelope could be addressed the next morning and dispatched from the office. He realised that Kate would not receive it for many weeks, but at least she would know the facts and there would be no danger of the letter falling into the wrong hands on the coast. Richard had said nothing of his decision to return, preferring to work on the details first.

As his gaze moved around the room, he realised that it was no longer the haven it had once been. He had changed and very little around him retained its previous attraction. He acknowledged for the first time that he was in love with Kate and had been since the moment he met her. For someone always so sceptical about love at first sight, this was a humiliating revelation, albeit a wonderful one.

* * *

Richard arrived at Leopard Chambers very early for the start of a new week. He had many interesting projects during the next few days and cases of an unusual nature. The post room staff gave him every assistance with the mailing of his letter, and it was dropped into the tray containing the outgoing mail for that day.

For Richard, George Steady's strange attitude at Friday's dinner had been forgotten, so when he was summoned to the senior partner's office, he had nothing but work on his mind, save perhaps his decision of the previous day.

To his surprise, the senior law clerk, Benjamin Blackstone

was in the room sitting off to Richard's right as Mr Steady waved him to a chair. Facing him across the desk, George Steady peered over his spectacles, a sign that Richard was going to be taken to task for some error of judgement or other. But why was Blackstone present?

"Richard, I hope that you will accept the presence of Mr Blackstone, for a serious allegation has been made and he should be witness to it."

"No objection at all," replied Richard, managing a smile for the aged legal clerk. "What sort of allegation George?"

"I'll get straight to the point," he said, clearing his throat and creating a pyramid with his hands. "The police objected to you being in Court on Friday, Richard. I questioned this absurd stance and was informed that there were circumstances under investigation. I have to know the circumstances and why they should merit investigation. Can you enlighten me, please?"

A frown had appeared on Richard's face as the situation became clear to him. This new development was ludicrous. He clearly recalled Rebecca's words in that distant seedy hotel: 'Radford has great influence which explains the cover up.' Radford had been a murderer, smuggler and a bull of a man, yet even in death his influence remained. Richard realised that he would find it very difficult to prove his story now. He felt trapped, looking across the desk at Steady's patient gaze and then at Blackstone's lowered head.

"Well, Richard?"

"George, this is a surprise, I assure you." Richard hardly recognised his own voice. "That such an incident should be magnified in this way." Richard paused, knowing that he must relate the whole story.

During the next thirty minutes, Richard gave the facts and stated his case. George Steady's eyes never left his face and Blackstone's stare was focused on a point around his feet.

Both listened impassively, and Richard felt that he was already in court giving evidence, a feeling borne out by the tone of Mr Steady's response.

"You say that you acted in self-defence, Richard. Was this accepted and established irrefutably?"

"The witness would have to admit that it was self-defence and the Sheriff accepted the facts as I gave them," he replied lamely.

"I imagine that you can forget your witness," said Steady, shaking his head, "And also the girl ... er ... Rebecca, was it not? So what defence do you have Richard? I wish that all my prosecution cases were as watertight as this one. I would have the noose around your neck in no time. I believe you of course, but you are in a pickle, my boy!" George Steady looked across at the clerk who was nodding his head solemnly. "What is your view, Mr Blackstone?"

"I ... I do agree with your analysis, Mr Steady. It would seem to me that if the police choose to take up this case, then there is no defence whatsoever. Mr Shaw's integrity and motives are not in question, you understand. However, the circumstances cannot help but sound implausible to us. Why should Mr Shaw use guns and take the law into his own hands?"

"Precisely so," agreed Steady, "When did you become a gunman, Richard?" The situation was becoming hopeless, and Richard likened it to recalling a dream, or a story told to one in the distant past. He made an attempt at describing the background to his ride into the mid-west. He suddenly remembered the drunk he had slain. What would they think of that version of self-defence? He left such extremes out of his account but even so he still saw the looks of incredulity on the faces of his listeners. The task of convincing his two colleagues was an impossible one.

"I shall probe into the extent of their enquiries," Mr

Steady concluded. "In the meantime, Richard, I will accede to the police request to keep you out of court." The interview was at an end. Mr Blackstone bowed jerkily to his employer and made for the door, hugging the wall whenever possible and giving Richard a wide berth, avoiding visual and physical contact.

Richard sat behind his desk, his mind made up. The trap had sprung and the net had closed in on him. There was no course of action left but to clear his name, and that could not be done in London. In any case, he was weary of Victorian England and its social charade. He longed to be with people who were themselves, for better or for worse, and who possessed no airs and graces save those with which they were naturally blessed. He knew that he must weigh up the alternatives and think over the possible consequences of his decision to emigrate. He instinctively knew that the disadvantages would have to be of enormous proportions to deter him from his resolve.

The rest of his morning was spent writing a letter of resignation to Mr Steady, dissolving their partnership and suggesting a figure for the financial settlement. He would stop work on the last day of the current month, February.

He left the chambers with a determined step and headed for the banks and finance houses, establishing that a sufficient amount of his wealth could be transferred to a foreign account and that with interest accrued, he should not want for funds. He then carried out his most impulsive act to date by booking his passage on the same ship in which Virginia was to return to America. Richard could hardly believe his own single-mindedness in making arrangements for his departure and felt elated. He returned to comparative sobriety, however, as he considered again the possible repercussions of his actions.

What of people near and dear, such as Caroline and his

father? What of his ultimate inheritance? His mother was sure to manoeuvre wills and legacies to his disadvantage. He would be leaving his home - his music. He would be wasting the opportunities in law for which he had studied hard and long.

At home in his room he dwelt on these reasons for not leaving, looking at each one closely. He commenced with the most difficult of them, Caroline. Richard knew that he would miss her and was sure that she would miss him too. They had been good friends for well over six years and lovers for most of that time. A wedding had been anticipated by the two families and most of their friends but never really taken seriously by either of them. He wondered now if in fact Caroline did harbour thoughts of marriage. He would not know, as he was not privy to her deepest thoughts and aspirations. Richard was very fond of her and looking back over the years could recall many good times when he had been proud to be her companion. He recalled moments of romantic fervour when he had decided to tell Caroline of his love for her and propose marriage in dramatic fashion. These impulses of youth had never come to fruition. Considering the future, he was uncertain how Caroline would take the news he must impart to her. Even if she was crossing the Atlantic on a fleeting visit, which he doubted. This, he accepted, was the most unpleasant aspect of his leaving.

His other main concern was his father. Richard was not certain how William Shaw would be treated in his absence, even living in his own house. Perhaps during the weeks that remained he could enlist the help of George Steady in providing a secure base for his father's remaining years. His father was, after all, only in his fifties. Richard was not sure whether leaving his father was going to be a greater wrench than saying goodbye to Caroline.

Other considerations were relatively insignificant. He

was concerned and apprehensive regarding his return to America, having been ordered not to go. He must be prudent, revealing his intentions and destination only to those he could trust.

A week passed, during which Richard handled nothing but the menial tasks of the partnership. He was happy to undertake this role knowing that his plans were gradually taking shape as each day passed. He had taken Mr Steady into his confidence, receiving his assurance that whatever Richard told him would be treated as confidential. Richard had confided in him only the fact that he had decided to cross the Atlantic again.

That particular Friday evening only two guests were to be entertained, they were neighbours and left quite early. Richard had retired to bed before his usual time, anticipating a full day's riding from the local stables. It was to be the worst night of his life.

He woke up suddenly, disorientated and startled. He was bathed in sweat and shaking with a fear that would not be identified. The darkness of the night was impenetrable. The dead face haunted him, eyes staring and motionless, the vision that had haunted him day and night. But this time there was a cruel twist as the face became blurred, gradually but inexorably taking on the features of another, bearded features, but still with those blank soulless eyes watching him. The two faces interchanged in a confusing manner, then he was sure there was movement in the death mask, a grimace, hideous and sinister. It was his own screaming at this apparition that woke him. He sat bolt upright, peering into the blackness, waiting for the next horror which mercifully did not come. He lit his bedside lamp, gaining sanity from the familiar surroundings, but his nightmare was a real, almost tangible thing, and he slept very little during the remainder of that night.

He cancelled his ride for the day and remained in the

house until it was time to meet Caroline in the little theatrical restaurant, only a short distance from her shop. He was bleary-eyed and still shaken from the experience of the previous night. He had with him her birthday present, a diamond brooch, not purchased at Jeffersons. He felt guilty at having to break his news to her on such a day.

Caroline had not arrived and he located a quiet table near the log fire. He stared into it, willing the flames to give him a sign. He now entertained no doubts as to his future, but would still have appreciated divine confirmation of his plans.

"Richard." Caroline was standing by his side, amused at his preoccupation.

"I'm so sorry, Caroline," he said, jumping to his feet. He took her coat and settled her into the confined space at the table. Was it his imagination or did she look even more wonderful tonight as she studied him quizzically?

"You look awful," she said frankly.

"Not sleeping too well," he offered.

"You were nearly asleep when I came in," she laughed superficially.

"I was miles away," he smiled apologetically.

"Three thousand miles away?" she suggested, keeping her gaze on him.

"What ... what do you mean?" he stammered.

"What is the problem, Richard? You've been living in another world for a long time now, I've only had part of you since you returned. I lost the old Richard two years ago. Mind you, I have been grateful for ..."

"Caroline, please." He could listen to no more. Had he really been so transparent? He found his voice, dismissing the waiter for a moment.

"Why did you not say something earlier?" he pleaded.

"I knew that our relationship was tenuous and I was afraid

to push you too far. I suppose, too, I was hoping to change you or make you forget." In response to his frown she put a hand on his arm. "She must be a remarkable lady Richard, this Kate."

"Oh Caroline, how ...?"

"Virginia," she said softly. He was near to tears and ashamed of showing his emotions in a public place.

"What did she say?" his voice was trembling.

"Just that you were in love," she whispered again, eyes moistening. Richard jumped to his feet and guided Caroline out into the night air, where they held each other closely. They moved wordlessly along the pavement, arms around each other. She let them into the rear door of the silent and dark complex which comprised the City Jewellers. Once inside, they kissed deeply, as never before, and there was something very ironic about the highly charged feeling between them.

Caroline lit a lamp in an inner room and they sat on opposite sides of the table, hands seeking each other's on the table top.

"Are you in love, Richard?" Caroline broke the silence between them.

"I suppose I am. I'd never considered it in that way, but she's with me day and night and I find it impossible to settle. Caroline, my life is a mess!" he exclaimed. She continued to watch him in the light of the lamp as he clung to her hands. He was hurting her but she didn't care.

"Caroline, I have to go back. I have to return to see if she feels the same. I have the impression sometimes that I dreamt it all, do you see that I have to be sure that those two days were not just a figment of my imagination? I have to go back, if only to clear my name."

"Yes, I see that." Her whisper was barely audible.

"I don't know what else to say to you, darling Caroline."

"Come and make love to me for the last time," she implored, wiping a tear or two from her eyes, "then take me back to the restaurant, I'm starving."

* * *

It was very late when Richard arrived at the manor. He was met by Bates and informed that his mother was waiting up for him.

"It's your father, Master Richard," Bates warned him.

"Thank you, Bates, goodnight."

"Is that you, Richard?" his mother called, hearing his knock on her door.

"It is, mother."

"Come in, come in." She sounded agitated, "Sit down, I have to talk to you." Richard was wary of her tone, it was different from her usual brevity and severity.

"What is it, why are you up at this hour?"

"Your father threw himself down the stairs, Richard. The nurse couldn't prevent it, it was a wilful act on William's part - you didn't tell him about Arthur and me did you?" She looked very old and haggard, certainly not his usual self-possessed mother.

"Of course I didn't. How is father, has he broken any bones?"

"All of them I should think, he's very ill. By the time he reached hospital he had lost consciousness. Richard, was I the cause of all this?" She was genuinely desperate and lonely in her independence. Richard had never before seen his mother like this. He went to her, hovering over her for some time before she came into his arms. She clung to him and sobbed violently into his shoulder.

Through his own tears he saw himself in her mirror and

cursed the cruel fate that had kept him waiting twenty-five years to embrace his mother, days before he was due to leave her.

Chapter 20

"It's time for decision-making all round it seems." George Steady had just presided over the week's agenda conference and had dismissed all the participants with the exception of Richard. The senior partner clasped his hands before his chest, as was his habit. "I'm going to retire, Richard." The large clock in the corner of Mr Steady's office became an intrusion into the stillness, its steady rhythm measuring the moments as the two lawyers faced each other across the polished desk. Richard, surprised by the announcement, found his voice.

"I do hope that I'm not responsible for you making this decision prematurely."

"Grace and I have, for some time now, been considering the prospect. As you know, we have a cottage in Dorset, Grace is tiring of the city and craves country life. You have simply brought things to a head and presented us with the ideal opportunity. I have to rebuild and restructure the firm or sell it. I have opted for the latter in the circumstances." Richard nodded sadly. "What would father think of us both, George?"

"I think that he would understand, Richard. He always said that he would get out before the business could affect his health, alas, he didn't see the signs."

"I am sure you are right," agreed Richard, "And we are both changing course as a result of the circumstances in which we find ourselves."

"Deal with the facts as they are presented. Quite right my boy." A rare smile crossed his features fleetingly as he pushed his chair back, both men moving towards the door. "By the way, your mother is dining with us on Friday evening, I do hope that you'll join us. As it is your last evening before sailing, perhaps you would care to bring Caroline, she would be very welcome."

"That is most kind, George. I will confirm her availability tomorrow. Uh ... George?"

"What is it Richard?"

"My mother - how is it that, well, I know how you have always felt about her - why the invitation?" George Steady considered long before replying, closing the door again softly. He waved Richard into a chair and occupied the adjacent one. Peering over the pyramid of his hands, he commenced speaking with typical deliberation.

"I have always held the view that William's most unhelpful influence was that of his wife, sad it may be, but very evident. That is the opinion of both Grace and myself regarding the lack of support she has given William in recent years. Yet last week your mother came to see us, pouring out her heart and desperately anxious to make amends in any way she could. The transformation is remarkable."

"Yes," confirmed Richard, "but how tragic that the change of heart should come too late for father. On Sunday morning at church, mother and I sat together, prayed together, conversed together with friends, even went for a drink together. She always wants to be in my company. How father would have rejoiced at the sight!" George unclasped his hands, raising them aloft, palms upwards.

"I know, Richard, I know. Life does take some cruel twists and turns. Have you any theories as to the reason behind the change in your mother?" Richard cast his mind back to a day two weeks earlier.

"Father's attempt at suicide brought about a remarkable change and she has mellowed with each day since then."

"Quite amazing!" exclaimed George Steady, getting to his feet again. He turned to face Richard as he rose from his chair. He placed a hand on his shoulder.

"Come on, Richard, let's get through as much work as possible in your last week."

For many years George Steady and William Shaw had met in this way, discussing the week's programme with employees. As they left the conference room, the two incumbents of the current and final partnership realised that they had done so for the last time. The close association of Shaw and Steady was soon to be discontinued.

* * *

It was just after eleven the following morning that Kate's actual letter arrived on Richard's desk, and by some inept act of fate, Caroline called at his office fifteen minutes later. Richard had received the transcript of the letter in the new year, but to hold the sheet of paper Kate had actually handled, and which contained her handwriting, was exciting. Staring at the envelope, he mentally envisaged its progress across land and sea. He was reading his letter for the second time when his secretary announced Caroline. Sliding the sheet into a top drawer, he rose to greet her just as she tapped on his door.

"Caroline, this is a pleasant surprise," he said, perhaps rather too enthusiastically.

"How is your last week going?" She resisted his attempt to embrace her.

"Still a lot to do," he sighed, as they took seats on either side of his desk. She came straight to the point, her manner cold, reminding him of occasions in the past when they had quarrelled.

"I have received this telegram from Virginia, you had better read it." Richard took it from her. The familiar typeface of the telegram he considered so impersonal, read as follows: 'Caroline, am delayed. Ask Richard to cancel and re-book three weeks later. Will you accompany me? Virginia.'

"Will you delay your departure, Richard?" Caroline was watching him as he looked up.

"I think not," he said, "I'll meet you at New York harbour when you both arrive," he added, "if I am a free man, of course." It was obvious from her reaction that Virginia had told Caroline of his problems, but at no time had she questioned him about them. "Before I forget, Caroline, we're invited to George Steady's for dinner on Friday. Will you come?"

"Your last evening, I have no choice," she said, rising.

They stood together on the pavement under the sign 'Shaw and Steady', feeling awkward as never before. The noise and the activity of the busy street seemed to isolate them, as though the world at large had run out of sympathy for their cause and was going about its business, immune to the turmoil within the young couple.

"I'll walk you to the shop," Richard said, finding his voice.

"That won't be necessary," she replied without emotion. "But I really must be going."

She glanced in the direction of the city. "You will book three passages for the last Saturday in March?"

"Three!" he exclaimed.

"My mother is coming with us," she shouted back at him, and was lost in the crowd.

* * *

The ever reliable Thomas Cook confirmed Richard's booking for Saturday and cancelled the one made for Virginia. The clerk did not anticipate any problems with the three ladies travelling on their chosen date.

"Not many choose to cross the Atlantic at this time of year," he said conversationally.

"This will be my third winter crossing," explained Richard.

184

"Urgent business, sir?" the clerk enquired routinely.

"Yes, that's it," agreed Richard. "That's it exactly."

* * *

That evening Richard and his mother were relaxing in the drawing-room. They had spent an hour at the bedside of William Shaw, though he had been incapable of appreciating the sight of his wife and son standing together over him, a situation that would surely have aided his recovery had he been aware of it. His body shattered and his mind gone, Richard's father was a mere physical shell, all grasp of life relinquished.

A log fire burned in the drawing-room. This was Shaw Manor as he remembered it before going off to university. He watched his mother, for whom he had always possessed a secret admiration. Her energy and resourcefulness were legendary among her friends and acquaintances, as was her sense of dress and awareness of fashion. What she lacked in natural beauty was made up for by the care and attention she lavished upon her appearance. Richard had inherited her dark hair and slim build. His father had been white-haired for as long as he could remember.

Mary Shaw put down her newspaper and looked across the room at her son, catching his gaze, which was still focused on her as his thoughts developed.

"If you decide to stay in America, I could take a few months off and visit you."

"That would be wonderful, mother." Richard was glad to leave his book for a moment - a classic recommended by Caroline, and heavy going. "I'm sure that Bates and the servants would manage until you returned." He paused, then added, "I may not be permitted to stay, we must remember that." Richard

185

had taken his mother into his confidence some days before and they had discussed the options available.

"Richard," she continued, "will you promise me that wherever and whenever you marry, I will be given the opportunity to be present?"

"I gladly make that promise," he said, smiling across at her. "My main concern is father. What if he regained some degree of normality? It would be dreadful if neither of us was available."

"I see William every day, and will continue to do so, Richard. I'll have a good idea as to the likelihood of that happening. I hope and pray that he will recover sufficiently to return home so that I can make amends. The nurse would not be required, only if I were to travel out to you." Mrs Shaw hesitated, gazing abstractedly at the ceiling. "I desperately need to talk to your father, Richard, please God I get the chance."

"It's unlikely, mother, but I pray for that too."

"Richard, please come here." She held out an arm to him, beckoning. He obeyed, and she took his hands as he knelt before her, feeling the fire's heat on his thigh.

"What is it, mother?" The moment was a precious one.

"Will you ever forgive me, darling? I must have been insufferable, I really don't know what got into me." She kissed his hands and her tears fell on his cuffs. He took her head into his arms and they remained locked in an embrace for some minutes. She pulled away, wiping her eyes with his handkerchief and regaining her composure. "Richard, there's something I must tell you, and time is of the essence with your imminent departure."

"Are you sure you want to tell me?" he asked quietly, not having a clue what it was she wished to tell him.

"I must, I must." Silence reigned as she struggled with herself. "Richard, I am ill, very ill. The day you flew at me over the dinner, do you remember?" He nodded, dread filling his very being. "That was the day I had the result of an examination. My headaches were becoming unbearable so I sought advice from my physicians in the city. It is their considered opinion that I have a growth somewhere here." She ran a hand through her hair, covering her skull. "So, Richard, now you know."

He held on to her hands tightly, ashamed of the cynical attitude he had adopted on so many occasions regarding his mother's sudden headaches.

"Mother, how long ...?"

"It could be years, Richard," she interposed, "I have medication to lessen the pain."

"If only you had explained earlier. It's you who should forgive me for my stupidity."

"Let's put all that behind us and look to the future," she said brightly. "Where is your travel list?" At his mother's insistence they turned their attention to the practical side of his departure and they noted his requirements concerning clothes and sundry items, paying due consideration to weight and suitability. Even in an onerous task such as this, Richard found joy in working with his mother.

* * *

The very next day Richard returned to his desk after lunch to find that a note had been delivered in his absence. The writing was appalling and barely legible, but an address was decipherable, as was the name 'Forest' at the bottom. Richard had to assume that he held an invitation to visit the new home of his cockney friends. He rejected any notion of going to the house that day. He had so many loose ends to tie up regarding his travel arrangements and the dissolving of the firm.

Wednesday was bright and frosty early, developing into a sunny and comparatively warm day, inviting a brisk walk. Richard left his Chambers at midday, taking the note with him, and within thirty minutes had located the house. The small dwelling was part of a smart terrace. Each house retained its own individuality, but conformed at the same time to the overall character of the terrace.

A beaming Henry Forest shook Richard's hand warmly and, accompanied by Mrs Forest (Richard had never heard her first name) he was given a conducted tour of the house. He was amazed at the transformation in the Forests' standard of living.

"I want yer to know, Mr Richard, that you and yours will allus be welcome in this 'ouse," announced Forest, proudly pulling out a new chair for him. "Yus, allus welcome." He poured whisky into three glasses and handed one to Richard, another to Mrs Forest and, picking up the third himself, proposed a toast to friends.

"Will yer stay for a bite t'eat?" Mrs Forest asked, turning to Richard and wrinkling her delightful snub-nose, a pleasant feature in an otherwise ordinary face.

"I would be honoured, madam, thank you," Richard replied as they eagerly awaited his response.

It was in this atmosphere of mutual respect and gratitude that the three passed the afternoon. The meal had commenced with Henry solemnly delivering a grace that must have shaken the very foundations of hell with its fervour. Richard was able to observe his friends at close quarters during the hours he spent with them. They were, in a sense, an unusual couple in that they resembled each other in so many ways, the most obvious being their red hair which was identical in texture and shade. They shared mannerisms, both facial and in body movement. The only difference in speech was the pitch which

188

betrayed their different gender. The way they both hovered over their guest attentively was quite natural and very genuine. In sight and sound, Richard considered them to be a perfect example of brother and sister. It seemed true that many married couples grew to resemble each other.

It also occurred to him, not for the first time, how much he was at ease with people from backgrounds less privileged than his own. He felt more at home with this couple than in his own house, grand though it might be. However, the atmosphere at Shaw Manor had changed for the better in recent days and he was grateful for that.

Richard gave the Forests a background summary of his intentions. Henry agreed to transport Richard and his luggage to the station on Saturday morning, together with his mother and Caroline.

"The missus an' me'll allus remember yer, Mr Richard," said Forest as the two men shook hands when Richard left. The sentiments were echoed by Mrs Forest as she too shook his hand, impressing him with her grip, unusually firm for a woman.

Chapter 21

Dinner on that last Friday evening at the Steadys' luxury city apartment was as good a send-off as Richard could have expected in the circumstances. As always, the hosts were kindness itself; realising the awkwardness of the occasion and sensing the mixed emotions of their guests, they did everything in their power to make the evening a happy one.

Caroline persisted with her distant approach to the proceedings and Richard had to admit that her attitude was fully justified. It disturbed him nevertheless.

"You won't forget us when you get to America will you?" George engaged Richard's gaze as he spoke.

"That would be impossible, George, but what makes you think that my destination is America?" A smile passed between them all.

"That is what I would have done at your age and in your position, Richard. Have no fear, I have no wish to meddle." He shifted his attention to Richard's right. "I understand Caroline, that you are not letting him out of your sights for long - when do you leave us?"

"In three weeks' time," she responded, throwing a glance in Richard's direction.

"I do hope that you will be careful dear," pleaded Grace Steady, "one hears of such dreadful things." Richard detected a trace of another smile on George's face as his wife expressed her genuine concern.

"I hope that he is going to invite his mother to visit him too," Mary Shaw added light-heartedly. "It occurs to me that I have never been out of England." Grace Steady threw her arms in the air in resignation.

"Nor have we dear, George has often suggested a foreign

tour but we never got round to it. Such a pity I feel. One's education is not complete unless one sees how others live, is it?"

"That is very true, Mrs Steady," Richard confirmed.

"A toast!" declared George Steady, "To Richard."

"To Richard," they responded in unison. Glass rang on glass and quality wine was drained by lips now more disposed to smiling as the atmosphere became convivial.

At the conclusion of the meal, the ladies left the dining-room and the two men of law were left to talk business over a glass of port. They had already established a date for the firm's closure and on the first of April George Steady would be a retired gentleman and the affairs of Shaw and Steady would pass into other hands. This decided, they had much to do concerning the timing and nature of the hand-over. They took off their jackets and made themselves comfortable.

"George, we were discussing mother's attitude recently; there is another aspect to consider, one of which I was not aware at the time."

"Yes Richard, I know."

"You know?"

"Your mother confided in Grace and me last week. She was determined not to tell you, not wishing to spoil your departure or to worry you."

"She told me last night, George."

"I'm so glad that she has. I did point out to her that I considered it unwise to let you leave the country unaware of her position."

"It explains a lot, doesn't it?"

"It does, Richard. I feel somewhat guilty at the thoughts I've been harbouring over recent years. It proves the folly of making judgements against people. Rather a good admission for a lawyer, what?" They laughed together.

"Will you look after the affairs of the manor in my absence, George?"

"I shall be retaining certain private clients, Richard. Your mother is one of them."

"And if anything should happen to mother?"

"Have no fear, I shall organise the maintenance of the manor until you return to make a decision." Both men simultaneously took the opportunity of a lull in conversation to drain their glasses. Richard refilled them, then put his brief-case on the table.

"So, let's get on with the business in hand, George." The older man slid his glass to one side carefully and reached for his own well-worn and bulging briefcase, extracting several files and stacking them on the table.

"Shall we deal with the demise of Shaw and Steady first, Richard?"

"That's the major task of the evening," Richard agreed.

Much later the two men rejoined the ladies, who were discussing their respective kitchens as the men entered the drawing room.

"It's difficult to keep plates hot, but essential," Mary Shaw was saying.

"There's nothing worse than hot food served onto cold plates," Caroline added emphatically.

"Hear, hear!" Richard exclaimed, receiving a reproving look and an impatient toss of the blonde head. From that moment on conversation became laboured as the participants tired and the hour grew late. Farewells were said, promises made and good wishes extended.

"Look after yourself, Richard."

"You too, George." They gripped each other's hands, bonded by the respect and familiarity of years. "Keep an eye on father," were Richard's parting words to the man who had been a second father to him.

Richard found conversation in the coach very difficult. His mother and Caroline had never been close, even less so since the involvement of Mary Shaw with her father. Caroline, by repute a conversationalist, made no attempt to encourage or develop Richard's sporadic remarks aimed at breaking the silence. His mother came to his aid with an unforgettable statement, winning his respect in the process.

"Caroline, I know that I've done much to disappoint you, and in the past not made you as welcome as I should have. I can only ask you to forgive me. I have spoken to your mother and now I can tell you both also that I shall not be seeing Arthur again. Now that he has been selected as candidate for a North London constituency, his politics are taking up more of his time and attention and we feel it is time that we both looked towards our families. Now, for Richard's sake at least, let's be affable, if only for one night. We will both have lost him tomorrow." There was complete silence of a very different order in the coach. It magnified the sound of hoofs on stone, the creaking of the suspension and the murmurings of the driver above them. Richard's eyes were still peering across the coach and through the gloom at his mother. There was not a word from Caroline on his right and he shot a sideways glance at her. She was weeping.

Richard alighted with Caroline on reaching the Jefferson house.

"I'll send the coach back for you, Richard," his mother promised, popping her head through the window. "Goodnight. Goodnight, Caroline."

"Goodnight mother," he said for both of them and the coach continued its journey to Shaw Manor. The Jefferson home was still well lit and there were signs of much activity. The couple moved into the garden and sat in the summer house. Caroline gave her eyes a final dab and returned Richard's handkerchief.

"Was that really your mother talking just now?"

"Yes, Caroline, amazing though it may seem." They huddled together for warmth, pulling coat collars up and thrusting hands deep into pockets.

"I was taken completely by surprise, your mother will think me utterly ill-mannered," she reflected.

"That has never been a fault of yours, anyway you can explain in the morning."

"Richard." Caroline was hesitant. "Richard, would you mind very much if I didn't come to the station?" He knew that she was watching him in the darkness. "I would rather say goodbye here, tonight. Do you understand?"

"I do understand, Caroline," Richard whispered, "In fact I feel very guilty where you are concerned - do you feel that I'm abandoning you?" In the stillness he could hear her fingers nervously scraping an object in her pocket.

"You made no promises Richard, and I gave none. I'm going to miss you very much and I don't know yet if I can accept you just as a friend. How will I feel when I see you with someone else? As I say, I really don't know, I'm confused. Let's see what happens. I'm committed to travelling with Virginia and mother is getting very excited at the prospect. I suppose I am too, it's just ... well, you being there and not being mine." Their faces touched and mouths came together as they kissed gently and completely without passion. Richard was reminded of Caroline's dramatic background and during the last few minutes had, rather unkindly, seen her, in his mind's eye, delivering lines at many a rehearsal he'd attended.

As they sat in the cold, holding each other closely, the lamps in the house were extinguished one by one. It was much later again that they heard the coach arrive in front of the house. The young couple got stiffly to their feet, suddenly aware of the cold night air. In the light of the coach lamp they stood, each studying the other's face, eyes locked and saying more than words could at that moment. In that familiar way she had, Caroline's head fell backwards and her face came up to him. Richard took it in his hands, his palms spreading over her cheeks. He kissed her and time stood still, the cold of the night was forgotten. They moved apart and Caroline ran from him without a word or backward glance. She went out of the circle of light and out of his life.

Chapter 22

The light was fading fast and Richard could just make out, in the grey of the evening, the darker grey which represented the English coastline. As he looked down at the ship's wake his emotions matched the turbulent waters. His parting from his mother had, miraculously, been the fond farewell between a normal mother and son, a situation inconceivable weeks before. Richard had loathed saying farewell to friends and colleagues. His parting with his father and with Caroline had been particularly distressing and, strangely enough, so had been the moment when in farewell, he shook the hand of the old butler. Both Bates and Richard were aware of the fact that they would probably never meet again. He sighed as the ship's acceleration increased the turbulence of the waters below him. He was now uncertain of the future and felt he was in a kind of vacuum between his past and whatever lay ahead.

Richard had boarded the ship without encountering any problems. He realised however, that it was always possible for him to be confined to his berth or even locked away somewhere should the ship be alerted. He was anxious to handle the situation his way and an arrest or a premature confinement would not help his cause. The one consolation amidst a welter of worries was the unequivocal fact that the ship was easing its way towards the woman who held his future in her hands.

Travel had always held a fascination for Richard as a boy and he had longed to visit distant places and meet other nationalities. He had already decided that if his dream concerning his return should be nothing more than that, then he would continue his travels, keep moving and explore each continent.

At this juncture Richard felt the need to keep a low profile once more. No familiar faces had presented themselves so it was more than likely that he was travelling with total strangers. It was indicative of his natural optimism that he spent the major part of that first week looking forward. He stood for hours beside the ship's huge anchor, bracing himself against the wind and peering across the ocean as though expecting the forbidden land to appear at any moment.

It was on the seventh day of the crossing that the storm hit them. The wind shrieked across the decks, down the hatches and along the gangways and passages. It defied anyone to break cover. The ship pitched and tossed like a cork in a swift running brook. Crew and passengers alike were in a constant state of sickness. Normal life below decks was impossible as the passengers' surroundings were constantly shifting, producing a state of disorientation. Richard wondered how Charlotte, Caroline and Virginia would cope should they encounter similar conditions.

The fact that the nearest land was hundreds of miles away did nothing to allay the fears of all on board. It was during that first night of severe weather that Richard became aware of the young mother and her two children. Sleep was impossible and passengers congregated in bars, dining areas and lounges. No doubt the desire for company and the fear of being alone was responsible for the communal existence. Richard had observed the young mother's inability to cope and had offered to assist her. Gradually he took the family under his wing, amusing the little ones whilst their mother, who was expecting her third child, took the opportunity of resting as much as circumstances would allow. Four year old Benjamin was so terrified that Richard took him back to his own bunk, whilst he occupied a couple of chairs. Much of the periods of darkness was spent re-assuring the lad and taking a nap only when the boy's eyes closed in sheer fatigue.

The storm continued for three long days, then, as suddenly as it had arisen, the wind abated and the ship became stable once more. Within hours however, the rain came. It lashed down out of grey clouds which enveloped the ship, making it impossible to define any demarcation between sea and sky. Visibility was down to a few yards. The ship had eased its engines and the depressed state of the passengers was deepened as the news from the Captain filtered through their ranks; the storm had blown the ship off course and a delay of two days to their arrival in New York was anticipated.

The ship moved into the murky blackness for the second night of incessant rain. No-one on board had breathed fresh air for some days. It was after midnight that Richard was disturbed as he slept. He was aware of a pounding on his door and he slipped on his robe to investigate. Benjamin was standing there wearing only his pyjamas, trembling and soaked to the skin. As the door opened, the youngster leapt into Richard's arms, crying bitterly.

"Where is Mummy?" Richard asked, repeating the question on hearing only a whimper. He carried Benjamin along the corridor to the berth the family occupied. The door was open and swinging gently with the swell. Richard became alarmed. The berth, the same size as his own, was empty of human life, but bedding, clothing and items of a personal nature were strewn everywhere. Richard took Benjamin to the ship's office.

The officer on duty was dozing fitfully as Richard tapped on the window. Making a remarkable recovery with the practice of years, the officer let him in and listened to the tale regarding the absence of the mother and her daughter. A search of the ship was immediately authorised by the Captain, who joined them in the abandoned cabin. It soon became obvious that Benjamin's mother and sister were not on board. The lad had buried his head in Richard's robe as he had tried to dry the youngster's tousled fair hair. The Captain pulled Benjamin away gently and sat him on his knee, then questioned him in an attempt to coax the truth from him.

"Where is Mummy? Where is Annie?" he asked kindly.

"In water," he mumbled indistinctly, but they all heard his words. The lad suddenly raised an arm and pointed out into the gloom. "In water," he shouted as if the horrific recollection had just come to him.

"Show me," the Captain said urgently, as he took hold of the little hand. They reached the side of the ship at the lad's direction, and again Benjamin repeated the same two words, pointing over the side of the ship.

"In water." Heads turned as they looked first at each other then into the grey mists swirling around them. The Captain sprang into action, yelling the order that was relayed in the distance by invisible crew members.

"Stop engines!" he roared. Richard was aware of the tiny hand gripping his own. What dreadful things has the little lad witnessed? The ship's Captain put into words the awful truth that was now apparent. "She must have gone overboard with the baby," he said with a look of disbelief on his face. The very next moment the huge engines stopped, the ship ceased its eternal shuddering and silence reigned. There was an eerie quietness as the mists drifted across the decks and the rain kept up its steady torrent.

A lifeboat was lowered and the sound of voices clear. The little boat headed back along the ship's route. The voices aboard could be heard for some minutes after the mists had swallowed up any visual trace of it. Richard left Benjamin at the ship's office and returned to his own cabin to rub down and dress in something more practical. He arrived back on deck just as the crew of the lifeboat became audible and, minutes later, came into view. The crew shook their heads solemnly. No one had expected to find the missing passengers, but nevertheless all were disappointed.

The ship eventually got underway again, the resumption of the pulsating vibration seemed obscene and incompatible with the mood on board.

"Another half-day lost," the Captain remarked, ducking into the office and acknowledging Richard as he sat with Benjamin on his lap. "I've checked the passenger list and apparently the family are - were Americans." Richard had guessed this from the few occasions he had spoken to Benjamin's mother.

"And that's all we know is it Captain?"

"Yes, Mr Shaw, unless you picked up anything." The Captain dropped wearily into a chair.

There's no husband - no father," Richard added, patting Benjamin's head. He struggled to recall bits of conversations, his brow furrowed in concentration. "She also said something about not being met on arrival. I think the lady was alone and afraid."

"She must have been to go to these extremes." The Captain took a mug which was offered him and flinched as he sampled the hot liquid. "Can you cope with the lad?" Richard felt the tiny body shivering in his arms and decided it was time Benjamin was in a warm bed.

"Leave him with me, Captain, if I need help I'll shout." The two men exchanged wan smiles as Richard led the boy to his cabin.

* * *

The seemingly interminable crossing came to an end one chilly morning. The mists rolled away in a stiff breeze and the coastline was suddenly apparent. Gradually it acquired detail and as Richard stood at the rail with a group of early risers, the dock buildings took shape, each piece coming into focus as the distance to the shore decreased.

The tragic events had eliminated any elation at arriving and solemn faces studied the emerging harbour, conducting conversation in hushed tones as though it would be irreverent to raise one's voice.

Richard now had to concentrate on his plan of action. He had not been apprehended thus far. On the contrary, he had won the respect of the ship's officers and crew, and was to accompany the Captain as he reported the loss of two passengers to the dock authorities. His disembarkation was to be nothing like the furtive slipping ashore he had imagined it would be.

Having organised his baggage, Richard collected Benjamin and they left the ship together. None of the youngster's effects could be taken, as the berth had to be left undisturbed. Richard had gained the boy's confidence mid-Atlantic and their relationship had developed to a point where complete trust kept the little hand anchored to his own. Richard's predicament was forgotten as his attention was taken over by the boy's requirements.

There were many questions and few answers, and the moment eventually came when Richard and Benjamin had to be parted. This was effected only by promises on Richard's part that he would return.

"I will come back, Ben," he assured the lad, feeling less confident than he sounded. After weeks of the ocean's movement, the stability of *terra firma* was a relief indeed and added to the joy he felt at setting foot on American soil.

As arranged, Nat Holland was waiting for him on the dockside. They greeted each other warmly.

"Three days late, Richard, what have you been doing?"

Nat smiled as they stowed away the considerable amount of baggage in the cart. "It was one of the longest crossings of the winter," Nat continued as he picked up the reins and they moved off along the coast road.

"I can believe that," Richard responded, his laugh reflecting his mood. "I'm lucky to be back in America again, for one reason or another."

"Was it that bad?" Nat grinned again as he flicked the reins, catching something of the Englishman's humour. He listened as Richard related the story of his crossing, an account culminating in his uncertainty regarding little Benjamin's future.

What a homecoming he received at the Holland house. Sarah was her old kind and maternal self and he felt very fortunate to have such friends so far from his home. That evening was spent catching up on news and during the course of it, Richard received an apology from both Sarah and Nat for not having been completely honest concerning their family background. They were not proud of their history. They visited the neatly-kept grave on which stood a vase containing early wild flowers. Staring down at the inscription, Richard found it difficult to believe, even after many months, that Dave was the one to whom it referred. Sarah was flanked by Nat and Richard, who both placed an arm around her shoulder. They stood there for some minutes, silently, each lost in private thoughts and memories.

As they returned home in the buggy, it was agreed that Richard should call on the Sheriff the next day to begin the process of clearing his name. Before they retired, Sarah took him into Dave's old room. It was just as he had left it the year before, his possessions piled neatly alongside that of his friend's. Standing there in that room brought memories flooding back. What a lot had happened since Dave's death nearly a year ago.

Chapter 23

The Sheriff had his back towards them as Nat and Richard entered the tiny office. Hearing their boots on the wooden floor he turned, recognising Nat at once. They shook hands and exchanged pleasantries.

"Do you recall this fella?" Nat waved a hand in Richard's direction.

"Can't say as I do," the Sheriff replied, squinting thoughtfully at Richard.

"Richard Shaw, Sheriff, I've returned from England." As he spoke, he moved towards the lawman, offering his hand and hoping the Sheriff would accept it. They clasped hands just as the name registered in the lawman's brain and the significance of it became clear.

"What in the name of tarnation are you doin' back here?"

"I aim to clear my name and I need your help."

"Guess I'm not surprised at that," the Sheriff concluded. "It would have been easier on you if you'd done it 'fore you took off though."

"I see that now, Sheriff, but I had urgent family matters to attend to." The Sheriff nodded and scratched his head, obviously bemused by this turn of events. He waved them into chairs and sat behind his desk, where he looked more comfortable and in control. He reminded Richard of Sheriff John Champion, as they were of similar build, stocky and a little shorter than Richard himself. They also shared the habit of waving their arms around in extravagant gestures, illustrating the spoken word with excited and animated movement. They had both been given the same Christian name, John. Perhaps, Richard considered, there is a particular type of man from which a Sheriff is moulded.

"I oughta lock you up," he said with conviction, "but I can't see any gain in that," he added reflectively. He glanced at Nat. "Is he stayin' with you?"

"Yep, until this is cleared up," Nat confirmed.

"Have I your word that you won't disappear again?"

"Sure, Sheriff, and thanks," Richard responded gratefully. "Can we ride over to the rail-head and locate one or two people who could assist my cause? That's my only hope of proving self-defence."

"No call for that," the lawman protested, "your friend here has given me a statement, so has his stepson Philip." Richard shot a questioning glance at Nat. The Sheriff continued; "I have a statement signed by four girls and written by er ..." The lawman hesitated, searching his memory, then through a pile of papers before him.

"Rebecca," prompted Richard.

"Rebecca it is," agreed the Sheriff. "She handed it in to the local lawman, God help him!" Their smiles were mutually indicative of the sympathy felt for anyone responsible for law and order in that place.

"Bless you, Rebecca," Richard breathed to himself. The Sheriff rose, kicking his chair back, giving himself room to stand and terminate the interview.

"So I can find you at Nat's place, my boy, stick around, leastways until I get this thing tidied up. I warn you, it could take quite a spell." Richard and Nat left John Maddox's office, but not before thanking him for his time.

"I'm optimistic Nat," Richard said as they climbed into the buggy.

"Me too," agreed Nat, shaking the reins and moving the team off in the direction of the headland. "Reckon you could be on your way before long."

"What's Philip's attitude, Nat?" Richard had expected

206

hostility from this quarter, not a signed statement in his defence. Nat's eyes drifted off across the ocean for a minute before he formulated his reply.

"I think that you'll be pleasantly surprised Richard. Philip is now a commissioned officer and a very responsible young man. He is very different from David of course, you'll see why the two of them didn't get along. Philip's ship is due in New York later this week, you'll no doubt meet him." Richard detected a note of pride in Nat's voice and was pleased that the depleted little family was now united.

The two men lapsed into general conversation for an hour, during which time they arrived at the tiny track which led off to the stables so familiar to Richard.

"Can we take a look at Valiant, Nat?" he asked eagerly.

"Sure thing," Nat replied, but continued along the trail to the coast. Richard was mystified but made no further comment.

Thirty minutes later they were in the drive of the Holland home. Richard gazed out across the ocean, which at this distance looked calm. The eye was able to reach the horizon and his thoughts travelled beyond it to his homeland. He had no regrets at this stage, just an inherent impatience, and a desire to be on his way west.

"Will you see to the horses, Richard?" Nat brought him back to practical reality and he nodded his reply, taking the two bays out of harness.

As he entered the stable, his mind had taken one of its habitual flights forward or backward in time. He halted in his tracks, the bays bumping into him. There in the first stall was the horse he loved.

"Valiant!" he exclaimed. The grey's whinny was a welcome indeed. Richard did his duty regarding the bays, then returned to his horse to effect a reunion he had anticipated over long winter months. Valiant looked healthy and well cared for, the winter coat almost groomed out. The horse had put on weight, but then so have I, Richard mused. The journey they were to make together would rectify that situation.

As Richard busied himself around the horse he talked to it, its big ears flicking in appreciation. If horses had not been good at keeping secrets, then all his personal aspirations would have been confidential no longer.

The Hollands could tell by the pleasure on Richard's countenance that he had spent time with his horse. In response to the barrage of questions Richard threw at him, Nat held his arms aloft in mock defence.

"He has been with us almost since you left," he explained. "I dropped in at the stables once or twice and it was obvious that your agreement was not being honoured. For the sum you left I bought Valiant back. He's yours, Richard."

"Nat, how wonderful!" Richard shouted excitedly, "You must have been confident of my return," he added with a grin.

Later that morning Richard became more restless than usual. He had promised to visit Benjamin, but he was aware of his house confinement. Sarah produced a solution with which they all concurred. Nat had to visit the docklands on business that afternoon and he would collect the boy from the authorities and bring him home, returning him the following day. Nat also agreed to send telegrams to London and Randolph stating that Richard had arrived in America and was hopeful of an early vindication.

Richard's mood mellowed considerably by the spontaneous action of a small boy. On arrival, Nat had lifted Benjamin down from the buggy and, seeing Richard coming down the path, the lad pushed open the gate and ran towards him as fast as his little legs would permit, jumping up into Richard's arms in breathless excitement.

"We can keep the little chap for as long as is mutually agreeable," Nat informed them over dinner. "There seems to be no trace of family, but there were documents in the berth which indicate that the boy's name is Benjamin Stowe, and that tallies with the passage booked under that name." Nat glanced at the boy seated next to Richard, too busy eating to take in the gist of the conversation.

"Any history of the mother?" enquired Richard, also confirming Benjamin's preoccupation. Nat nodded, chewing for a moment.

"She had a record of mental instability in Manchester they say, but why she lived there and the reason behind her return is not known."

"Poor little fella," sighed Sarah, "what's to become of him?"

"He's prone to tantrums apparently," Nat continued, "They are quite concerned, but are happy for us to look after him until a solution is found."

"Well, I haven't perceived any ill-temper," offered Richard, running his hand through Benjamin's fair hair and receiving a rewarding grin.

Later that evening, Richard went to the boy's bedroom as Sarah was tucking him in. Their little guest was very sleepy, but before his eyes closed in final submission Richard promised to take him riding on Valiant the next morning.

The morning in question was wet. Once again the ocean was lost to view and the headland enveloped in a dank and depressing mist of drizzle, like that which had proved the last straw in a depression suffered by the mother of the boy currently in their charge.

Richard became restive, a feeling that was constantly near the surface. His goal was Randolph. He had achieved half of it in treading American soil, now there was an inward urge and impatience to fulfil his ambition. He endured visions of all kinds of situations prevailing at his journey's end. One night on board ship he had dreamt of Kate in bridal attire with a stranger at her side. He had opened his eyes, fearful and bathed in perspiration as though expecting to find his dream a reality. Richard's composure was not enhanced by such provocation of his heart and mind.

Life in the Holland household was never dull. There was a continuous stream of visitors, all acquaintances and business associates of Nat's, and their arrival was unpredictable, as was the time of their departure. This damp evening was no exception. Sarah responded to a hammering on the front door returning with a telegram which she handed to Nat.

"Abel Horricks is coming later tonight," he informed them all.

"Oh, really?" said Sarah unenthusiastically.

"I know, I know," Nat agreed, "but he has influence, my love."

"Abel really is the oddest man," she said uncharacteristically, and shaking her head in Richard's direction. Richard thought no more of the impending visit until the man actually arrived. Astonishment was still apparent on Richard's face as he was introduced.

"Haven't we met before?" Abel Horricks remarked as they shook hands, and his brow creased as he made a visible effort at recollection.

"We were passengers on the same ship last winter," Richard informed him, recovering his equilibrium. After a moment, during which Abel Horricks covered his brow with the palm of his hand, his face lit up.

"Yes, of course, it was David who invited you over in the first place." The three men talked for an hour before Nat took his colleague into his study, and they were not seen again that night. Sarah's eyebrows moved heavenward as she emerged from the study after providing the men with refreshment.

"He's staying the night," she whispered, "Would you believe he's Nat's new manager at the docks, what have we done to deserve that?" Richard bade her goodnight and climbed the stairs to the sound of muffled voices coming from the study.

The sun rose on a day in complete contrast to the previous one. Gone were the mists and the ocean sparkled. Valiant plodded around the garden carrying Richard with Benjamin seated in front of him. He felt optimism rise as they rode through the spring flowers which covered the ground like an exotic carpet. Each tree and bush was in bud and Richard was almost a contented man. They eventually left the garden to tackle the rather more demanding cliff path. Occasionally Richard would dismount, leaving the boy in the saddle, watching him closely as he led the horse at walking pace. The four year old sat quite naturally in the saddle, showing no signs of anxiety.

"C'mon Vajunt," he would shout, leaning forward in the saddle as if to encourage impetus. Valiant came through the exercise with flying colours too.

Returning to the stables at noon, Richard observed that an additional horse occupied the stalls. He knew that Abel Horricks had left early that morning.

"I wonder who owns that horse?" Richard said aloud to himself, causing both Benjamin and Valiant to turn their heads, unanswering. "Come on." Richard took the little hand in his, "let's find out, eh Benjamin?"

* * *

Philip Holland was a rugged, handsome young man, immaculate in the uniform of ship's officer. Even though they were not blood relatives there was a resemblance to his late brother which Richard found difficult to define. Whether it was in mannerisms or features, he didn't know at that moment. Richard gratefully accepted Philip's hand and returned his firm grasp.

"I'm pleased to see you at last, Philip, but I must confess to some considerable apprehension concerning our meeting." A smile transformed the tanned face and Richard immediately placed the resemblance. It was the infectious grin he had seen so often and which had been Dave's greatest asset in winning others to his cause.

"Your reputation depicts a totally conflicting picture of you, Richard," the seaman answered in a strong voice, raising a hand to deter Sarah and Nat from leaving the room. "Please stay?" he requested gently. The four of them settled into chairs, fully aware of the tension which prevailed. Benjamin slept in a fifth chair, defeated by the morning's fresh air and excitement.

"Richard," Philip began, "if I may speak, then if you will tell me in your own words exactly what happened last year." Richard nodded and Philip, after a moment's thought, continued: "I am not proud of my paternal heritage but the man was, after all, my father. I took a transcript of your testimony and did some investigating of my own, visiting that dreadful place where father insisted on conducting his business. The reason for his choice is now obvious, of course." Philip leaned forward in his chair, clearing his throat in the silence. "I went to the shack he occupied and found it to be just as you described, his bloodstains still evident on the floor by his desk. There was no trace of father's workforce, which didn't surprise me, as his company folded after his death. I did find your friend Rebecca at the hotel. She was in very poor health, but she gave me her account of the incident exactly as you had recorded it. So, Richard, I am convinced of the truth of your story; people and places tally and I now have a clearer conception of my father's activities." Philip swung his glance away from Richard and his eyes rested on his mother and step-father. "It will come as no surprise to you that I had a low opinion of my brother. I considered him to be a wastrel and his flagrant and clandestine relationships were a disgrace. I do, of course, regret his death and the circumstances surrounding it, and appreciate the friendship which built up between you and him, Richard. What you all will not know is that the last woman Dave chose to flirt with was, at that time, living with my father. To Captain Radford, a proud man, that evidently was the last straw, but as you stated, Richard, there was no justification for a killing, either on father's part, or yours." Richard and Philip held each other's gaze unflinchingly. "Do tell me, Richard, why a gentleman like yourself had to gun down my father, I must hear it from you."

The frankness of Philip's approach was, initially, the cause of discomfort; gradually, however, his listeners began to appreciate his honesty. Richard was prepared to present his case and did so in the manner in which he'd been trained.

"I had no intention of using a gun," he concluded, "but when you are staring down a barrel, you react instinctively and quickly. I had no options open to me, I had to shoot."

In the ensuing silence, each person in the room digested the facts as presented, and everyone came to their own conclusions. There was a general feeling of relief that the affair was now out in the open and that grievances had been aired. Sarah courageously broke the awkwardness of the moment; "Shall we eat now, gentlemen? I have prepared a cold buffet." It was, incredibly, a high-spirited party that moved into the dining-room. As the voices lifted and became lighter, the volume was sufficient to wake Benjamin, who had remained asleep during the previous hour's deliberations, conducted in under-tones.

At the table they ate the light midday meal, made all the more welcome by its delay. Philip suddenly dived into a pocket, producing a telegram.

"Sorry, Richard, I should have given this to you earlier. It arrived at Nat's office this morning." The envelope was handed around the table to Richard, who eagerly tore it open.

"Richard," it read, "your letter and telegram received. You are in our thoughts and prayers. God speed. Kate."

The dawn had heralded a beautiful day and Richard had responded with optimism. Now he considered it a wonderful day and looked forward to the remaining hours with a happy heart.

Chapter 24

The days were lengthening perceptibly and the trees made their inevitable transition from bud to blossom. Birds, flashing colours, skimmed the hedgerows and twittered and bustled within them, making their contribution to the announcement of spring. The small meadow at the rear of the house was covered in a carpet of colour, its green backcloth of grass taking on a richer hue by the day. Even the mighty ocean looked attractive, as if in an attempt to dispel and apologise for the bleakness and hostility of its winter guise.

With his impatience gradually mounting, Richard had spent many hours each day preparing for the time when he and Benjamin would ride west. Sponsored by Nat and with the backing of the ship's Captain, Richard had signed provisional adoption papers, which indicated his willingness to take responsibility for the boy. He was convinced that he was doing the right thing in taking Benjamin with him, for Richard had, rightly or wrongly, become Benjamin's sole conception of a parent. It was odd how the loss of his family seemed to have little effect on him, but Richard had noticed his independence, resulting no doubt from his having had to fend for himself.

At Richard's request, Nat had purchased a mule, so as the weather became kinder and the going firmer, they rode the cliff paths within sight of the Holland home, Richard astride Valiant and Benjamin clinging on to the mule, which was suitably packed as though on the journey proper. A lead rope led from the pommel of Richard's saddle to the collar placed over the mule's head like a bridle. The rope was attached to the collar under the mule's chin. This measure of independence was enjoyed by Benjamin whose excited shouts of "C'mon mule" could be frequently heard but appeared to have little impression on the animal, which remained imperturbable.

At first Richard regularly glanced behind him, but in time was pleased at the realisation that young Ben was proving to be a natural rider. As they moved along the clifftop, Richard reflected on his motives for keeping the boy. To begin with, he had feared the outcome of their parting, but the more he considered the matter, the stronger his resolve became not to abandon the young orphan. Benjamin was backward with his speech and Richard was convinced that this was due not to a lack of intellect, but to the absence of a father figure, resulting in little attention being afforded him by an overworked and inaccessible mother. Richard was also of the opinion that their conversation on a one to one basis was bound to improve the lad's vocabulary. Teaching him to write would be more difficult, but certainly not impossible. It was a challenge and would prove to be rewarding as he witnessed the slow maturing of the young man.

However, Richard was aware that there was more to taking a young boy under his wing than the mere response to a challenge. As they returned from the stables that day and Richard ran his hand through Benjamin's hair, he knew that he loved the boy and that on no account could he leave him unprovided for.

Sarah was horrified at Richard's intention to take Ben with him and made it clear that she was willing to care for him until a permanent arrangement could be made. Richard did not doubt her competence or kindness, but felt it an imposition on his part, particularly as he knew of Nat's reluctance to revert to his paternal role.

They crossed the meadow from the stables together, Benjamin's tiny hand firmly clinging to his as they engaged in elementary conversation. Richard could not help but consider the irony of his change in fortunes. Less than a year ago he had departed in disgrace, his problems following him home across the Atlantic. Now he had returned, illegally, yet was held in high esteem, confident of winning a pardon from the authorities of this vast country of opportunity.

Two significant items of news came to Richard's attention on that glorious April day. Nat returned home early, having seen Philip off on his ship at the end of his shore leave. He handed Richard a telegram which had arrived at his docks office that same morning. 'Richard,' it read, 'Virginia staying in Germany. Has met Manfred, an engineer. Caroline and Charlotte not sailing. Father no change. Keep in touch. Love Mother.' Richard had been eagerly anticipating the arrival of the ladies during the next few weeks and was somewhat disappointed that it was not to be. He was surprised at Virginia's decision and knew that Caroline and her mother had been looking forward to travelling. Thinking about Virginia's friend, he realised that in the next few years there was going to be tremendous opportunity for trades such as engineering as the country developed. Perhaps she was bringing her German across with her, for there were many Europeans working in America fulfilling many kinds of roles. It was, Richard admitted to himself, a selfish thought that was uppermost in his mind regarding the news, that of diminished complications concerning his future plans. He visualised his father in that distant hospital bed and considered the knife-edge on which his mother was living.

The second revelation of the day was brought to him by Sheriff John Maddox that evening. The lawman invariably managed to arrive in time for dinner and on this occasion, as always, he was invited to partake. They were all relaxing after one of Sarah's particularly good meals when the Sheriff announced:

"Got some good news for you, young Richard." He exhaled and cigar smoke drifted into the eyes of the three expectant adults. He dug into a pocket producing an official but crumpled document, which he waved in Richard's direction. "It says in this 'ere notice that you are free to travel anywheres." He paused as Richard moved round the table, shaking hands vigorously. "Furthermore," he held his hand aloft, waiting for silence which quickly came, "furthermore, Richard, your intention to study American law has the blessing of the authorities, judges are required up and down the land, 'specially so out West." Richard did the rounds again as excitement grew. "And furthermore." The Sheriff was enjoying this and savouring every moment. There was silence once more. "And furthermore, I'll have in my hands in a day or so papers assigning the young 'un to Richard Shaw from England."

The Sheriff, his duty done, joined in the celebrations, accepting a glass of whisky and downing it with a flourish. Richard held his glass high and motioned towards Sarah and Nat. As he looked at them, something Dave had said to him flashed through his mind. It was in the days before he had even met them, when Dave had described his father as 'a great man.' Richard agreed completely. Sarah, Dave had decided, 'was an angel'. Richard wouldn't quarrel with that either.

"My thanks to good friends here." Richard and the Sheriff toasted the Hollands.

"And to you, Sheriff." The lawman became the centre of attention. "I'll buy you a box of those damned cigars." They all laughed together and Richard threw an arm around Benjamin, who peered up at him, not understanding the significance of the occasion.

Richard was now free to make the journey west, for which he had made adequate preparation. His frustration was replaced by anticipation as his way became clear. He knew, however, that there was one thing he must do before leaving the coast.

It would mean a delay of several days and involved returning to a place which would revive unpleasant memories. He headed north-west, just as he had the previous year on his mission of revenge. The rail-head had then been unknown to him, but was now all too familiar. The trail he recalled had been a mere thread winding its way up and down the hilly terrain. Now it was a well-worn highway as the rail-road persuaded more merchants to move their goods and wares inland from this growing terminus. Richard decided that however much this trail might change, he would still recognise it, as every twist and turn was imprinted on his mind, particularly the final hilltop view of the place before the track ran down the slope and disappeared into the huge unplanned and shapeless development.

As his destination drew nearer, so his dread of it increased until it was almost tangible. Richard passed the stables in which he had housed Valiant and rode on down the slope into the teeming complex. The main street still throbbed with life and activity in many forms. Keeping to the centre of the street, he made his way carefully but purposefully to his destination, throwing just a cursory glance in the direction of the Golden Nugget saloon as he passed. Richard did not anticipate being recognised, but his feeling of discomfort kept him moving. He was very conscious of the fact that on this occasion he wore no gun.

The hotel was smaller than he remembered it, looking insignificant in an equally forgettable row of buildings. Richard tied Valiant to the sagging rail, cleared the steps in a bound and crossed the tiny lobby. He took the stairs two at a time, pausing outside the familiar, still unpainted door. He listened, ear to the keyhole, for a sign of movement within. He broke the quietness with a firm double tap, detecting a noise which he loosely construed as an invitation to enter. Richard stepped inside.

Chapter 25

It took several minutes for his eyes to adjust to the gloom and in light afforded by a single window, he eventually made out the form of Rebecca, lying on the bed wrapped in a blanket. Richard realised immediately that she was a mere shadow of her former vibrant and independent self.

"Rebecca, do you remember me?" Richard stood by the bed. There was an unmistakable yet indefinable odour of sickness. Rebecca's eyes opened wide, registering surprise and recognition. She nodded. Those eyes, once so mischievous, now appeared too large for the pale face with its sunken cheeks. Her scrawny neck had lost its slim beauty and the hands lying at her side were more bone than flesh. Her hair, once fair with a healthy fragrance, now hung limp in dull disarray. As Richard took in her condition, she struggled to a more upright position and surveyed him with a penetrating stare.

"I'm surprised you recognised me," she said weakly, with just a glimmer of her old humour. "What brought you back?"

"Heard you weren't well - and to say thank you," he replied lamely, upset at her situation.

"That's nice," she whispered, "thought I'd been forgotten by the world." She looked away, tears filling her eyes.

"Not so, Rebecca, what can I do?" Richard pleaded earnestly. "Are you being looked after?" She smiled wanly at his concern.

"Nancy will be in later, but I'm very hungry Richard. My money has gone, you are all alone when that happens." Richard did not trust his voice, so he gently took her emaciated hands in his, managing an unconvincing smile. He stood up, then left the room.

Richard found a store nearby and bought a hot steaklet

with some modest garnish. His own appetite had deserted him. He hurried back to Rebecca and watched as she painfully but avidly devoured every last morsel.

The door opened and a young girl came into the room. Richard guessed her age at eighteen at the most.

"Are you alright, Beckie?" She eyed Richard with suspicion.

"You must be Nancy," Richard said as he rose to his feet.

"S'right," she snapped, "and who are you?"

"An old friend of Rebecca's." Richard knew that his accent had the girl mystified. "How long has she been like this?"

"Month or two now, I comes in now and ag'in to see that she's comfy."

"Thank you, Nancy. Would you like to help by making some coffee then?"

"Sure," she said and crossed the room to pour water into the billy-can, returning Richard's smile as her tension eased.

"Richard." Rebecca beckoned him nearer and he leaned closer. "I don't want to die here - please help me." The sequence of events which followed were to remain forever in his mind, a mental monument. Firstly there was the silence which surrounded Rebecca's heart-rending plea, followed by the ring of metallic mugs behind him. Then silence again, punctuated only by soft weeping from the bed. Finally the intrusion of the clatter made by a couple on the stairs outside the door, then silence again. Time itself had stood still.

Richard was suddenly aware of Nancy at his elbow. She handed him a mug of steaming liquid, left one at the bedside and took a seat across the bed from him.

"Do your folks still live in New York?" Richard found his voice, hoarse and unfamiliar. Rebecca took the mug from Nancy in both hands and turned back to him.

"Only Ma is left," she said, her voice trailing away so

that Richard needed to bend low again to catch her words. "My brother and sister left home before I did - when Pa died." She looked away again and stared at the tiny window. "Perhaps Ma has gone now too." Richard there and then made up his mind.

"Let's get you out of here," he said resolutely, "Can you ride d'you think?" He immediately realised what a stupid question that was, but he had to consider the practical side of his decision. "We'll have to get you down to the street, how does that sound?"

"Better than lyin' here," she replied, forcing a weak grin. Richard looked across at Nancy.

"Can you get Rebecca dressed?" The girl glanced down at the bed, receiving a nod in the affirmative from Rebecca.

"We'll try," Nancy said. The thin hand Richard held squeezed his own, very lightly, it was the only response possible at that moment. He replaced the hand on the blanket and stood up.

"I'll bring a meal back with me," he promised, and left the room once more.

Valiant was in skittish mood as Richard untied and mounted him. This place is disturbing the horse too, he reflected, not without humour. He rode on down the main street, eventually in completely unfamiliar surroundings. He needed to make a purchase and, finding himself riding between the shacks of traders and merchants of all kinds, did not take long in effecting a transaction. He bought a serviceable buggy for less than the original asking price after haggling energetically. He acquired a harness which he placed around Valiant, putting his saddle and bags into the buggy. Next on the shopping list were blankets and a thick winter coat with high collar and warm hood.

By the time Richard had visited the food store and

returned to the hotel, there were only four hours of daylight left. Rebecca, now clothed, looked marginally better as the three ate around the tiny table.

"Richard," Rebecca breathed, "could we take Nancy with us?" He raised an enquiring eyebrow in the young girl's direction.

"I've had it with this place," she offered, "And there could be work in New York, right?"

Richard was mulling this over in his mind - it would be tight in the buggy. "And I can help you with Beckie," she added, seeing his hesitation.

"Well, I guess the buggy will take the three of us," he conceded, "Be ready within the hour, Nancy."

"Sure," she said, diving out of the door.

* * *

An hour later they pulled away from the hotel and were waved off by a couple of girls who happened to be around their rooms at that hour. They cleared the main street and negotiated the gradient that would take them up and away from the dreary rail-head. Richard kept Valiant at a steady walk and they were soon in open country. There had not been a backward glance between them.

Rebecca was sitting snugly with Richard on her right and Nancy on her left, affording her as much protection and warmth as possible. Richard had been saddened as he placed the two bags in the buggy. They represented the sum total of the girls' possessions, inside was everything each had accumulated over the years. Walking Rebecca down the stairs and onto the street had been a slow and difficult process, but her determination had guaranteed success.

Richard found it momentarily irksome to be travelling in

the opposite direction and moving east, but put such thoughts behind him for the moment as he considered his present situation. The sun was falling low in the sky behind them and he realised that a night stop would be necessary. The Holland home was within reach, but he could not take advantage of Sarah's kindness. He opted for the small stage post just beyond Nat and Sarah's house, overlooking the ocean, where he had spent the night at the end of his ride east the year before. A couple of hour's ride the next morning would see them in New York.

Chapter 26

"I will not hear of it, Richard. You must all stay here tonight. Book into a hotel indeed! I shall be offended if you do." Richard had not expected such an outburst from the gentle Sarah. He had called simply to allay their anxiety and to update them on his movements.

"But Sarah ..."

"I'm going to prepare the beds Richard, please bring the girls in before they freeze!" Richard was caught in mid-sentence with arms outstretched in protest. He lowered his arms wordlessly as Sarah bustled off in the direction of the bedrooms.

So Rebecca and Nancy were installed in the spare rooms and three extra places set for dinner. Nancy arrived in the dining room with a look of wonderment on her face.

"What a lovely room, ma'am." Then, seeing the vacant space: "I don't think Rebecca is strong enough to join us." As the first course reached completion Sarah excused herself and left the room to coax Rebecca into eating some of the excellent broth they had enjoyed.

"All that girl needs is good food and fresh air," Sarah later announced, waving the empty bowl.

"Do you not feel that her illness goes deeper than that?" Richard asked her.

"I'll get Doc's opinion in the morning," she answered, returning to the table. She studied Nancy, who was sitting opposite her. "And you could do with fattening-up too young lady." Nancy smiled, mildly embarrassed.

"How did you girls get into this state anyway? You both have obviously had an education." Nat had been quiet up to this point, but his curiosity got the better of him. Nancy gazed around the table at each face turned towards her. She saw only kindness and genuine concern in those faces, and lost her reticence.

"My story is typical, Mr Holland. I left home last year. As one of eleven children I wasn't greatly missed, in fact it was one less to feed. Ma was left to run the farm when Pa went off into the city to find his fortune. He was never heard of again, leastways, not before I left. Then it's a case of drifting. Catching a ride here, bedding down there until you find yourself in a place like the one you found us in, Richard. In such a place everyone is in a similar situation, and you pull together, home from home, sort of. And you make money where you can, from anyone you can." She paused, somewhat sheepishly, and surprised that her audience was still attentive. Her voice lightened. "And now Beckie and me's going to make a new start, there must be work in New York." She looked at each face again, enquiringly.

"It's possible," Nat said encouragingly.

* * *

The days were now bright and becoming gradually warmer. Richard and Benjamin continued their trial journeys on horse and mule respectively. Their route now took them much farther afield and on occasions they were gone for several hours. On this particular morning the sun shone out of a clear sky and the ocean was in its most attractive mood. The on-shore breeze had diminished and it felt warmer. The five of them were sitting in the garden (or yard, as Nat would have it) watching Benjamin romp around in his fantasy world. Rebecca was well wrapped up and with her hair washed and combed by Sarah and Nancy, was looking more like her old self by the hour. A faint touch of colour had crept into her cheeks and Richard began to accept Sarah's prognosis of the previous night.

The doctor, however, had not been too sure when he called early that morning. He had spent considerable time with Rebecca and had taken many samples and conducted many tests.

"Her malady," he told Sarah, "is common among girls with her lifestyle." He left appropriate medication and departed announcing, "With care and attention and regular treatment she'll pull out of it - she's young and resilient."

April was passing quickly and Richard's impatience to be away was restrained somewhat by his current obligations, but his dilemma was nevertheless evident to at least one observer. As they all left the garden to prepare for lunch, Sarah put her arm around his shoulder.

"Why don't you be on your way son? Rebecca won't leave here until she's well, I promise." Richard took her in his arms, touched by the presence of a great lady who had called him her son. He was proud to accept that role.

"I'll leave on Monday Sarah, bless you." He knew that moment would remain forever in his memory, together with many other remarkable and momentous occasions. Richard had the absurd notion that Dave was looking down, approval showing on his eternally young face. Richard sighed. He still missed Dave. For all his faults, he had been Richard's best friend during those years at university and the two years after graduation. He sighed again. There was only one person he missed more and he was taking steps to rectify that after the weekend.

* * *

Three events strengthened Richard's resolve to leave after the weekend. Nat left with Nancy on Friday morning and returned without her. He smiled at the concerned looks he encountered on entering the house, infuriating Sarah by his secrecy.

"She's on a ship," he said, "it sails tomorrow morning for Liverpool."

"What?" they said in unison.

"Nat, be serious!" Sarah exclaimed, annoyed now at his frivolity.

"I tell you, she's one of the crew now, signed on as a stewardess. She is delighted and sends you all her love."

"But what if she doesn't like it?" Sarah's voice was softening now.

"As the girl herself said, she can't get off the ship mid-Atlantic, so she'll have to learn to like it." They all laughed, but Richard made a mental note that the joke would not be at all appreciated by Benjamin when he grew up.

"I think she's the type to enjoy the life," Richard added with conviction, "as long as she can accept a constantly tossing and heaving world." They moved into the house and Nat held Richard back as the ladies walked on.

"Richard, I was going through your arrangements with John Maddox today. Everything was fine until I told him of your plans for Benjamin, and that you intended to take him with you. The Sheriff was adamant. The boy has to remain in this neighbourhood, at least for a few months in case a relative should be discovered, Sorry." Richard exploded, bitter disappointment showing on his face.

"Nat! After all my preparation, this is ridiculous!" The two friends stood glaring at each other and for the first time anger simmered between them.

"Be sensible, man, you can't take a lad that age halfway across the country on a mule!" Nat had never been known to raise his voice in the house and Sarah had arrived at her husband's side, alarmed. The two men still confronted each other, hostility dying and ebbing away as Sarah now stood between them.

"It *is* for the best Richard, really. I know that you're frustrated and saddened by the decision, but we'll work something out." Richard embraced her and took Nat's hand.

"I'm so sorry," he said quietly, "there was absolutely no reason to take it out on you, to behave as I did in your house is unforgivable."

"You're forgiven," Sarah whispered, "and in any case, this is your house too." They moved into the house to join Rebecca just as a knock at the front door announced the arrival of a visitor, John Maddox. Nat brought him into the lounge, where he paid his respects to the ladies and crossed the room to Richard.

"I know all about it, Sheriff." Richard pre-empted the lawman's question.

"About what, son?"

"Taking Benjamin with me."

"Oh sure, can't be done for a while. No, my callin' is to give you this, my boy - not good news I'm afraid." Richard took the telegram from him. Its size and appearance were now very familiar, but he still felt the same apprehension each time he received one, even after being forewarned of its contents, as now.

'Richard.' it read, 'father died yesterday (Wednesday). Funeral Monday. I shall miss you. Mother'.

Richard, message in hand, walked out through the meadow and onto the clifftop way above the great ocean. His gaze covered the expanse of water, trying to identify an horizon in the evening haze. He momentarily had the insane idea of joining Nancy's ship in the morning bound for England. Then, his thoughts coming more logically, he realised that no ship would get him home for his father's burial. In those minutes as he stood on that promontory, his long shadow before him, Richard paid a brief but impassioned tribute to his father. His thoughts ranged through the happy years of adolescence when his father's influence was so vital, to the encouragement and financial backing he had received on going to university. Then he recalled their music-making together in those days when the atmosphere at Shaw Manor had been convivial. Richard and his mother would play piano and cello respectively to accompany the powerful, if undisciplined, baritone voice of William Shaw, whose major achievement had been to sing in 'Messiah' on one occasion. Frequently such recitals ended in side-splitting laughter as his father sang on, totally oblivious to the fact that the accompaniment had ceased and his wife and son were in hysterics. Richard smiled to himself as he recalled those good days. Then a sadness entered his thoughts. What had happened between his parents in their latter years? His father had become distant and immersed in his work, and his mother house-proud to a fault, devoid of emotion, her coldness often frightening Richard by its intensity.

The development of a shadow beside his, then a soft footfall brought him back to the reality of the clifftop in his adopted country.

"Are you all right Richard? I'm so sorry." Rebecca stood before him as he turned, looking as though she could topple over at any moment.

"Rebecca," he greeted her, smiling, "did you make it on your own?"

"Sarah brought me through the meadow, isn't it wonderful?" She waved her arms excitedly and lost her balance on weak legs. Richard caught her as she lurched forward and they laughed together.

"You know that I must leave?" he whispered, his mouth close to her ear.

"Yes, I know that you must." She looked up at him as he held her securely. "How can I ever thank you, Richard?" She buried her face in his chest as his gaze took in the house behind her.

"We owe much to so many," he said, "and you can thank us all by getting better." He shivered. "C'mon, there's a chill in the air, let's walk." His strong arm supplied her needs of the moment, support, warmth and companionship. The wind behind them scattered her now healthy fair hair across her face and he heard her giggle. They moved into the protection of the meadow, leeward of the lifting wind as it struck land after thousands of miles of unhindered progress. Richard pushed her hair from her face.

"It's wonderful to see you returning to health, Rebecca."

"I have never known such kindness," she replied. "Why did you return for me Richard, was it simply from a sense of obligation?"

He laughed. "I took my turn in plying you with broth and recalled another such occasion. I was in trouble, remember, and needing a friend. I was helpless too. Now who was it supplying the broth and aid then?"

"But how did you know that I was in need?"

"Philip." She looked puzzled, He continued: "The sailor who called on you a month or so ago. He asked about Captain Radford."

"Ah, hah," she nodded comprehendingly, "But I thought he was a representative of the authorities - was I right?"

"Rebecca, there are things that I must explain regarding this household."

"I'm staying on in this household, Richard."

"I beg your pardon?" he said stupidly.

"Sarah has asked me to remain, if I wish, to help around the house. She intends to accompany Nat more as his travels take him farther afield. I've accepted. Do say that you're pleased, Richard." He knew that Sarah would welcome the assistance Rebecca was able to give her. Nat's business associates were becoming difficult for Sarah to cope with.

"It's great news Rebecca," he said genuinely, "let's walk to the house or we'll miss dinner - you're not cooking tonight are you?" he asked in mock alarm. They laughed again and his arm remained as her support until they reached the door of her room.

"By the way, you and I must get together after dinner and I *will* give you some Holland family history - essential now that you are staying."

"You're not going to scare me off, are you?" she asked with a grin.

"On the contrary, madam," he replied, returning her smile and opening her door. "See you at dinner," he said, closing the door softly behind her.

Richard stood there for a long moment, his back to the door. There was now no reason why he shouldn't concentrate all his energies on achieving his goal of reaching Randolph in time for Josh's birthday late in May.

Chapter 27

It was all hands to the plough that weekend in the Holland household in order that Richard could be on his way at sun-up on Monday. Sarah and Rebecca handled the practical side of the preparations, rejecting Richard's argument in favour of travelling light. Essential items were produced and stacked in one corner. Adjacent piles contained items of a more useful or desirable nature. There was equipment to be checked and cleaned, boots to be relaced and preserved. Richard and Nat oiled and inspected the two revolvers and rifle, during the course of which Nat divulged that he had, in his youth, been a gunsmith. It explained to Richard why his host had such a thorough knowledge of weapons.

Richard chose to wear a far less austere outfit than on the last occasion, with the intention of merging with a crowd rather than standing out from it. He rode Valiant to the local blacksmith where shoes, bridle, saddle and accoutrements were carefully checked and replaced or strengthened as necessary.

Richard dispatched two telegrams, one to his mother and the other to Kate, courtesy of the Hilltop Hotel. The simple message in both cases was that he was leaving the following day, destination Randolph.

Dinner on that last Sunday evening was high-spirited despite the fact that not one of them was really looking forward to the imminent farewells.

"Family and friends will be passing through from time to time," Richard was saying, "and I have no doubt that I'll be back this way, probably to pick up this young one here." Benjamin stared at Richard, the point lost on him, but the very look reached Richard's heart, cementing his resolve in that regard.

"Do let us know as soon as you arrive," pleaded Sarah, "And should you find the girl of your dreams out there, remember, there's no wedding without Sarah being present." They laughed together as Rebecca echoed these sentiments and Nat raised his eyebrows to heaven.

"Women," he moaned, "and now I've got two of 'em!" The mood of the diners remained good, perhaps artificially so, but each was making an effort to extract a modicum of normality from the day.

After dinner Richard escorted Benjamin to bed and explained once more that he had to go away but would one day return and they would go for a long ride on Valiant. With that the tired eyes closed and Benjamin was soon asleep. Richard stood over his bed for many minutes, gazing fondly at the tousled head and angelic face of the sleeping child. He mentally arrived at the analogy that the hair of Benjamin and that of Josh could be compared to silver and gold, such were their hues. Sarah joined him quietly and they remained for a few seconds before leaving together and closing the door softly behind them.

"We'll give him the best that two old people can until you're settled, Richard," she said as they joined Rebecca and Nat in the sitting-room.

"I have no doubt about that." Richard said gratefully. "Thank you both for taking him on and of course the girl here." Rebecca aimed a mock blow at his head and they laughed together again until Nat proposed a toast and glasses were refilled.

"To you, Richard. Your future happiness."

"Richard!" they echoed, and Richard felt good in the knowledge that he had such friends.

Sarah and Nat retired early in order to be up next morning and Richard and Rebecca sat facing each other at each end of the settee, still with glasses in hand.

236

"Richard," she began falteringly, "if there should be nothing for you at the end of your journey, would you spare a thought for me?" He studied this girl who had made such great steps towards a remarkable recovery. His memory ran over the events of the previous year and of her kindness. He recalled her incredible optimism and energy, her leadership ability and complete honesty. He found it amazing that she was just as much at home in this middle-class environment as she had been in the cheap hotel where they had met. "I'm still waiting for an answer, Mr Shaw." she reminded him.

"Sorry," he said with a smile, "I was day-dreaming."

"Was I in it?" She smiled too.

"Yes, actually, I was back in that awful place ..."

"Don't Richard, it's all in the past. Thanks to you I can now forget it all and live like a human being. I'll never forget you."

"You'd better not." he chuckled, then, kissing her softly, assured her that she would always be close to him whatever the future had in store.

* * *

Richard set off very early. Benjamin was allowed to sleep on and Rebecca had preferred to say her farewell the night before. So it was just Sarah and Nat who waved him off as he rode away on Valiant with the mule following behind, a guide rope between them.

Richard noticed the tip of the sun emerging behind them over the ocean and he would always remember them that way. As he negotiated the bend in the road they were lost from view. He was on his own now with a mission, the outcome of which was to shape the rest of his life.

He snaked his way from the coast, moving steadily along

the winding track. Richard was aiming to catch the first of two rail-road relays that evening and judged that his easy pace would achieve this. Nat and he had calculated that his chosen route would result in Richard riding just over half the distance, a vast improvement on the interminable trek of the previous year.

He arrived at the rail-head some two hours before the train was due and installed himself atop his saddle and baggage. The two animals, now relieved of their burdens, stood by almost gratefully. Richard took his diary from his saddle bag and idly flipped through its pages. He was horrified to realise that his habit of a lifetime had ended on the day he left Randolph almost a year ago. He took up a pencil and entering the date at the head of the next clear page, recorded that he was now heading back to the town and its people he had so foolishly abandoned.

* * *

By the time the coaches lurched into motion, Richard had housed Valiant and Captain, (the latter named by Benjamin as a result, no doubt, of his contact with the ship's officer). The evening was cool and Richard dallied between the coaches, gripping the rail. His thirst drove him to the rear of the train where, it was advertised, a restaurant car could be found.

Richard had always been of the opinion that travelling on trains was the place to meet people, as they were thrown together in close confinement and usually bored and seeking company and solace from fellow sufferers. This had been his experience both at home and in America. Now, with only a few hours to spend on this particular train, he met the Judge from Kansas City.

Approaching what passed as a restaurant car, Richard overheard the white-jacketed waiter refer to the only occupant as 'judge'. Curiosity compelled him to sit at an adjacent table

238

facing the man. He fitted Richard's conception of a judge as he was well-dressed, mature in years and sported a moustache which covered the majority of an otherwise clean-shaven face. The moustache twitched as he munched on a slice of bread, deciding thereafter to dip it with little enthusiasm into what appeared to be a cold bean soup. Richard had already decided not to eat on the train and ordered a whisky, dividing his attention between the scrubland through which they travelled and the lawman opposite him.

The judge pushed the dish away from him and dabbed his mouth with a handkerchief, which he produced from an upper pocket of his jacket.

"Like a drink, judge?" Richard offered, holding his glass aloft.

"Sure would, young fella," he replied, "need to wash that swill down with something." Richard smiled and summoned the waiter. "I was in England year last fall," the judge continued conversationally.

Richard nodded and explained, "This is my second spell in America, I too am in law." He paused as the drinks arrived and he paid the waiter.

"Where are you headed?" the judge enquired as he studied his glass. Richard told him and the moustache jumped as the judge raised his bushy eyebrows. "I'm from Kansas City you're a ways north of there, maybe our trails will cross, young fella." He motioned for Richard to join him at his table. They discussed variations in the law concerning their two countries and Richard learned much from him. The judge was kind enough to outline the adoption laws for him, and even offered to be responsible for Richard's training, but this was after several whiskies. They agreed subsequently that distance would probably make such an arrangement impossible. "Just you look-a-me-up if you need me, young fella." They shook hands and

Richard thanked him, accepting a piece of torn paper from the Judge's wallet on which, no doubt, he had written an address. He then returned to the stable coach in order to make preparations for leaving the train.

* * *

It was midnight as Richard cleared the town and the rail-road. He rode for an hour then set up camp for the remainder of the night. His hunger had got the better of him, and he made a fire and shamelessly indulged in large portions of bacon and several eggs with steaming coffee to follow. Feeling relaxed and contented, he appreciated the solitude and gazed up at the stars. He was soon asleep.

Richard was on the move again as the sun appeared, announcing a new day. His next date with the rail-road was five days' ride away and progress with the mule was, by necessity, a steady one. He momentarily wondered how he would have coped had little Benjamin made the journey with him. He concluded that perhaps Sarah had been right, although it would have been good to have had the little boy's company.

He reached the rail-head after days of uneventful riding. He was weary and secretly looking forward to a couple of days on the train. Once again he had to wait a few hours and, having unloaded the animals, lay dozing in the heat of the afternoon. He was suddenly aroused by the arrival of the train and just had time to purchase his ticket and get his luggage, horse and mule on board. Manoeuvring horse and mule up the ramp into the coach was never easy. Richard's frustration was not diminished any by the taunts and grins of locals standing by. Whereas Valiant was used to such an operation, it was evident that the mule was not, and Richard had frequently to leave the horse and concentrate on getting the stupid and obdurate creature into one of the boxes. Only when both animals were settled and fed, and Valiant groomed, would Richard stow away the saddle bags and leave the stable coach.

Richard strolled into the first passenger coach and found a seat next to the window. He dropped into it as the train got under way to the usual accompaniment of clanging metal and flurries of steam, which for a moment obliterated everything from view. He noticed then that sitting opposite him was a wizened old negro whose face lit up with a welcoming smile. Richard nodded. "Hello." he said, alarmed at the very Englishness of his greeting.

"How-di," drawled the negro, "Yo aint from these parts, ah knowd afore yo opened yo muth." Richard retained his smile and raised his eyebrows questioningly. "Yo sittin' wid a nigga, boy, dat aint smart." The huge smile had evaporated and was replaced by a look of deep sadness. The old man got to his feet with a great effort. "Good day, suh." Richard jumped up and placed a restraining hand on the negro's arm.

"Please sit down, I beg of you, if anyone is to leave it will be me." Surprise and a deal of suspicion registered on the black face as Richard guided him back to his seat. The old man slumped into his seat without a word, unsure of the situation. "The journey is a long one and I wish to talk to you." Richard went on in an attempt to allay the fears apparent in the features of the man facing him. The black head shook slowly from side to side in protest and bewilderment. "Why are you travelling today - where do you live?" Richard asked pleasantly.

The train was moving swiftly and the old man's eyes wandered to the window and the ever changing scene beyond it, but the gaze was fixed and registered incomprehension. There was no answer for some time as the seconds ticked away to the accompaniment of the wheels drumming on metal and finding the joints in the track with regular monotony. Suspicion gradually left the old man's face as he perceived Richard's genuine interest.

"Ahm a lookin' fur mah boys," he said almost to himself. "Ah had me five boys. They wus fightin' fur the Yankees. Mah boys dey never come back, suh, all mah chillen gone. Mah missus gone too suh, so I's jus' lookin' fur mah boys." Richard was speechless for a moment as he considered the implications of the man's quest.

"You have been looking for over five years?" Richard eventually managed.

"Five years suh, an' I'm still a lookin'," the old man confirmed.

"Have you anything to go on - where are you looking?" Richard asked incredulously.

"Jus' a lookin' fur mah boys," the old man repeated, his gaze again drifting out of the window at nothing in particular. "Ah just knows ah will find 'em suh." His voice tapered off, making it difficult for Richard to hear. The enormity and futility of the mission rendered Richard incapable of logical thought and there was silence as the train's brakes were applied erratically, announcing the first of many stops.

Richard pulled himself together and excused himself from the old man, who was still gazing distractedly out of the window. Richard had developed the habit of keeping an eye on Valiant each time a stop was made. Rumour had it that many a quality horse and much personal baggage had been taken from the train on these occasions by unscrupulous dealers or thieves. On returning to his seat as the train shuddered its way out of the town, he found that the negro had gone. It became obvious later that he was no longer on the train. The old man was continuing his search.

It was dawn when the train reached its most westerly

point and Richard negotiated the ramp for the last time. He considered discarding the mule there but realised that he would have to jettison much of his possessions if he did. He moved urgently out onto the trail and when clear of civilisation, made a brief camp to brew coffee and eat. A feeling of excitement was enveloping his whole being, taking his appetite away. He was within three days' ride of his destination and with impatience also mounting, he wasted no time in breaking camp and getting underway with the prospect of a full day in the saddle.

Richard was suddenly aware of familiar landmarks and realised that the trail itself was known to him. He was back in the mid-West, travelling for the second time into Randolph. He rode ever onwards, his weariness consumed by a nervous energy which tempted him to go beyond his own limits and those of Valiant and the mule.

At his final camp sleep was evasive. Richard moved out of the fire's glow and circled it in a wide circumference, speaking to the animals as he came upon them. He decided to pull out at the very first suggestion of the new day. What a day it was to be, one for which he had longed almost from the time he had left the town in that mad homeward flight. The long night passed and Richard discerned streaks of grey off to the east, fingers of pale light pushing away the darkness. He quickly but methodically packed his gear onto the animals and, turning his back on the rising dawn, picked his way up into the hills that stood between him and the town he hoped would mark the end of his quest.

Chapter 28

Richard urged Valiant up the grassy slope at the side of the trail. At the top he halted and, shielding his eyes from the glare of the high sun, could just make out the hills beyond Randolph. The heat haze made them shimmer and his eyes quickly tired. He tried to focus on the shifting horizon but could not locate the town or valley, both still hidden below him. His weariness left him as he rejoined the mule on the trail, impatiently resuming his westerly course.

Richard watered Valiant and Captain at a small farm about an hour's ride from Randolph. He had only to top that familiar rise, a mile or so ahead, and the scene of many a dream would unfold before him. He learned from the couple at the farm that there had been a shooting in town some days before. The drifter that imparted the information had given no details. Richard had a flutter of anxiety, then the story left his mind as he headed up the slope, waving a hand of thanks to the good folks behind him.

Richard slowed Valiant to a walk as the crest of the hill drew near. He felt a nervousness that now pervaded his entire frame. His heart pounded, and he became breathless, finding co-ordination difficult. Diagnosing his malady, he gazed down at Randolph, which now appeared, spread out below him as he topped the rise. Doubts began to assail him. What if the Mack's had sold up and moved out? What if he was not welcome? What sort of reception awaited him? What if Kate had married? His condition worsened despite the absurdity of his thoughts. Below him was the scene exactly as he had left it. The town snug in the valley with highways running east and west, like trails of thread at this distance. The backdrop of hills shortened the horizon. Narrowing his eyes Richard could just detect movement on the streets, townsfolk emerging as the day cooled.

The light breeze in his face carried the sound of the bell to him even at that distance, the church bell presumably. Recovered now from his nervousness and with a new resolve, Richard spurred Valiant into action and, shouting to the mule to keep up, descended into the town. The doleful single tolling of the bell was now clear and insistent. As he got closer, the activity became more detailed and it was obvious that a funeral was taking place, with people in dark clothing gathered around the church. Richard remembered briefly the shooting that was alleged to have taken place, and his concern grew. He reached the edge of the town and dismounted, walking the animals forward. He brushed as much dust from him as he could, but felt very much out of place at that moment. As he moved still closer Richard recognised faces in the crowd.

Josh saw him at the precise moment Richard arrived at a spot opposite the church gate. His heart leapt as Josh ran across the wide street, shouting his name and crashing into him with arms encircling his waist. He hung on tightly and Richard held the boy's head, not trusting himself to speak. As they stood together for what seemed an age, Samantha, searching for her brother, caught sight of them and, uncertain of herself, ambled in their direction. Richard held his free arm out to her and she came to him, the three of them silent, but complete in their happiness.

Richard looked over the heads of the two young people and off across the street. The hearse was drawing up outside the church, its two bays stamping the ground as if impatient to be free of the onerous task allotted to them. Josh followed Richard's gaze and whispered in his ear; "Old Jeb". Relief washed over him. He was sorry indeed that old timer had gone, but the fact that he hadn't seen Kate, only her family, had pushed his worse fears to the fore.

"Mother is in the church", Josh continued, looking up into Richard's face. "She's only got Auntie Jackie with her".

"Will you take Valiant and the mule to the hotel for me?" Richard asked them both as they continued to peer up at him. They nodded their agreement. He thought they might not be too willing to make the journey out of town to the graveyard anyway. Josh took the reins as Richard's arm dropped from his shoulder, Sam however, remained a few seconds longer with her arms around him. She eventually moved away, smiling through her tears. Her likeness to her mother had become even more pronounced in the intervening months.

"Ma will, 'preciate you being with her", she said, then ran after her brother. Richard realised that she was now a young lady, grinning to himself at the revelation. He also wondered how he could have left these people once he'd discovered them.

Richard was very much aware of his own aching body and pushed his tired frame in the direction of the hearse. He was acutely aware, too, of the dust which had become encrusted in his clothes, and the stubble on his grubby face, accumulated over the last few days on the trail. It had always been his intention to tidy up at the hotel before seeking out Kate, but events had determined otherwise. Sweeping off his hat, he strode purposefully past the stamping horses and up the pathway, nodding to people in mutual recognition. Richard slapped his hat against his thighs, observing with dismay the cloud of dust coming from both it and his trousers.

He ducked into the porch just as the coffin was being brought out of the church. Standing back, he allowed the procession to pass. Two of the pall bearers were known to him, one of whom offered a sober, toothless grin as he passed, which Richard acknowledged. He remained crouched in the confines of the porch as Kate and Jackie moved by, instantly recognisable, even though their heads were covered, by their bearing. The Champions and the Bennetts followed close behind, and Richard was struck by the deterioration in John Champion.

Richard straightened stiffly, and fell into step beside Kate as they cleared the porch. Jackie gasped open-mouthed as she saw the tall figure. Kate was aware of the sharp intake of breath to her left and tug on her arm. Jackie's stare prompted Kate to investigate and, suddenly, for the first time in almost a year, Kate and Richard came face to face, eyes riveted, and displaying at the same time, relief, joy, and another ingredient yet to be identified. They were motionless, lost in each other as the tiny retinue passed by them. A discreet cough ahead prompted the couple to join the waiting mourners, having uttered not a word save to breathe the other's name in those first magical seconds of their reunion. They stepped up into the buggy with Jackie and once again Richard found himself in the company of the two women that he had driven, on a happier occasion, around the town, listening to their infectious chatter as they waved to the schoolchildren. Now there was a strange silence between them, highlighting the creaking of the buggy and the sound of hooves on the packed earth. Anxiety once more gripped his heart, only to be dispelled moments later as he shot Kate a glance across the buggy. Her smile said all he would have wanted to hear and put his entire being as ease. That smile, he later reflected, would have melted an iceberg.

* * *

Richard took the two mugs of coffee from Kate as she sat down beside him on the homestead veranda, handing one to her as she settled.

"We're going to have a houseful when your family and friends arrive, Richard", she remarked as he joined her. "But with Jackie's help, I am sure we will manage".

"Sure we will", Richard responded, producing a document from a file beside him. "This guest list must be complete now. Sixty in all. You are coming to the wedding I hope, Kate?" She elbowed him playfully, and he winced, his ribs still giving him occasional discomfort. Kate took the list from him and studied it, frowning slightly.

"Well," she said eventually, "I cannot think of anyone we've left out. I do hope that Virginia and Manfred make it back. I'll never forgive her for getting married in Europe!" Richard smiled as she continued; "I am looking forward to meeting the Holland's, but your mother?" She sighed, returning the list.

"You'll get on wonderfully together." He prophesied confidently. His mother had sold Shaw Manor, Bates having gone to live with an aged sister. Richard felt no sense of loss regarding the Manor, just a tinge of sadness as he thought of the demise of his father and family's roots. Mary Shaw was to stay in Randolph for the rest of her life, however long that might be. Richard turned his attention to happier things. "As far as young Benjamin is concerned, Josh and Sam will be the best teachers he could have at this stage."

"He sounds adorable, Richard. Oh I do hope they'll all arrive in time."

"Nat will see to that, don't worry," he replied, laughing.

Kate stared at her mug cradled in her hands on her lap. "Will you take the sheriffs' job, Richard?" She asked after a moment.

"How do you feel about it?"

"Very proud, but apprehensive."

"It will keep me out of mischief until I qualify for this circuit judge thing," he joked, "you are going to be married to a lawman which ever way you look at it."

Kate sipped the steaming liquid and leaned back with a

contended sigh. He watched her and a smile developed on his clean shaven face.

"You sound happy, Kate," he remarked, testing his own coffee.

"I am." Her head fell sideways on to his shoulder. They gazed out across the land and off to the river, glinting in its constant movement. They would have to move soon as the sun was travelling around the heavens, shortly to invade the shade of the veranda on that side of the house. For the moment, though, they were comfortable, the silence between them saying more than words ever could.

Kate wriggled beside him, and he knew from the little experience he had of her she was about to speak. "Richard," she began tentatively.

"Yes," he encouraged softly. She straightened and looked him full in the face, each pair of eyes again engaging the other.

"Don't leave me for a moment."

"Never," he managed to answer as they burst into laughter and further words were impossible. The sound of their happiness echoed on the porch and across the meadow, through the barns and along the trails. The whole valley resounded to the joy of two people who were to shape its future and whose union would guarantee that such sounds were commonplace.

THE END